My heart trembled with remembering...

As Alex pulled his giant black horse upward, the animal threatened the air with his heavily shod hooves. Thwarted, I reined Lady to the right only to meet again my black-clad tormentor and his warlike horse. Whichever way I turned, he blocked my way. I screamed with frustration and fright. I wouldn't let this man get the best of me. When I pivoted again to the left, the black horse was a jump ahead of me. Again the animal reared. My brave mare shuddered beneath my legs.

"I hate you Alexander Dominican!" I shrieked through tears.

Alex's horse turned in an agitated circle. "No you don't."

"Yes, I do! This marriage is damned! I want to get away from you." I started forward once more.

Slowly, like the view from a slow motion camera, the black gelding reared again. Just as slowly, Alex toppled off. Already unbalanced, the horse fell on his side amid a wild thrashing of hooves. In seconds, the black animal regained his feet, yet Alex remained silent and still on the ground. Lady stood immobile beneath me. My palms were wet inside my gloves.

Dizzy waves washed through me. Like so many other things, this had happened to me sometime in the past. Not in this particular way, not in this same manner, but it had happened. My heart trembled with remembering. My body ached with a longing and an anxiety retained from some previous time. Some unfathomable force pulled me toward Alex in a way I couldn't control. I fought it. A fierce battle raged within my mind and spirit. I convulsed with it. I opposed the certainty growing strongly within my being that I could not leave without knowing if my husband was alive or dead. After all, he was my reason for existence.

What people are saying about Tangled Memories...

4 Star Review, Romantic Times Magazine 2001

Finalist 1994 RWA Golden Heart Contest

Jane Toombs:
"Not only gothic lovers will find this a marvelous and rewarding read - any reader who enjoys suspense mixed with romance won't be able to put this book down."

Patricia Kay:
"Lush, vivid writing. Tone, style and voice are all original and quite wonderful. The mood is nicely maintained, with just enough brooding suspense and Gothic overtones. Reminiscent of Mary Stewart."

Teresa Medeiros:
"Jan Scarbrough gives romantic suspense a fresh twist in her compelling first novel Tangled Memories. Her strong, provocative voice is one I look forward to reading more of in the future."

Harriet Klausner review:
TANGLED MEMORIES is a wonderful gothic romance complete with a foreboding castle, a helpful housekeeper, strange visions, and an insane antagonist. Told in the first person from Mary's point of view, readers feel the same fears that the heroine experiences. Jan Scarbrough has written a modern day gothic that will delight fans of this growing sub genre.

Tangled Memories

by

Jan Scarbrough

Tangled Memories

Contact Information: info@thewildrosepress.com

Cover Art by *Rae Monet*

The Wild Rose Press
PO Box 708
Adams Basin, NY 14410-0706
Visit us at www.thewildrosepress.com

Publishing History
First Faery Rose Edition, 2008
Print ISBN 1-60154-270-4

Published in the United States of America

Dedication

For Bill, my husband.
I've waited centuries to find you again.

CHAPTER ONE

His eyes were gray. I had never noticed before. They weren't the color of slate, but smoky and mysterious. Down the silent aisle, I walked confidently toward him—chin high, very lady-like in posture and demeanor, a trace of a smile upon my lips. Inside I didn't feel confident, swallowing the hard knot of dread that had surfaced in my throat. A cloying scent of gardenias assaulted my heightened senses. How curious the delicate white flowers should be so over-powering. Just like the man in front of me. Just like the deep, heady gray of his eyes.

I extended my hand. As he took it, I drew a breath and held it, the firm feel of his fingers surprising me.

"Friends, we are gathered together in the sight of God to witness and bless the joining together of Mary and Alexander in Christian marriage."

He was tall, so tall I was forced to look up into those mesmerizing eyes. My breathing started again—erratic and shallow. I didn't understand the sense of familiarity I felt about him, because I certainly didn't know this man. How ironic. I was marrying again for the second time in my life, and for the second time, my reasons were more practical than romantic.

I glanced briefly at the Methodist minister. Although he wore a white stole symbolic of purity and love, his black robes matched my intensely somber mood.

"I ask you now," he said, "in the presence of God and these people, to declare your intention to enter into a union with one another."

Jan Scarbrough

To enter into a union. Heaven help me. Would it be a union? How could it be? It was a business arrangement, plain and simple. I understood that. Somehow though, sadness clutched at my heart.

Reverend Watts looked at me. "Mary, will you have Alexander to be your husband to live together in holy marriage? Will you love him, comfort him, honor and keep him, in sickness and in health, and forsaking all others, be faithful to him as long as you both shall live?"

My stomach burned. I felt Alex's gray penetrating gaze upon my upturned face as I concentrated on the minister's receding hairline. "I will."

"Alexander, will you have Mary to be your wife?"

From underneath my lashes, I watched him. He wore his jet black hair swept back and long and curling at his neck. A stray lock touched his forehead and set off his eyes. His high cheekbones and jawline gave him a classic look. His lips were full and inviting. Enigmatic in his formal black tuxedo, crisp white shirt and bow tie, he seemed a brooding Byronic hero. Handsome, though austere, his masculine good looks belonged on the cover of a romantic novel.

I often wondered how different my life might have been if I hadn't become pregnant at eighteen...if I hadn't married Bill...if I hadn't miscarried. What if I had met Alexander Dominican under different circumstances, before life had touched me so harshly?

"I will." His deep and resonant voice grabbed my attention.

Turning from the minister to me, his eyes brightened as his gaze captured mine. Out of habit, I licked my lips, but nothing eased the tension I felt, which I knew I somehow communicated to the self-assured man who held my hand. Did he feel the hypocrisy of our oath? Or was he simply content with a marriage of convenience? Daring him with my stare, I narrowed my own eyes in challenge to his casual acceptance of our deceit before God. His black brow lifted to meet my dare. He cocked his head to the side as if to tell me I could still back out. I could walk away a single woman. Poor, but single. I shifted my gaze, unable to continue our silent joust, knowing full well I couldn't back out. Bill's death had made sure of that.

2

"Let us pray. Eternal God, creator and preserver of all life."

I bowed my head, but I couldn't shut my eyes. It didn't seem right. Nothing seemed right these last few weeks. Not since the dark-clad police officer had come to my door, telling me my husband had been killed in a car accident.

When the prayer ended, the minister motioned us to face each other and join our hands. I gave my bouquet to my friend Gail, who took it with hesitation. Alex's grasp was warm and determined. The grip of his fingers transmitted a vibrant fire through my arms coursing straight to my heart. Trite as it sounds, I felt my heart skip a beat. Had I read my emotions correctly? It had been a long time since I had felt sexual attraction, and I certainly had not expected to feel ardor toward this tall man I was about to marry. What good would it do? We had an arrangement. A platonic arrangement. I'd mother his infant daughter. He'd pay my debts. I berated myself because our stark and concise agreement left no room for this unexpected play of emotion.

"I, Alexander, take you, Mary, to be my wife."

To be my wife. My throat constricted. I had met Dr. Alexander Dominican eight years ago. The partner of my doctor, Alex had been on call the night I had lost my baby. I had been such a foolish teenager. Straightening my shoulders at the thought, I caught the slight narrowing of his eyes, and turned self-consciously from his scrutiny. What did he really think about me? Did he remember that scared child-patient of eight years ago? I had changed. At twenty-six I was now a woman. Did he know that?

The minister nodded. Summoning all my willpower, I looked at Alex and in a hushed voice, repeated the same vows. My hands were damp when he released them to turn to Dr. Bramwell, his partner and best man. At the same time, Gail handed me a thin gold band. Unable to meet Alex's gaze, I took his left hand, and slid the band across the third finger. In a different time, I believed he would have bowed and kissed the back of my hand. As it was, he held onto it, and firmly slipped my own wedding band into place. Hastily, I glanced up to find his eyes

3

appraising me. As I tightened my lips, my returning gaze did not falter. The weight of the ornate, gold ring nudged into my flesh, and created a link between us I was hard-pressed to comprehend.

"Bless, O Lord, the giving of these rings, that they who wear them may live in your peace and continue in your favor all the days of their lives."

Alex smiled a slow, half smile, as if he understood something I had failed to discern. The smile softened his stern features, bringing back my recollection of the gentle doctor who had once comforted and cared for me. I offered a smile in return, and was gratified to see his eyes lighten in response.

The minister joined our hands together again, and symbolically wrapped his white stole around them.

"Now that Alexander and Mary have given themselves to each other by solemn vows," he said, "with the joining of hands, and the giving and receiving of rings, I announce to you that they are husband and wife; in the name of the Father, and of the Son, and of the Holy Spirit. Those whom God has joined together, let no one put asunder."

A surprising disquiet pricked my scalp and traced down the back of my neck. I swallowed once, to ease the dryness in my mouth and then looked away from our joined hands. We were husband and wife. It seemed so appropriate, so right. As if it were meant to be. But how could it? Under the strained circumstances of our compact, we were nothing but business partners.

"Are you going to kiss the bride?" I heard amusement in the minister's voice, because he expected us to be a conventional couple.

Alex released my hands. I felt oddly bereft. When I looked up at him, I found him staring down at me, his eyes shadowed by coal-colored lashes. I read the speculation in them. He lifted his hands, and I fixed my gaze upon them, charmed by the beauty of his tapered fingers. His hands lingered in the air briefly, and then I felt them raise the thin veil from my face. His breath touched me. My gaze now held spellbound by his, I watched his eyes as he gently elevated my chin with a fingertip, and caressed my cheek with his thumb. My heart hung suspended in my chest, for an instant, and then dropped into a relentless beat. For some reason, I welcomed the touch of his hand upon my skin. Dreamily, I smiled.

His focus was only on the mere movement of my lips. He stood so very close. I could see the flecks of dark in the lighter gray of his eyes. My own eyes widened in dismay as Alex lowered his lips to mine, tenderly touching them with a kiss so poignant that it pierced into my soul.

The kiss startled us both. I could tell by the way he hesitated, seeming to gasp for breath. With his left hand, he still caressed my face, connecting us to each other in an untold way. I found it hard to breathe. I found it hard to move. In the recesses of my mind, warning bells clamored.

I straightened my shoulders and lifted my chin away from his touch. We may be married, but his kiss was not appropriate for two people with a business arrangement. Awkwardly separating, we held each other's gaze an instant. I felt dazed, swaying from side to side. Alex set his jaw, and glanced away.

"Congratulations." Reverend Watts pumped Alex's hand.

Gail gave me back my bouquet, and offered me a swift hug. Her face was strained, her lips pursed. "I hope you'll be happy, Mary."

"Thank you." Holding on to Gail's hug longer than was necessary, I then stepped back, embarrassed. I knew she was still upset with me for doing this. My friend had tried to talk me out of remarrying so soon after Bill's death. My reasons were wrong she had said. I was being purchased like a broodmare for the price of a gambling debt. A significant gambling debt, I had tried to remind her. Bill had charged more than fifty thousand dollars, and I had no other way out. Gail and I had argued. I wasn't surprised we now had so little to say to each other—that Gail and I treated each other like birds ready to take flight.

Dr. Bramwell warmly congratulated Alex. Dr. Hilliard, Alex's other partner and our only other guest, came forward and loudly slapped Alex on his back. "How do you capture the pretty ones, my man? How do you do

it? You've got a beauty here for a wife. I ought to know...."
He finished his sentence with a meaningful wink.

I thought his remark crude. He was my gynecologist, after all, and of course "knew" me as no other. But I overlooked it, and allowed him to congratulate me with the obligatory kiss for the bride.

Tasting bourbon in his mouth, I ended the kiss abruptly, tossing my head as if to fling the flush from my heated face. "Why, Dr. Hilliard, you certainly have a knack for exploratory surgery. Did they teach you that in medical school?"

He laughed. "Yes, Alex, I love a woman with spunk."

"Or is it just *my* woman you love, John?" My husband's tone was slick ice.

Blinking with astonishment, I tried to assess the undercurrents swirling around me, but found Alex's staid demeanor unreadable.

"Please step into my office to sign the marriage certificate." Reverend Watts interrupted our conversation to lead us out of the quiet sanctuary.

Alex took me possessively by the hand and tucked it under his arm to place it on his sleeve. He kept hold of my fingers, his own hand warm and sure. I had no trouble keeping up with his deliberate pace. There was something strangely comfortable about the way our strides matched.

"He's been my doctor for eight years," I muttered, "but I never realized Dr. Hilliard could be so obnoxious."

"You've only seen him on his best behavior at the office. Thank goodness my esteemed partner doesn't usually come to work under the influence of Maker's Mark."

I glanced at his firm features. "He's not an alcoholic, is he?" I asked, thinking about my late husband.

Alex's fingers pinched through the fabric of my simple, linen wedding dress. "Let's just say he's walking a fine line where I'm concerned. Dr. Bramwell and I've been watching him. For some reason, he's gotten a lot worse in the past three months since Allison's death."

The minister's office was hot. Summer sunshine strayed through open drapes. We all crowded inside while Reverend Watts went to the window air conditioner and flipped it on. A blast of cool air erupted into the room.

Returning to his desk, the minister shuffled papers for what seemed an eternity, finally producing a formal-looking document. When he nodded at us, Alex released me and stepped forward. Standing slightly away from him, I watched my new husband bend over the minister's desk and put his signature on the paper. It all seemed so unreal. My best friend was upset with me. I had just learned my trusted doctor had a drinking problem, and I was married. *Again.*

A high-pitched ringing sound shrilled loudly in my ears. I wondered if something was wrong with the air-conditioning unit. The noise grew in intensity, blocking out all other sounds. Alex turned toward me, offering me the pen. His mouth moved, but I couldn't hear him speak. Sweat beaded on my upper lip. I felt so light—as if I was floating. Somehow the stuffy little office was growing hazy. Like Fourth of July fireworks, pulsating lights of exploding colors shot before my eyes. I closed them. In the distance behind my shut eyes, I saw a young girl dressed in a strange yellow gown. The room vibrated....

****

ENGLAND, 1327

Mary de Mandeville confronted her father. Frowning in anger, she placed her hands on her hips.

"I will not go!"

Sir Robert regarded her. "Ye have no choice in the matter, my girl," he said quietly, looking down at the offer he held in his hand. "The deal has been struck, and you are to leave on the morrow. This marriage proposed by the earl is fair and well-met."

"No! I will not marry that old man. All he wants from me is to produce an heir." Mary twirled around to gaze glumly into the fire.

"It's the way of the world, Mary. Perhaps if your mother had lived, she could have made you understand."

Mary didn't answer. She understood all too well. Her throat tightened with hopelessness.

"You are already fifteen. I've been sympathetic long enough."

Sir Robert's firm word spoke her doom. Mary knew she had lost, but she didn't want to admit it. She didn't want to leave her home or the father she held so close to her heart. Yet she wasn't blind. Her father had grown gaunt with disease these past months. Gellis had told her she must face the unavoidable truth. He was dying and he had to provide for her. Yet why would he send her away? Why would he not want her with him during these last days? Her heart ached with the dismissal, for she knew it meant her father held her in scarce regard. Why else would he make her leave when he needed her so?

"The earl will permit you to bring Gellis," Sir Robert offered hopefully.

"Allow me to bring my maid! Wonderful! I'm to be at the man's very beck and call!" Disheartened, she struck out once more.

Mary heard her father sigh. "The lord is a very comely man. He is but seventeen years my junior, and not so very old." When Mary didn't respond, he tried another tactic. "I know you had your heart set on the Warwick boy. But for the terrible accident at the lists, you would already be his bride. Because of his death, I've been generous with you, not pressing you because of your grief. Yet the time is nigh when you will make a marriage, and do as I bid."

She turned to face him, her unnaturally dry eyes desolate in despair. Lifting her chin, she looked straight at her father and nodded in submission.

The strange vision shifted.

It was her wedding night, but Mary felt none of the excitement a young girl should feel. Instead, her emotion bordered on dread. Thank goodness they all were gone, those women who had witnessed her wedding. And her dreadful mother-in-law. They had stripped her naked, shaming her with their wanton talk, as they had prepared her for bed. Her servant Gellis had brushed her long blond hair until it snapped and sparkled. Then the good maid had touched her body with scented water, and while the other women watched and gossiped, tucked her securely into bed draping her flowing hair over her shoulders and breasts to cover them.

For some time Mary had sat alone in the lord's great cold bed, her fingers clutching the linen sheets. Her father had only been trying to provide for her.

Unfortunately, this *was* the way of the world. Mary was realistic enough to understand. Besides, what did it matter whom she married since she couldn't have Richard Warwick?

Lowering her lashes, she squeezed her eyes as if to shut off the tears threatening to spill down her cheeks. It worked, for by the time she heard her husband and his men coming toward the solar, her eyes were dry.

"Now, my good fellows. You have seen me safely to my chamber where my little bride awaits me. Pray you, take your leave so I may go alone inside."

Outside the raucous laughter of the male wedding guests drifted through the shut door. A couple's wedding night was known for the bedding ritual, and that, among other baser things, was scaring Mary to death. She listened intently to her husband's voice, for she could hear him clearly. Was he not drunk like the others? He didn't sound it.

"Yea, yea," her lord was saying. "But I'm not a green lad going with wobbly legs to my wedding bed. You forget. Many of you have ushered me to this same room some twenty years past. Humor me now, as I try to honor my young bride. She's newly come from her home, inexperienced and frightened. Let me go alone so as to spare her sensibilities."

Amazingly, the noise of the celebrants faded as they apparently retreated to the great hall where they could continue their merry-making. Mary knew they would let their lord make merry in his own way, for there was good wine to be had and wagers to be won and their own women to be bedded.

He came to her then, across the quiet chamber. Mary heard him undress and slowly approach the great bed. When he pulled back the linen hanging, cold air washed over her face before she turned her gaze away from him. His great weight sank the side of the feather mattress as he lifted the fur coverlet and crawled in beside her. He smelled of good Bordeaux wine and mustard. She could hear him breathing regularly.

"Look at me, my wife," he said, touching her chin with a forefinger, and drawing her head around.

Wide-eyed, Mary gazed at him as she was told. He

9

was still very good looking for a man of thirty-five. His arms were muscular and his chest full of dark, thick hair. Thankfully, Mary couldn't see the rest of his body, but she could feel the heavy weight of his hairy leg resting against her own. His head was bare. She'd never realized the blackness of his hair. Even in the candle-lit gloom of the solar, she could see it shine with a luster of its own as it fell to his shoulders. His nose was straight, his face classically drawn. Most importantly, his soft gray eyes were kind. They spoke a gentleness she had never associated with the great lord she had been forced to wed.

"I know you are frightened," he said to her. "I'm not a randy youth. I will not hurry our union, for it is much too important."

Her pale lashes lowered over her eyes as Mary remembered the reason for their marriage. Her warrior husband had failed to get his first wife with child. Success on the battlefield certainly did not herald success in the bedroom. Her great lord needed an heir, and just months after the death of his first wife, he had contracted with her father, hoping his child-bride would prove a good breeder. Mary shivered as she envisioned him running his hands down her legs, and pulling back her lips to check her teeth. She didn't want to be a broodmare. She wanted to love and be loved.

"I've left the curtains parted so I can see you," he explained in a hushed voice. "For tonight I am content just to look at you and hold you—to let you grow accustomed to having me near you."

Mary was dumbfounded. How could she be so fortunate? She had expected the very worst, knowing it was her duty to submit, if not willingly, then passively. Now she had a reprieve and she was indebted to this man by her side.

Still averting her gaze, Mary spoke quietly. "I thank you, my lord, for granting to me more than I deserve."

When she looked at him again, he was smiling, his eyes lit with approval. Charmed, she reached up and touched the dimple that graced his chin. The touch startled them both, but he caught her hand and reverently kissed her palm. Then he wrapped her in his arms, and drew her down in the bed, and just held her.

He was so warm, and after the first awkward moments, Mary felt so safe and good in his bear-like embrace. Hearts beating as one, the rising and falling of their breasts in unison, they snuggled together, and after such an eventful wedding day, fell asleep.

****

PRESENT DAY

"Mary, are you all right?" Alex's voice came to me as if from a deep, deep abyss.

I was in a daze, that nethermost world between full awareness and oblivion. Slowly I became aware again of my physical body. I was standing, hardly able to keep my feet. Had I been dreaming? Blinking, bemused by what I had just witnessed, I looked at my new husband's clouded gray eyes. Ironically, the vision of the young newlywed and her mighty medieval lord had been like clear crystalline.

Swaying, I struggled to regain my composure. What had I seen? I stared for a moment at the ceiling, the shaft of bright light from the window making mockery of my memories. I believed my senses, but what did the man in my vision, who tenderly held his new bride, have to do with me? Why would my brain be playing games with me this way? More importantly, why in the here and now would my heart seem so unwieldy with a yearning that weighted my very soul? I throbbed with longing, and glanced above me. In the silhouettes that danced across the ceiling, I saw the shadows of another time. I was bewildered and afraid.

Lowering my gaze, I realized an oppressive silence had settled over the room. Everyone was watching me. Solicitous, Gail's face loomed near mine. Alex gently gripped my wrist to take my pulse. His fingers were like an unholy conflagration upon my skin. I felt a flush mount in my cheeks. Never in the long years of my previous marriage nor in the hasty, giddy days of my youth had I wanted a man as much as I now wanted my husband. I wanted Alex, now—forever. It was an unexpected desire and it troubled me. Swallowing, I tried to ease the dryness in my mouth.

"Sit down, Mary," he ordered, propelling me backward until I felt the edge of a chair touch my legs.

Alex lowered me, holding my upper arms until I was seated.

"It's the strain," Gail said. "She's been under so much stress."

The minister offered me a glass of tepid water that I forced myself to sip.

"I'm okay," I said, lifting my chin with a boldness I failed to feel.

I handed the glass back to Alex, and our fingers touched again, sending sparks straight up and down my body. What was wrong? Why couldn't I control the ebb and flow of my emotions? My body told me one thing, but my mind denied it. I had committed myself to another loveless marriage, and although I needed the money, I was unsure now why I had married Alex. For better or worse, though, I would keep my bargain. It would be hard. I would pass my wedding night in a cold, solitary bed. The child-bride of my vision had experienced a finer honeymoon than I would have. I wanted so much more out of life.

Even with the breath of cool air from the air conditioner, the room was still stifling. Finding it much too bright, I lifted my arm to hide my eyes from the light of the sun strafing the room. Unfortunately, I couldn't hide from myself.

CHAPTER TWO

Mrs. Alexander Dominican. My new name had such an exotic sound. I repeated it under my breath as Alex's finely tuned BMW thrust me away from Louisville, Kentucky, and ever closer to my new home.

"Are you feeling better?" Alex's voice was like the contented purr of a cat.

I glanced at him, drawn by his classic, almost austere profile. Sunlight spiked through the driver's side window, and glimmered off his swept-back hair.

"Yes," I replied, but my wispy voice lacked conviction.

Our recent wedding ceremony had become a blur. I suppose most women remember their wedding day unclearly. Yet this one held a measure of unreality that still caused my head to spin. Not to mention the other thing that had happened to me today. That was even more inexplicable—and even more frightening. I tried again to understand what I had seen and felt in the minister's stuffy office. No reason came to me, so I accepted Alex's logic. Although I hadn't fallen, he said I had blacked out a few seconds, perhaps because of the heat.

A few seconds? Was that how long it took to witness a marriage night somewhere back in time?

Alex's gaze briefly darted my way. I caught it out of the corner of my eye and turned to him. His white knuckles gripped the steering wheel. Was he as nervous as I felt?

"I want to thank you for the sacrifice you're making."

13

The muscles in his jaw moved.

"You paid my bills. I'm grateful," I answered tensely.

"Yes, I know, but my part of the bargain is over and done with. Your part lasts forever." He seemed unsure of what to say. Glancing my way again, he added, "It won't be easy for you."

"Life isn't easy. We all do what we have to do."

"Oh, a philosopher as well as an expert kindergarten teacher," he drawled, a quirky smile animating his expression.

I didn't know how to take his remark. Was he trying to ease the tension? Or was he slamming my profession? "You can learn a lot of important things in kindergarten, things like sharing and obeying rules. Someone even wrote a book about it."

"You're too serious. I must remember that," he said, almost to himself. "There's so much I don't know about you, Mary."

When I stiffened, Alex covered my hand with his. The beat of his heart pulsed through his fingertips into my own. A peculiar, but not unwelcome, warmth sought the recesses of my femininity. I suppressed a shudder.

Gail had not wanted me to marry this man, her own cousin's widower. Although a strange misgiving coiled tightly in the pit of my stomach, I had never admitted my doubts to Gail. She was my best friend, not to mention my co-worker at Kinder Day, but I didn't want to confess that some undeniable force was driving my actions, controlling me in some inexplicable way. It was almost like that childish compulsion that had driven me to seek out Bill's bed. My desire for approval had gotten me nowhere but pregnant. That's why this new desire frightened me— frightened me so much that I had become defensive. Was I repeating the past?

"Well, I *am* going through with it. I have no choice," I had told Gail the night before the wedding.

"This isn't like you, Mary." My friend had been blunt. "I don't know why you're so hardheaded about this. It's as if you're on some sort of divine quest."

"As I've said before, his child needs a mother and I need my debts paid. It's a simple business arrangement, not a holy crusade."

"But to marry a man twelve years older, a man you don't even know."

"I do know him. Alex was your cousin's husband and my doctor's partner. He's kind and gentle. His intentions are honorable. He needs a mother for his child." My list of reasons sounded trivial even to my ears. Glancing away from her, I had mumbled, "Besides, I probably know him better than I knew Bill before I married him."

"And that was really a good marriage," she had retorted. "You rushed into that one too."

"I was pregnant."

"That's beside the point. Why can't he just hire you as a nanny? You're qualified. Why does he have to *marry* you?"

My gray cat Munster had curled around Gail's legs, his loud purr muffling the strain in her voice. But I had heard it. As if to quell her own anxiety, she had gathered Munster up in her arms and stroked his silky fur, running the palm of her hand along the silvery wisp that was his tail.

"Alex said something about never having had a mother himself. He wants one for his own daughter." My voice had sounded small.

"I still don't think you should do it."

"Oh, Gail, you worry too much." I had shrugged my shoulders.

I remembered our quarrel now as Alex squeezed my hand, drawing my attention back toward him. He tipped his head, as if he wanted me to look forward as well.

"Your new home—Marchbrook Manor."

That's all he said. The tinge of pride in the tone of his voice made me straighten as I followed his gaze. He squeezed my hand once more, before again gripping the steering wheel with two hands and turning it as we came around a sweeping, tree-lined curve. The massive house was breathtaking. Contemporary in design and built of stucco and Indiana limestone, Marchbrook Manor had high vaulted windows pointing skyward. Gray and impersonal, one wing angled to the left and lost itself beyond a tangle of shrubs. The house seemed out of place on the Kentucky hillside, a brusque trespasser where a homey cabin or four-column colonial should have stood.

Jan Scarbrough

"Alex, it's magnificent!"

"I thought you'd rather like it."

His smugness was somehow endearing.

"It's so large, and, well, English-looking, in a modern sort of way." I fought to express my reactions to Marchbrook Manor.

"That's because it's patterned after some eighteenth century replica of some medieval castle."

When I questioned his explanation with a skeptical raise of a brow, he smiled.

"Really, my father wanted something old-fashioned, but my mother favored the contemporary. They sort of compromised, but my father still insisted on naming the house as they do in England."

I had never lived in a house with a name. What had made me think I could carry this off?

When the car stopped in the wide circular driveway, Alex threw open his door and jumped out. I had a moment to collect my wits before he opened my door and handed me out. I looked askance at him, and wondered what other emotions hid behind his dark glasses. Alex's mouth was set into a straight line, a slight film of moisture beading on his upper lip. His clear-cut profile was magnetic, the upsweep of his raven locks an enticement. Yet he was in some way untouchable, holding himself away from me, even as he intimately grasped my fingers.

"Mrs. Garrity is the housekeeper and has been tending Elizabeth since her birth. The other help is Rufus. He sees to my father. Guy is an invalid and somewhat irritable. It's best not to disturb him, so you must stay out of his wing."

I nodded, receiving my instructions as an obedient servant might. But, I was a servant wasn't I? I had been bought and paid for.

For some reason, I felt vulnerable. Even with my fingers entwined with those of my husband, I longed for some unspeakable thing—something to fill my soul—something I had never found. And something I doubted Alexander Dominican would ever be able to give me.

Alex dropped my hand and removed his sunglasses. "You'll love Elizabeth."

Hearing the softness in his voice, I reminded myself

16

again what had impressed me about the man I had agreed to marry. He was a caring, competent physician who had helped me through a dark time in my life. Despite Gail's misgivings—once making a bargain, I stuck with it.

"Yes, I think I will," I answered with a smile.

Alex favored me with a smoldering look. Glancing away at the wide expanse of grass and the nearby house, I felt hot. The five o'clock sun was still sultry, and I regretted not removing my linen jacket. The fabric captured the warm air and held it intimately next to my body. Ever honest with myself, I realized the perspiration now staining my underarms had nothing to do with the heat of the June afternoon, and everything to do with the man I had just married.

"Good. Let's go find my daughter."

I followed Alex up stone steps to an oaken door of mammoth dimensions, darkened by weather and age. He opened it and ushered me inside, giving me a moment to acclimate myself to the expansive and unexpected grand entrance hall rising to an impressive forty-foot domed ceiling trimmed with aged wood. A vision of some remote past, its blinding white walls and pristine marbled floor tiles gave the room a special allure. What made the foyer even more extraordinary were the myriad tapestries adorning the walls. The ancient-looking hangings were vibrant multicolor depictions of medieval scenes—knights in shining armor, fire-breathing dragons and damsels in distress. The handiwork was superb, everything embroidered in what appeared to be fine stitches. To top it off, actual metal armored knights stood along the walls, giving the place the look of a set for an old Three Stooges movie. Although I had been in awe of the impressive room, when I visualized my favorite comics running from lifelike, ghostly armor—I had to laugh.

"What's so funny?" he asked, not unkindly.

"Your knights in shining armor. I just imagine them chasing Larry, Curly, and Moe."

He looked at me as if I'd lost my mind.

"Now, who's too serious," I quipped, feeling a flush in my cheeks.

"Touché."

17

His gray look held me spellbound. My heart seemed suspended in my breast, and then fell back into an unsteady beat.

"It looks as if your father won on the inside of the house," I remarked, trying to mask my reaction to him.

"Yes." He appeared sad. "Since my mother's death, my father has had a long time to decorate his own way."

I was sorry I'd reminded him of his mother who had died so tragically in a car wreck only a week after he was born.

"Dr. Dominican."

A sharp voice arrested our attention. We both turned to find the housekeeper holding baby Elizabeth. Mrs. Garrity wasn't what I had expected. Not the staid, gray-haired, motherly type of so many movies, she was lithe and angular with a cap of black hair styled in an old-fashioned pageboy. Her aquiline nose drew my gaze to her thin lips and shadowy eyes. Pale freckles splayed across the bridge of her nose. I guessed she was in her late forties.

"Oh, let me see Elizabeth." I stepped toward them, my hands outstretched.

Mrs. Garrity shouldered past me, and gave the child to her father. Taken aback by her rude actions, I was still too unsure about my role to offer comment. Instead I stared while Alex cradled his daughter in his arms. Pulling back the blanket, he grasped her tiny hand. I saw her fine fingers curl around one of his. The look in his eyes was soft satin. For a moment, I was jealous.

"Has she eaten well, today?" he asked.

What followed was an exhaustive description of the three-month-old's bowel movements, diaper changes, feeding and sleeping habits. *With this woman around, why does he need me?* As if he had heard my unspoken question, Alex turned to me, inclining his head in invitation.

"Come see your new stepdaughter."

Mrs. Garrity's stance suddenly went rigid. Her hostile black eyes bored into me as I came forward and took the wiggling bundle into my arms.

Elizabeth smiled at me. I guess it was a smile and not simply gas pains. I shifted her weight, supporting her

18

head carefully, and drew her close to my breast. She seemed to belong there—like the child I had lost and the children I could no longer conceive. Her bright eyes, blue like the aquamarine of the sea, penetrated my heart. I swallowed once in wonder, a thin cord of longing tying me to her.

Like many small children, Elizabeth's features were indistinct and undeveloped. She had a pug nose and a bow mouth and pencil-marked eyebrows. She didn't favor her father, but was stockier and fair. What hair she had was blond.

"She's beautiful, Alex," I said, glancing up.

"I'm quite partial, but I think so." I was gratified that his soft gaze now included me. "She's very like her mother." A far-off look came into his eyes.

"I see." Smiling uneasily at him, I noticed the housekeeper studying me through narrow eyes. I had to remember I was the interloper—that Alex had recently lost his wife.

"It's Elizabeth's bedtime." Her tone permitted no discussion.

Alex shifted his stance. I thought he acted bemused. He searched my face as if hunting for some long-lost thing, but pulled himself together quickly.

"Why don't you go on upstairs, and Mrs. Garrity will show you the nursery. After that, she can take you to your room."

"Won't you come with us?"

"No, I have to check with my answering service. I may need to go into the hospital this evening."

I was dismissed. As Alex stroked his daughter's cheek once more and then turned toward a dark doorway, I caught the fleeting glow of triumph in the housekeeper's eyes. I stiffened, and Elizabeth began to whimper.

"Let me have her."

Relinquishing the child into Mrs. Garrity's eager grasp, I followed dog-like behind her up a graceful, winding staircase carpeted in red.

"Mary!"

I stopped at the landing, and turned to find Alex clutching the polished banister and staring intensely at me. The distance between us was vast. Gazing down at

19

his black-clad physique, his princely features and raven hair, I wondered at the beauty of the man I had married. I too grasped the slick, mahogany banister, more to keep myself from going to him, than to steady myself.

"Yes?"

"It's early yet, but you've had an eventful day. I think I'll tell you goodnight now. I may be busy later."

"All right." My voice fell. "I'll see you tomorrow." He turned to leave. "Goodnight," I whispered as his broad back disappeared through a nearby door.

****

Out of the silky cocoon of half sleep, the wail of a hungry baby awakened me. Instantly, my adrenaline kicked in, and I jumped out of bed. I was surprised at the excitement I felt about something that mothers normally consider drudgery. Wrapping my white satin robe around my sleek, silk nightgown, I trotted across the darkened hall to Elizabeth's room. Gail had given me the negligee as part of my trousseau. I don't know why she had bothered.

A single nightlight pricked the darkness. I felt for the wall switch, and flicked on the overhead lights. No expense had been spared in the child's room. Colorful Mickey and Minnie characters decorated one wall while the two walls nearest Elizabeth's bed were painted a soothing amethyst. White wicker furniture added a feeling of femininity. I noticed the daintiness was deceptive, for all the furniture was sturdy and serviceable, able to withstand a growing child's needs. Because the baby's room was so far from the kitchen, a convenient cabinet hid two helpful appliances: a refrigerator and a microwave.

"My, my. We are just crying too much," I scolded the infant with mock gravity.

At the sound of my voice, she paused a moment, but seeing a strange face, began to complain even louder.

"Just hold your horses. You'll feel better in a minute." I started to change her. "What a mess you've made, sweetheart"

"I always change her on the table." A cold voice startled me.

Glancing over my shoulder, I noted the disapproving

20

face of Mrs. Garrity.

"This was more convenient," I explained.

She marched toward me, the flap of her flannel robe dropping open to reveal serviceable pajamas.

"She'll fall off the bed."

"No, the rail doesn't go down low enough."

"She doesn't like being changed in her bed."

Doomed to lose the power struggle, I backed off, letting the housekeeper finish the task I had started, and wondering again why I had been included in the household.

"Get the bottle in the refrigerator."

I raised my eyebrow at the command, but did as she bid, bringing the cold bottle from the small appliance in the corner.

Mrs. Garrity jerked her head to the side, indicating the nearby microwave. "Turn it on for forty-five seconds, put on the nipple, and then test it on your arm."

When I brought the prepared bottle to her, I refused to surrender it. "I'll feed Elizabeth and put her to bed."

The look she threw at me was as brittle as a January night. Angry, I raised my chin and held my ground.

"Elizabeth is used to me. She doesn't know you."

"But this is my job now," I reminded Mrs. Garrity, my back ramrod straight. Strained moments passed as we measured each other.

"Yes, I suppose it is." Her smile was twisted and condescending.

Round one won. Carefully taking Elizabeth from Mrs. Garrity, I settled down in the rocking chair while the housekeeper busied herself straightening up.

"The child's own mother never even got to hold her," she muttered. "This just isn't right. I don't know what the doctor is thinking of."

I held my peace. Offering Elizabeth the nipple, she took it greedily.

"Don't let her drink more than six ounces."

"All right."

She stood at the door like a drill sergeant. "Elizabeth will go back to sleep quicker if the lights are off."

Mrs. Garrity flicked the switch, throwing the room into darkness.

"Thank you for your help," I said, slowly rocking back and forth.

I thought I heard an offended 'humph' as she closed the nursery door.

Elizabeth Allison Dominican. I sounded the baby's name to myself. Christened for her grandmother and her mother, it was a big name for such a tiny child. I rested my head on the back of the chair. One pinpoint from the night light cut the blackness of the room. Mrs. Garrity was right. The soothing darkness and steady clack, clack of the rocking chair were comforting. And there was something primal and basic about the suckling child in my arms. Warm and cuddly, she depended on me. *Just as I depend on her.* The thought struck me like a dagger. I did rely on Elizabeth. Without her father's need for a mother, my debts would have gone unpaid. But there was something more fundamental about my need for this child. I could sense it as I pulled her nestling body to mine. I had lost a child once. Maybe this is what I had been seeking all my life. Maybe little Elizabeth would fill the void I knew to be in my heart. Shutting my eyes, I let the notion ramble around in my mind until I drifted off to sleep.

****

ENGLAND, 1327

He came to her dressed all in black. She couldn't see his face clearly, for his head was swathed in a hood. Some sort of cape with ragged ends fell over his shoulders. His jacket was velvet and he wore black hose and strange pointed shoes. She shivered in his presence, her heart hammering in her breast.

"Mary, I'm sorry to do this. You disobeyed me, and a man has the right under law to punish a wayward wife." His voice was firm.

She looked up at him with wide blue eyes. "Forgive me, my lord."

Nodding his head he acknowledged her repentance. "I know you're young, so newly come from your father's house. But I must teach you my ways. We live on border lands, and riding out is dangerous."

The phantom man raised his hand as if to strike her. "It goes against my grain to hit a woman—no matter that your stubbornness could have caused your death as well as those who serve you."

"No!" she cried. "Don't beat me!"

She knew he was right, but it troubled her to admit it. She shouldn't have ridden away from the castle, forcing her husband and his armed men to search for her. Luckily, they had arrived in time to deal with Welsh intruders who had surprised her. Unfortunately, her presence prevented the knights from finishing them off, and the raiders escaped. Her father would have beaten her for her willfulness. Mary expected the same from her husband.

"I won't hurt you, Mary. Not this time, but you must never disobey me again." The sound of his voice glided away like a dying summer day.

The man in the vision advanced toward her. Suddenly its character changed. No longer was it a tall, black-cloaked man, but a delicate woman with black-plaited hair. A thin veil covered her head, enhancing her reproachful eyes. Her light blue dress, the color of the cold winter sky, was long and tight, and trimmed in luxurious fur.

"Stupid child, you were lucky nothing worse came from your folly. You were wrong to go against our lord's word and disobey him." The woman's voice was severe.

"I don't like his ways," Mary said with a pout. "He angers me."

"Stupid child." As fast as the strike of a snake, the older woman raised her hand and struck Mary across the mouth. "My son may not punish you, but I will."

Mary reeled from the force of the blow. Her head spun and her mouth smarted, but she righted herself, pulling the shreds of her dignity around her. With square shoulders, she faced her mother-in-law, eyes bright with anger.

The woman must have recognized Mary's outrage, for she smiled her contempt. "It matters not if he angers you. You are here to do his bidding and produce his heir. What if you had been killed? You are bound in the eyes of God to be a good wife."

"I don't want to be a good wife. I don't love him." Mary was defiant.

23

"Love has nothing to do with it. Women love their sons. Rarely do they love their husbands." Her strong but graceful hands moved to Mary's shoulders. Shaking her hard, the woman's tapered fingers bit into the young girl's gentle flesh. "The sooner you learn to obey him and conceive his child, the better off you will be."

"That's crazy!" a voice protested from deep in the murky haze. "This whole thing is a nightmare! I want to wake up!"

The vision shifted once more. The hands touching Mary were now the work-worn hands of Gellis, carefully soothing her bruised lip with a decoction of knapweed and rose water.

Gellis' brown eyes were gentle. "Noble women such as you, milady, don't have much choice in the matter. You marry whom your father bids."

"It's so unfair. I hate my husband."

"Listen to me. I've known many women who often come to love their husbands and make good marriages, especially if their husbands are as generous as your lord. He is a good man. Remember, you told me how kind he was to you on your wedding night?"

"He isn't kind. Tonight he humiliated me."

"Tonight he honored you with Christian grace. He did not punish you, as is his right."

"Yea, but his mother did." Mary frowned. "I know she hates me."

Gellis began to loosen the plait in Mary's long blond hair. "She's jealous of your beauty and your youth."

Mary nodded in agreement. "Yet there's something more. There's another reason she hates me. I just don't understand."

"Don't worry about her spitefulness. Once you please your husband, you'll have nothing more to fear from her."

Sighing, Mary closed her eyes, allowing herself to enjoy her maid's attentions to her hair. "It would be much easier if I loved him or he loved me."

"So it was with your gracious mother when she came to your father's hall." Gellis bobbed her head at the memory.

"But my mother loved my father," Mary said.

"In time."

Cocking her head to the side, Mary smiled. Gellis comforted her troubled heart with such wise talk. Maybe it would be so with her and her own black lord, for he was a kind and forgiving man.

White mists swirled around the features of the two women. The figures faded away, into the gloom that was deep sleep, only to return in different forms. The blue-clad mother-in-law, disdain in her eyes, was there in the room with her. Turning to a black specter standing behind her, the lady spoke in a brittle whisper. Mary screamed, fearing her mother-in-law's presence as well as the loathing and triumph that now glittered in the woman's eyes.

CHAPTER THREE

I shot into full wakefulness like a bullet entering its target. Trembling, I wondered if I had cried aloud. I was wet with sweat. Fearful, I glanced down and found sweet Elizabeth still bundled against my breast, her mouth making sucking motions in her sleep. Her empty bottle lay on the floor.

Slowly the fear began to ebb, but not the clarity of my dream. As if suspended in time, the actors on the stage of my vision were tangible. There was something gut-striking about the young woman's anger and humiliation. And her fear.

Dazed and shaken, I took the baby back to her crib. Placing Elizabeth on her back, I covered her gently with a thin cotton blanket. She sighed, a tiny mewing sound hardly penetrating the hushed silence of the night. I clutched the railing. Palms moist, heart racing, I fought the darkness surrounding me. What was happening? I'd never before dreamed dreams like that one. It was like viewing act two in the play of a very unhappy life that had ended long, long ago. A life that somehow seemed like my own.

The thought snaking through my mind frightened me. Tentatively, I took a step backward. I felt if I stayed longer, I would somehow infect Elizabeth with my insane idea. Turning on my heel, I hurried from the room, the caricatures of Mickey and Minnie on the wall appearing to smile at my flight. My own bedroom was hardly a haven. Grossly feminine with Victorian lace curtains and small-flowered print wallpaper, the room was done in blue, and reminded me of the color of the medieval woman's dress. It wasn't my room at all. It had belonged to Allison.

I knew it as clearly as I knew the thread of fear and confusion that wove its way through my consciousness. This room was Allison's. The child I had cuddled was Allison's. I had married Allison's husband.

My hand halted on an inlaid brush that lay face up on the dressing table. Strands of pale gold hair tangled in its bristles. Allison's hair. Allison's brush. My throat dry, I licked my lips. But Allison was dead. Tragically, swiftly, hopelessly dead. Through the shadowy gloom, I glanced at my reflection in the ashen mirror. Dark circles smudged my eyes. The blue of my eyes seemed stony. My honey-colored hair hung in straight strands.

I picked up the brush, and drew its fine bristles through my own hair. I brushed and brushed the shoulder-length strands, the repetitive motions somehow stilling the race of my heart. Alex's present wife and Elizabeth's new stepmother, I had the right. This room was mine now....the brush mine. Dark blond hair mingled with fine gold curls, and I swayed as if in a trance.

Maybe the guilt I felt caused the dreams and the fear.

My palms wet from nervousness, the brush slipped soundlessly onto the plush azure carpet. I clutched the hard edge of the dresser, my fingers smearing the polished surface. How else could I explain the strange dreams? Guilt. It was an honest emotion—a human emotion—something I could grasp like the cold handle of the brush. It had no grotesque implication. Not like the thin thread of suspicion that the dreams had really happened.

****

Watery sunlight slipped through low, gray clouds and created a forlorn pattern on the white marble floor of Alex's medieval entrance hall. The promise of rain hung heavily in the air. If you don't like the weather in the Ohio Valley, all you have to do is wait twenty-four hours, I mused as I hesitated at the foot of the stairs and clung momentarily to the banister. The farcical suits of armor now seemed menacing to me, the multicolor wall hangings somehow portentous. Maybe the overpowering images of the foyer had affected my subconscious. Maybe that's why I fell asleep to dream of ancient times. Irrational guilt and the power of suggestion. However impractical, the explanations were plausible. Somewhat heartened by the thought, I straightened my shoulders and stepped across the glass-like floor, deliberately ignoring the real question. Why had my first vision come to me at the church?

The cozy aroma of coffee and bacon wafted from somewhere deep inside the house. I followed my nose, so to speak, and found my way to the large family kitchen. Shiny white appliances and stark white walls produced a severe effect. The only interruption to all that white were small touches of country blue in the cafe curtains, the crocheted place mats and napkins, and the ceramic floor tiles. I was left with the impression of coldness. Had Allison decorated the room in blue and white as she had decorated her bedroom? Did it reflect her personality or that of her husband?

"Good morning, Mary." Alex's voice was warm with welcome.

I blinked once, focusing on the elegance of his upraised hand and the dizzying gray of his eyes that studied me over a mug of steaming coffee.

"Good morning to you," I said, crossing the threshold.

For the space of a breath, our gazes held, and then I looked away to see Mrs. Garrity standing at the stove and Elizabeth safely strapped into an infant seat and propped up on the kitchen table.

"Up so soon?" I did not expect an answer to my question, but at my approach, the baby's whole body squirmed in welcome. I captured a waving hand and stroked its softness with my fingertip, silently glad Elizabeth remembered me.

"She awakens at 6:30 every morning." Mrs. Garrity refilled Alex's coffee mug. Her face was a stone mask.

Alarmed, I glanced at the wall clock to find it was 7:30. Only then did I glance back at my new husband. "I didn't hear her. I'm sorry."

"You needed your rest," he replied. "We have a

sophisticated intercom system, and I simply turned off the speaker to your room."

Feeling the flush of surprise on my cheeks, I murmured, "Thank you."

His gaze quickly strafed my face, and I read the silent "you're welcome" in his eyes, before he returned to his *Wall Street Journal*.

"You look tired. Did you sleep well?" He spoke from deep within the newspaper.

"I was up with Elizabeth," I answered, not wanting to tell him about my dream and the trouble I had going back to sleep.

Mrs. Garrity had her back to us. Water ran in the sink.

"Have a seat." Alex glanced up again and tipped his head toward the empty chair by his side.

Noting that Mrs. Garrity had not offered me coffee, and was not likely to, I first went to the fancy coffee maker, and poured some into a mug I found conveniently turned upside down on a nearby blue towel.

As I slid into my seat, Mrs. Garrity mumbled, "That belongs to Mrs. Dominican."

"I *am* Mrs. Dominican."

Angry, I glanced down at the mug to find "Allison" scripted in blue on its surface. Eyeing the housekeeper, I lifted the mug to my lips and defiantly sipped the hot liquid.

"Help yourself," Alex said again from behind the paper, unaffected by his housekeeper's rudeness. "Helena will fix you some eggs and bacon if you want."

Like hell she will, I thought. "No thanks. This will do fine." I reached for a homemade bran muffin and butter and the bowl of sliced cantaloupe.

As I slowly munched a muffin, I stared at the barrier of newspaper between us. Like some television lampoon of a married couple, we sat silently at the table—nothing to say to each other, as if we had been together twenty-five years. I found the analogy depressing. Licking the greasy butter off my fingers, I longed for something to say to my husband. I didn't know him well enough. I couldn't ask about his coming day, because I knew nothing about his routine. I didn't know how he spent his leisure time. I didn't even know what type of toothpaste he used.

The cantaloupe was sweet and juicy. I used my fingers, biting into the slippery slice, the juice dribbling down my chin. I grabbed the cloth napkin and wiped my mouth, noticing for the first time the entwined "A's" embroidered on one corner. Allison and Alex. I almost choked, feeling a flush of embarrassment rise in my cheeks.

To cover my dismay, I asked, "Are you going to work today?"

Silly question. Alex was dressed in a steel gray, three-piece suit. I thought him quite handsome.

"Umm," he muttered, lowering the newspaper and folding it neatly into place. He surveyed his watch. "Yes, and I'm going to be late."

He stood and I did the same. Ill-at-ease, I clutched the blue napkin like a lifeline. "I need to go to my apartment and collect some more things. My cat is 'home alone,' and I don't want the neighbors turning me in." My little joke sailed over his head. And he thought I didn't have a sense of humor.

"Why don't you wait until this evening, and I'll drive you there," Alex offered, his voice cool and neutral. "That way you can bring your car back."

"I suppose Munster can last a little longer. I gave him plenty of dry food and water before I left." I said with a faint smile.

"A cat! You're not bringing a cat into this house!" The strident voice of Mrs. Garrity reverberated throughout the kitchen.

Startled, I felt my hackles rise in defense. I turned on the prudish woman. "Alex knows about my cat. He has no problem with me bringing Munster here."

"Dr. Dominican, surely you aren't going to let this woman bring a cat into your house."

"It's her house too, Helena."

"But Mrs. Dominican is allergic to cats." Mrs. Garrity's eyes flashed hatred.

A chill trickled down my spine. She spoke of Allison in the present tense.

Alex used his best bedside manner. "There's a new Mrs. Dominican now. You know Allison died in March." I watched in fascination, happy to have him champion my cause.

"But the baby. She may be allergic."

"Munster won't get around Elizabeth," I volunteered. "I'll keep him in my room."

"Cats smother children."

"Oh, my gosh! You believe that old wives' tale?"

Alex stayed me with his hand. Sparks kindled where he touched my arm, igniting a glow in my heart.

"Helena, I have given Mary permission to bring her cat. I want her to feel at home here."

The subject was closed. My side won. Mrs. Garrity understood and spun around to face the sink. A skillet clanked. Steam rose from the sudsy dish pan.

"Thank you," I said and followed Alex as he left the room.

He stopped to pull a rain coat and umbrella out of a closet. Turning to me, the gray in his muted eyes was unreadable.

"Helena, Mrs. Garrity, is a very caring woman," he told me. "She means well and was very loyal to my first wife."

I nodded, feeling I had been reprimanded. *Get along with Mrs. Garrity.* I made a mental note.

"When will you be home?" I asked as he paused at the door to put on his coat.

"I'm not sure. Babies don't keep schedules. Sometime before dinner, I hope." His hand on the doorknob of the ornate wooden door, he paused for one last look at me. "Get some rest. You look tired."

I nodded.

"When you feel like it, explore the house, but like I said, stay out of the east wing."

"All right."

"Take care of yourself."

I nodded again and he was gone, damp morning air blowing in with the opening and closing of the door.

Damn. I hated this ambivalent sensation. It was as if I were a desperate housewife, seeking the approval of a detached and unloving husband. Well, I was, wasn't I? Alex didn't love me. He had loved Allison. I swallowed hard and stared at the closed front door.

31

But I refused to be desperate. Never that. I wasn't helpless either, and I didn't need to be talked to like a school child. After all, I quite efficiently handled a classroom of five-year-olds every day. I'd even handled Bill. He'd never made me feel this way—unsure of our relationship maybe, but never unsure of myself. *Get a grip. You asked for this. It's just that hateful woman, the newness of the situation, the strangeness of the dreams.*

My gaze careened over the knights in shining armor. I breathed deeply of the scent of the summer rain and the muskiness of antiquity. This foyer spooked me. I tossed a stray strand of hair from my eyes and stepped quickly across the vastness of Alex's entrance hall. After all, I had a baby to tend, and a house to explore.

****

Mrs. Garrity assured me that Elizabeth slept from nine o'clock until noon every day. If she awakened, she could be heard from any place in the house through Alex's elaborate intercom system. So, after I put Elizabeth down for her morning nap, I felt free to look around.

Aside from the kitchen and Alex's library, the main floor appeared to be a curious mixture of various sitting rooms all emanating from the central medieval entrance hall. One was especially poignant, for I guessed it to be Allison's retreat. Decorated in pale blue and crisp white, the color she seemed to favor, it was a delicate room. Lace curtains restrained the view from the outside. I pulled one back to find a rose garden swathed in the gloom of the rainy day. The furniture was a mishmash of styles, warm cherry and pristine wicker. I particularly liked the window seat with its plush cushions and throw pillows. I envisioned the former Mrs. Dominican sitting there on rainy days. Did she read? Or was she into needlework as the embroidered napkins suggested? What kind of person was Allison? What qualities had Alex loved about her?

The second floor of Alex's house contained eight bedrooms, only three of which were occupied. My room was across from Elizabeth's, and Alex's was next door to mine. When I realized I had entered his room, I quickly retreated, flustered, feeling an unwanted trespasser. Tight-lipped, I walked the cool and dimly lit hallway. The sumptuous carpet muffled my steps. At the end of the hall, a closed door taunted me. The east wing. Off limits. I paused and glanced around. Tired of feeling out of control, I longed to take charge of my life again. In my marriage to Bill, so many things had often been out of my power. Past frustrations, not yet buried and put to rest, tempted my sense of honor. Ever sensible, I almost turned away. But I couldn't. Something beckoned to me from behind the closed door, something I yet again had no control over.

Like an unruly schoolgirl, I dared myself to disobey. Hesitating, my hand wavered near the doorknob. I pulled the lower part of my lip in and worried with it. When I touched the cold brass, a salient sensation of dread touched the back of my neck. I suddenly felt imperiled. My damp fingers fumbled with the knob. Abruptly, without giving myself more time to consider, I turned it. But it was locked. Then and only then did I realize I had been holding my breath. Expelling it slowly, I withdrew a step...right into the solid but yielding flesh of a human body.

Needless-to-say, I jumped like the long-legged and much celebrated jumping frog of Calaveras County. My heart threatened to leap out of my chest as well. Whirling around to find a small, hunchbacked man peering up at me, I stifled a scream. The little man's oversized head and bulbous red nose were hideous. His hands and feet seemed too big for his tiny body. He wore a red jersey turtleneck shirt and dark trousers. When he removed his stocking cap, revealing a bald head, to sweep me a bow with great flourish and ceremony, I thought I glimpsed a speculative spark in his dark eyes.

"Who are you?" I croaked, watching the gnome-like hunchback in horrid fascination.

"That's Rufus."

I jumped again at the imperious sound of Mrs. Garrity who appeared from out of the gloom.

"He doesn't speak or hear."

"I'm sorry." It was a stupid thing to say, but right about then I wasn't in a position to sound smart.

A gap-toothed grin greeted my rueful glance. Rufus cast an impudent wink my way, stuck his cap back on his head, and mutely jostled past me. At the closed door, he produced an old-fashioned key from his pocket, unlocked it and disappeared within. Dismayed, I gaped open-mouth after him, hard-pressed to know what to think.

"You were told not to go into the east wing." Mrs. Garrity's sharp indictment annoyed like a paper cut.

"I didn't." I turned to face her, a guilty edge to my voice.

"But you tried. I saw you. Don't you know not to go against Dr. Dominican's wishes?"

What could I say? She was right. I had tried to enter the east wing. I swallowed slowly, appraising my accuser.

"Speak up. I'm talking to you, girl."

Déjà vu. A French expression. It suddenly took on new significance. I felt like the young wife of my recent dream, berated by her new husband's hellish mother. My whole body began to tingle as I looked at Mrs. Garrity. Her figure blurred as my eyes refused to focus. I wobbled, wondering if my legs were going to collapse from underneath me. Deliberately, as if I climbed the hard edges of a rock cliff, I pulled myself back. Mrs. Garrity's stern form came clearly into view. I lifted my chin.

"For one thing, I'm not a girl," I told her, my tone as hard as that rock cliff. "I'm twenty-six years old. I'm Dr. Dominican's wife, not his servant. You'll do well to remember that."

With my cloak of defiance around me, I stalked back to my room, eager to regain my only sanctuary in this bizarre household. How ironic I sought refuge in Allison's room, a room I had last night considered alien.

It wasn't such a bad room. Allison's bedroom contained a measure of femininity and quiet grace. The regal canopy bed with its elegant paneled headboard was luxurious. Soft azure-colored fabric flowed to the floor and matched the quilted floral bedspread and the color of the carpet. A generous triple dresser was antiqued in a fruitwood finish along with its tri-fold mirror. In another corner stood an armoire topped with an arrangement of blue and white silk flowers. Two companion Queen Anne chairs completed the decor, making the room plush and cozy.

I circled the bedroom, flicking on every light I could find. Tired of dark hallways and lurking hostile servants, I frowned at the glaring lights. No, I wouldn't second-guess my decision to marry. I'd just try to make the best of it, and make this room and house my own.

With that thought in mind, I decided to unpack. That's when I found my suitcase inside the closet. The outside had been slashed, shreds of navy canvas pulled from the sides. Incredulous, I couldn't move, couldn't react. Drawing a deep breath, I knotted my hands. Who could have done such a thing? And why? Finally able to kneel beside the suitcase, sweet smelling cologne overwhelmed me. My clothing was soaked with it. The fragrance was foreign to me. Fear prickled my skin. I licked my lips. Mrs. Garrity...or Rufus?

I straightened. A cathartic stab of ire purged my fear, and I sought out the irrepressible Mrs. Garrity.

"Did you have anything to do with ruining my luggage and belongings?"

She stood at the kitchen sink peeling potatoes. When she turned to face me, her eyes hard, her hand holding a paring knife, the force of her hatred struck me like a punch in the mouth.

"What do you mean?"

"Someone slashed my suitcase and went through my things," I told her, watching her dark eyes as I spoke.

"Why would I do something like that?"

"I don't know. I'm asking you."

"Well, I certainly have no reason to disturb your belongings. Are you sure you aren't mistaken?"

I felt defensive. Her quirky smile and smirk questioned my sanity. I stiffened. "Someone ravaged my things. Maybe it was that Rufus."

"You don't know anything do you?" Her remark cut like her paring knife.

She turned her back on me, dismissing me as unimportant. I made up my mind to speak to Alex.

"Thanks to someone in this house, I'm going to have to do laundry. Where is it?"

She answered me by jerking her head toward a closed door. This one wasn't locked, and when I opened it, a cool, musty smell assaulted me. Black as an exposed sepulcher, the gaping opening to the basement beckoned me. As a raw-edged sensation stabbed at my stomach, I shut the door firmly and retreated from the housekeeper's lair to gather my clothing.

Something as mundane as washing clothes should have calmed my nerves, which were vibrating like a bowstring, but not today. Taut with anxiety, I finished my task in the dark shadows of the basement, and then casting about for something else to do, I wandered into what appeared to be Alex's office or library. Countless leather-bound volumes graced the bookshelves. The room smelled of rich books, quality bourbon and fragrant wood from the unlit fireplace. Roaming the library, my fingers strayed along the edge of his mahogany desk. I touched the back of a corduroy, easy chair and slightly moved its ottoman with my foot. Reading glasses lay on top of the end table next to a book that was open and turned upside down. Preoccupied with my thoughts, I picked up a leather-bound book, kept the place with a finger, and rotated it in my hands. *The Three Edwards, Thomas B. Costain.* A history of England. The fourteenth century. The Middle Ages. Wonderful. History had been my least favorite subject in college.

Settling into the cozy chair and propping up my feet, I relaxed for the first time that day and gazed at Alex's domain. It was a man's room. A sanctuary. I belonged here. I knew it as clearly as I knew my name. I tilted my head back against the corduroy cushion. This was Alex's chair. This was where he came to get away, to read. And he needed reading glasses. The thought was somehow comforting, making him seem more human, more approachable. I smiled to myself, and opened the book at Alex's place. From what I'd seen of his house, I expected Alex to be reading a history text. Fighting drowsiness, I glanced down at the page and as the shadows lengthened in the room, began to read.

****

"Dr. Dominican won't be home for dinner."

I wrenched awake, my neck stiff and my senses dimmed. The leather-bound book toppled to the floor.

Blinking at the shadowy form of Mrs. Garrity, I asked. "When will he be home?"

"He's not sure. He has an emergency. He said for you to go ahead and eat."

I sat up and put my feet on the floor. "We were to go

over to my apartment." I couldn't keep the disappointment from my voice.

She seemed to gloat. "Well, you just won't be able to, will you?" Mrs. Garrity turned to leave. At the door she turned back and leveled a sharp glance my way. "I've already changed Elizabeth and fed her supper. She's in her room."

Great. She had thwarted me again, using my own inexperience against me. As the housekeeper left the room, I released a long breath of frustration. Well, at least I hadn't had another dream. The emotions I felt were today's emotions, not something left over from an over-active imagination.

Rising, I stood motionless. What would I do about Munster? He had to be fed. Moving slowly, trying to get my bearings, I went to Alex's desk. How would Gail respond if I called? We hadn't parted in the most amicable of terms. But it couldn't be helped—I needed to talk to her. Taking a deep breath, I dialed my friend's phone number.

"Gail, it's Mary." Clinging to the receiver, my fingers cold, I clenched my teeth and waited for her reply.

She hesitated a moment. "How's it going, kid?"

Gail's voice was warm liniment. Until I heard it, I had not fully realized the isolation of my situation. How could I tell her about the dreams, the hateful Mrs. Garrity and the strange character, Rufus. How could I explain my confusion about my husband?

"Oh, it's a little slow. I'm just learning my way around."

I must have transmitted my tension, for she paused again before replying, "It is a big house."

I took a deep breath. "Elizabeth is a darling. I'm enjoying her. I think we'll get along fine." I hoped my tone sounded brighter.

"I haven't seen her lately, not since shortly after her birth."

And Allison's death. Gail didn't have to say it. I knew what she was thinking.

"Look, I have a favor to ask."

"Sure."

"Do you mind going by my apartment and feeding

Munster? I'm stuck here without my car, and Alex won't be home this evening."

"Sure," Gail said again. "Now you know why Allison was often unhappy. Alex's practice kept him away from home a lot."

Her words hung heavily between us. But he loved Allison, I thought. I had seen him at the funeral home. He had looked like death.

"In a few months, I'll have enough to keep me busy. Elizabeth won't be an infant forever."

"Um, I guess not."

"What did Allison think of Mrs. Garrity?" I asked, realizing Gail was trying to mollify me.

"She loved her. Mrs. Garrity was very loyal to Allison."

That confirmed Alex's comment, and perhaps explained the housekeeper's reaction to me.

"Did Allison wear perfume?" I was almost afraid to ask.

"Sure, why?"

"I think I've been given her room. Some of her things are still in it. I just wondered." I tried to sound nonchalant. "Was there anything special about it?"

"About what?"

"Her perfume."

"Oh, I dunno. It was overpowering, as if she used too much of it."

"What did it smell like?"

"A summer flower garden—really sweet."

I closed my eyes and let the revelation hum through my mind. Had the sweetly smelling perfume in my suitcase been Allison's? Who had put it there? And why? Gail promised to run my errand for me and said goodbye. My arms were dead weights as I placed the receiver back on its cradle.

I needed to pull myself together. The emotional roller coaster of the past two days had bankrupt my practicality. Drawn by the need to reestablish my sanity, I went upstairs and found Elizabeth awake in her crib. She waved her tiny hands, her eyes focused on her fingers. When I picked her up, she squirmed and gurgled.

"Hello, sweetheart. Did you miss me?"

Elizabeth smiled her vague smile and puckered her button mouth. I drew her to my breast. She was warm and vital, the promise of a life just begun. This thought somehow stabilized me and brought me back to reality. I sat in the chair and began to rock. Elizabeth liked the motion, simulating the movement of her mother's womb. A mother who never saw her. A mother who died so tragically. I rocked and pondered my life, and the short life of Allison, the first Mrs. Dominican, as I cuddled her small child in my arms.

CHAPTER FOUR

Like a molten cascade, hot water splashed over my naked body, surrounding me in soothing steam. I liked the enveloping steam, and the feeling it gave me that the world was far, far away. I stood a long time lost in the water, just letting it wash over my hair and face and soak away the tension that knotted my neck muscles. With my eyes shut against the deluge, my head bowed, I opened my mouth to breathe.

I wished I really could block out the world, disappear into a vapor of warmth and comfort. But it wasn't possible. Not since my marriage two days ago, I thought, as I stepped forward a bit, poured lavender shampoo into my hands, and lathered my hair.

Why hadn't Alex come home? Since I planned to let him know about my slashed suitcase, I was jittery about seeing him again. What would his reaction be if I accused his employees? Whose side would he take? Not mine, I supposed. But, doggone it, this is my home now. As I rinsed my hair, I knew I needed to assert myself so I could establish my place in the household.

Just as I needed to assert myself on this hair on my legs, I thought with disgust. Reaching for the shaving cream and plastic shaver, my mind wandered away from my own problems. When had women started shaving their legs? I guessed those medieval women I'd read about in Alex's history book didn't have to worry about that sort of thing. After all, their long skirts covered their lower limbs. Did women back then even bathe? If they didn't, how unpleasant for them. A long, hot shower certainly could soak away a person's melancholy.

Melancholy. Such an old-fashioned word. But that's how I felt. Melancholy, as if some great entity had been carved away from my inner being. I didn't understand my feelings. Perhaps it was the strange dream I'd had the night before. Or the housekeeper's hostility or little Rufus. Perhaps it was because, no matter my determination to be assertive, I continued to feel not in control.

Damn. I jerked as I whittled a chunk out of my leg with the razor. Couldn't I even shave my legs without doing myself bodily harm? Turning off the flow of water, I pulled back the shower curtain and grabbed a towel. The heavy cotton fabric felt good to my body as I dried myself. I wrapped another towel turban-like around my hair, and then I tore a small piece of toilet paper from the roll and stuck it on my bleeding leg.

Still naked, I padded out of my bathroom into Allison's blue and white room. Sheathing myself in a robe, I crossed to the dresser, unfettered my hair, picked up a comb and hauled it through the long, wet strands. I wished its blond color were not the color of honey, but pale gold like gossamer. Like Allison's hair?

There I go again. Making myself sick with this brooding fascination about Alex's dead wife. I resolved to put her out of my mind. Taking the heavy bulk of my hair, I coiled it into a knot, holding the pins in my mouth until I fastened the hair into place. Cocking my head slightly, I looked at the angle of my high cheek bones and the curve of my jaw. With all my hair pulled back, my face seemed thinner and more angular, my nose straighter, and my blue eyes deeper set. To my estimate, I wasn't beautiful, but I did possess a certain lanky stature and a sophistication that had always stood me well in my teaching career.

Before I finished my hair, a high whine pierced my consciousness. As the noise grew in intensity, it suffocated all other sounds. I scowled at my reflection in the mirror. *No. I'm not asleep. This can't be happening again.* Feeling so weightless, as if my body was buoyed on a placid lake, my vision suddenly blurred. Intense colors, like a child's fingerpainting, smeared in front of my eyes. The room quivered...

****

Water poured roughly over Mary's head. "Ouch! That's hot!"

"You said you wanted it hot," Gellis said, not minding the objections of her mistress.

Rarely did Mary get a bath. The last time had been before her wedding day. She luxuriated in the feel of the warm water upon her skin. Gellis lifted her heavy hair, and used a linen cloth to rub the lavender-scented soap across her shoulders. She stroked in circles, loosening the tension of Mary's muscles and restoring her body to its youthful glow.

"Ah, Gellis. You do that so well," Mary murmured, growing drowsy.

The serving woman abruptly shoved the cloth into Mary's hands. "We've no time for you to idle," she said, her voice mellow but firm. "Our lord's mother is come to dinner."

With a sigh, Mary finished washing the lower parts of her body with soap her mother-in-law had recently brought from London. For a moment she had forgotten. Now the misgiving returned. Her lord's mother had made it clear the reason for her marriage. Nine months later and still no baby, Mary sensed she had failed although her husband had not made it an issue.

She was sorry she hadn't conceived, for she had come to regard her husband with warmth and wished to give him what he wanted. He wasn't a bad man. In fact, he was better than most. She had been lucky in that. She just wished he'd look upon her with a little love. Yes, her husband had honored her most graciously in many ways, but only because of the services she was expected to provide. She wished he respected her for herself.

Mary stood up in the wooden tub, the water sloughing down the length of her body. Gellis, her round face pleasant, brought a linen towel and began rubbing her dry. As Mary allowed her servant to minister to her, she chided herself for such wishful thinking. She had a nice life, more pleasant in fact than she had expected. Why want more? A woman's lot in life was to be submissive to her husband, see to his household and bear his children. It was unnatural to expect more from a man. "Love" was a word associated with the minstrels and romantic poetry. Few real women found it in marriage. Eleanor of Castile had been so loved by her husband, but she had been a queen who had given her lord many children. It was too much to envision for a mere noblewoman like herself.

Mary stepped out of the tub, aware only of a deep sadness within her heart. Telling herself to be thankful for what she had didn't help. Her lord had only scolded her once, and that early on in their marriage. She had been wrong and willful, and didn't hold the reprimand against him any longer, but something was missing from her life, something that pierced her being like the icy honed blade of a knife. Mary sighed, fearing the emptiness inside herself would never be filled.

"Milady!" Gellis spoke sharply. She had brought Mary's shift, and having stripped the towel from her hands, glimpsed her naked body.

Startled, Mary watched Gellis reverently run calloused hands over her slightly rounded belly. Her servant's warm fingers felt good and strong upon her skin.

"I seem to be putting on weight, and I haven't been eating well lately," Mary said.

Her brown eyebrow raising in speculation, Gellis asked, "When were your last monthly courses?"

Mary's own eyes widened. "Do you think…"

"Of course, silly lass. Your lord's been in full attendance to you." She let the implication hang in the air.

Catching her servant's hands, Mary squeezed them. "Oh, Gellis, can it be? I had wondered about being late, but was afraid to hope." Her heart soared like a bird taking flight.

The realization she was probably with child pleased her. She allowed Gellis to dress her as she quietly savored the thought. Over her shift, Gellis helped her put on a kirtle, an undergown that fitted her figure closely to the hips, falling from there in a wealth of elegant folds. The sleeves were very tight, but practiced as she was, Gellis took only a brief time to button them from wrist to elbow.

How soon would her figure expand? She would have to make another gown.

Mary's surcoat was saffron with exaggerated sleeves attached at the elbow. They hung three feet toward the floor and were banded with fur. When her hair was dry, Gellis brushed it until it sparkled. She parted the heavy locks at the center of Mary's head and confined them in plaits over her ears. Then she covered the plaits with an ornate net, and topped her head with a delicate veil.

"Beautiful," Gellis murmured, clearly proud of her young charge.

Mary smiled, feeling suddenly excited. Like a child who can't keep a secret, she felt as if she'd burst. "Should I tell my lord?" she asked Gellis, for the woman was a trusted friend as well as a servant.

"Yea." Gellis nodded. "What could be better with his lady mother dining at the same table? You must take full advantage of this public announcement."

"Oh, Gellis," Mary whispered, knowing she spoke the truth. Then hugging the older woman to her breast, she went down to the great hall.

The servants had set up the trestle tables and covered them with cloths. Places had been laid with steel knives, spoons, dishes for salt and silver cups. Trenchers, a thick, day-old piece of bread, and wooden bowls were in place to receive the food.

This efficiency was her mother-in-law's work, Mary knew. The old woman had a way of taking over, ordering Mary's people around, as if she were still the lady of the house. Mary stiffened with anger as she glanced to the head table. In most households, a dowager was sent away to live. She wouldn't be allowed to remain, a thorn in her daughter-in-law's side.

Her husband permitted his mother to stay, so Mary's predicament couldn't be helped. *Yet.* Mary lifted her chin high, and walked among the tables down the length of the room, greeting people as she went. She had grown quite popular among the castle folk, for she was young and beautiful. The former lady had been ill and sour because of her barrenness. Tucking her secret close to her heart, Mary smiled as she looked up to the head table where her lord sat speaking with his mother. She had done what her predecessor could not, and she was proud.

When Mary approached, her lord rose from his great chair and handed her around the table where she shared his seat. Still attractive for a woman her age, her mother-in-law looked beautiful in her sumptuous gown and wimple of soft blue. She smiled at Mary and inclined her head in mock welcome. Mary wondered why the woman's smile only stained her lips, never touching her eyes.

She proudly returned the smile as the procession of servants bearing food began. First the pantler brought the bread and the butter. He was followed by the butler who poured the wine and beer. As her lord attended her meal—breaking the bread, serving it to her, and passing the cup—the hall buzzed with the latest gossip.

"So Mortimer was tried and hanged at Tyburn?" her husband questioned his mother.

The lady had recently come from a trip to London and so was the source of all news. She nodded in response. "They say Edward has banished his mother from court. How Isabella will hate it," she said with a malicious snort.

Her son cut the roast with a knife, and as was customary, offered a piece to Mary. "Edward is truly in charge. I am glad."

"Yes, they say he helped get his men into Nottingham Castle, but refused to watch as they captured Mortimer. He honors his lady mother, even though they say she had something to do with his father's death."

The rumors did not interest Mary. It was enough to know handsome Edward Plantagenet was now in control of England. Hopefully, he would prove a better ruler than his ineffectual father. Mary's everyday flow of life would not change because of the politics of the new king and his relatives. More momentous to her young existence was the discovery of her own fertility. She couldn't help the smile that curled her lips as she sipped wine from the cup.

"Mary, is all well? You only nibble at your food." Her husband's voice was kind, but concerned.

Raising her gaze to look into his gray eyes, Mary grinned shyly. "Yea, my lord husband. All is truly well with me." She lowered her lashes, and coyly inclined her head. "My condition has affected my appetite."

"What condition?" His tone was hushed.

"I suspect I'm with child."

Mary was suddenly the center of attention, the previous gossip forgotten. Her lord took her hand into his great grasp and sat silently a moment. She knew his first wife had not once suspected the fact, and so hearing her words seemed to have taken his speech away.

"Is it true?"

Mary nodded. "Gellis thinks so, and I have failed to have my courses."

He squeezed her hand, his finely chiseled features alight with anticipation. "You have given me happiness, my lady. Not only are you a gentle and good wife to me but a kind mistress to my people, now you have granted me my greatest gift."

Still holding her hand, he announced to the assembled hall the happy news. The joyousness that erupted around Mary was rightfully loud and lengthy. Amid the comical jugglers and minstrels singing her praise, Mary glanced smugly at her mother-in-law who sat pale and silent, her bejewelled hand gripping a wine goblet.

Yea, you have something to fear, Mary thought, raising her goblet in a mock salute to her husband's mother. *Perhaps you shall be sent away just as the king sent away the hapless Isabella.*

Turning back to her lord, who still held one of her hands in his, Mary cherished her fruitfulness to herself. If she couldn't have his unconditional love, she would have her husband's approval. Perhaps that and the child growing in her womb would fill the void she knew to be in her heart. Mary smiled to herself in hope.

****

I blinked once again at my reflection in the mirror. My limbs felt unwieldy and lethargic. Even standing, clutching the wooden edge of the dresser, I was oddly uncomfortable, the happiness of the woman of my dream still swirling mist-like in my mind. For the first time, it all seemed so strangely real and viable, as if I had experienced it in another life.

Tangled Memories

A thread of unexpected fear wove its way through my mind. What was happening to me? I hadn't been asleep. How had I envisioned those images from the past? My past? *Certainly not.* Sweat prickled the palms of my hands. I didn't believe in reincarnation. That kind of new age stuff wasn't real. I glanced down at my rounded breast peeking through the gap in the terry cloth robe. Jerking the robe around myself, I wrapped it and my arms around my body.

The book. That was it. I'd been looking at Alex's history book. That made sense. Perfect sense.

Except that the dream had been about the same young Mary of my previous visions.

Heart pounding, my breath coming in gasps, I cursed myself for my delusions. Swaying, I fought my body. I fought my mind. I was like an animal caught in a trap of my own weakness. Slowly, I steadied my emotions. My breathing stilled. When sufficiently under control, I lowered my arms, my unknotted robe falling open again. I balled my fists at my side.

Faraway in the blackness of the hushed night, I heard a car door slam. The heavy front door opened and closed. Alex's shoes made brittle sounds on the unyielding floor of the foyer. Moments prowled past as I waited for his footsteps in the hallway. I shut my eyes, and opened my fists when I realized he wasn't coming to his room. Deliberately, I dropped my robe from my shoulders and stared at my naked body. Unbidden, my hands strayed to my abdomen, caressing the flat, muscular contours, my fingers touching my body like ebullient bubbles in a soothing bath.

I had to go to him. My reasons were practical. Alex needed to know one of his servants had slashed my suitcase. Deep in my heart I knew I sought him as a mewling kitten seeks a mother cat. My reason, my need, was axiomatic—obvious.

Safely encased in sensible long pajamas, slippers and tightly knotted robe, I left my room and traversed the upstairs hallway and front entrance hall to cautiously push open the door of Alex's library. A lone light illuminated the room.

"Come in, Mary."

Much as I had imagined, he sat in his easy chair, long legs stretched out before him. His discarded suit coat draped the back of a chair. Tie loosened, cuffs unbuttoned, Alex looked up at me as I took a tentative step forward. He was wearing his glasses, the history book open in his lap.

"I read some of your book today," I told him as I crossed the room.

"Really? I was wondering who had moved it." He took off his glasses and lay them on the table.

"I'm sorry if I disturbed your things. I tried not to lose your place." Carefully balanced I sat on the edge of the sofa several feet away, my robe tightly screened my legs and my torso.

His smile was tired. "No. I don't mind. It's your house too."

I wanted to protest that it wasn't my house. Although I tried telling myself it was, it wasn't. *Not yet anyway.*

"Do you read much history?"

Alex closed the book, and moved his feet to the floor. Leaning forward in the chair, elbows on his knees, he rubbed his eyes. Spellbound, I watched his graceful fingers make circular motions.

"When I get the chance." He glanced up at me.

Fixing my gaze on his smoky, gray one, I longed to tell him about my dreams and strange waking visions. I wondered what it would be like to feel his arms around me, comforting me, telling me not to worry. But I couldn't expect that. Not now. Probably never.

"I was never much interested in history," I said.

Still leaning forward, he stared at me with fervent eyes. "Too dull and boring, huh?"

I inclined my head to acknowledge his insight. "I prefer a heart-stopping mystery or a juicy romance."

"Well, I imagine you'd like Thomas Costain. His books read like novels."

"I never have much time to read."

"I know what you mean. With all that's gone on these last few months, it's been hard to find the time." Alex's gaze wandered away. His fingers locking in a pensive clasp, he paused several moments. "This is the second time I've read this particular book." His remark was offhanded.

I didn't know how to evaluate his mood. "Really? Why's that?"

My question hauled his attention back to me. His eyes lightened as he smiled reflectively. "I don't know. I just like the time period."

"Tell me about it." I wanted to hear more of his voice.

"Let's see. It's about the three King Edwards of England who lived more than six hundred years ago." He picked up the text as if to refresh his memory. "There was Edward I, the soldier king, who loved his beautiful wife Eleanor of Castile. She bore him fifteen children, and when she died, Edward raised crosses along the route of her funeral procession."

Long cords of suspicion tightened around my heart. I swallowed, my gaze never leaving Alex's fascinating lips as he continued to speak.

"Edward II, the first Prince of Wales, was murdered by servants of his wife Isabella, and her lover Roger Mortimer. Edward III arrested the infamous Mortimer, hanged him at Tyburn, and banished his mother, Isabella, from court."

The actors in my dreams had spoken about these people. Disconcerted, I plucked at the fabric of my robe as Alex's deep and vibrant voice tormented me.

"This youngest Edward was the victor of Crécy and Poitiers, battles that proved common English soldiers with longbows were better bets when facing mounted French knights."

His words left me dazed and shaken, as the black whirlpool of my mind fought for control. Now I understood. *If these kings and queens had actually existed, maybe my elusive actors had lived as well.*

"Mary, are you okay?"

Alex's query cut into my reverie. Bemused, I let my gaze slid over his face. He had lapsed into silence and studied me with curiosity. I wavered like a child on a seesaw.

"Mary?"

My cold fingers fumbled with my robe. I didn't understand my recent fantasies. I needed time to think.

My vision blurred. My irregular breathing troubling me, I felt my face drain of color. Afraid I'd slip into another trance, I battled back. Rallying, I seized upon the reason I had intruded on Alex's privacy.

"Someone took a knife and slashed my suitcase today." My quiet and controlled complaint hit him like a summer storm.

His gaze never left mine as he climbed to his feet. "How did that happen?"

"I don't know." I straightened, my voice rising. "I thought maybe one of the servants."

"No." He spoke sharply, swinging away from me and seeking the cold fireplace. He rested an arm on the mantle.

My heart shuddered for him. He looked so exhausted and world-weary. An irresistible rope pulled me toward him, but I remained seated.

"Mrs. Garrity doesn't like me, and that Rufus is certainly strange." My accusation hung inertly in the air.

"You can't think one of them did something to your suitcase?"

"They're the only ones in the house, except Elizabeth and your father, and you said he's an invalid."

"My servants are loyal and trustworthy," Alex said, turning to face me. His gaze was hooded. "You just don't know what you're talking about."

That was the second time today my word had been questioned. "I know someone slashed the canvas on my suitcase. Someone trashed my things. I'm not crazy. I know it happened."

"But I'm telling you my servants weren't responsible."

We jousted silently, our gazes never shifting. He set his jaw. I lifted my chin. "How can you be so sure? You're never home, and they're having a tough time adjusting to Allison's death and a new mistress."

"I assure you, my servants are not involved. There are things you don't understand."

I looked away, breathing deeply. "Well, then explain it to me. Tell me bout this house, about you, about your first wife."

Glancing back, I found him measuring me. He

lowered his arm, and stuffed his hands into his pant's pockets. "What do you want to know?"

"What about Rufus? He frightens me."

"Rufus wouldn't hurt a fly. You're just put off by his disability."

Ashamed, I acknowledged his observation with a tip of my head. "He startled me."

"That's why Rufus hardly ever goes out," Alex continued. "Too many people react to him like you did. But he's excellent with my father—probably because he can't hear the old man when he cusses him out." His eyes lightened at the thought.

"And Mrs. Garrity?"

Alex shrugged. "She's been with me for ten years. I took her on just as my father's mind started to wander, and when Rufus came to relieve her, Helena took on more of the household duties. She was a godsend when Allison got sick."

"I suppose she resents me," I mused. That could explain her reaction to me, but didn't justify it. "What about Allison? I know she had cancer...." My words trailed off.

Alex seemed to shrink. His voice went flat. "When Allison was about seven months pregnant, she developed a rash on her chest. Until then, she had been healthy, her pregnancy normal. I prescribed some ointments, but the rash persisted. Soon afterwards, she had trouble breathing, but I told her it was a common problem during her stage of pregnancy. I was distracted by my work. I didn't check her out."

His eyes took on a haunted look. I wished I hadn't asked. My problems were pale in comparison to what he had endured.

"This all happened within the span of a week. By the end of the week, Allison was really sick," he went on. "Her lungs were congested and she was extremely fatigued. I ordered some blood tests, and brought in an oncologist." Alex hauled a hand through his black hair. "Allison had acute myelomonocytic leukemia, a virulent, rapid form of the disease. Her white-blood-cell production was out of control. Toxins attacked her lungs and other organs. She died just hours after Elizabeth was taken by C-Section.

Allison never had a chance."

As he spoke, I'd chewed on the knuckles of my right hand, emotion welling up in my chest. How horrible for him...for Allison...for little Elizabeth. "Nothing could be done for her?" My question whispered between us.

"Only ten percent of patients with this form of leukemia are alive at the end of five years."

"So nothing could be done."

Alex didn't answer. He turned from me and strayed to his desk.

"Alex?"

I stood and followed him to his desk. We faced each other across it.

"You don't blame yourself, do you?"

His eyes were stricken when he raised them to meet my gaze.

"You do," I stated with simple conviction. The very vulnerability in his manner was gut-wrenching. I clutched the edge of the desk. "Could her pregnancy have caused it?"

"Pregnancy itself had nothing to do with her disease. It's rare for a pregnant woman to have AML."

I nodded. "And it spread so quickly there was nothing *anyone* could do."

"Don't you understand? She was my wife. I should have been able to do something."

"How could you?"

"It's my job. It's why I became a doctor."

"So much of our life is out of our control," I murmured, my gaze roaming away.

"Don't talk in platitudes." The anger in his voice caused me to glace up at his dark and enigmatic eyes. "There should have been a way. I should have been able to do something."

I thought of my own life—full of "shoulds" and self-recriminations. What right had I to try to assuage my husband's guilt when I had so much difficulty handling my own? The revelation hit me like a strong gust of wind.

I swallowed convulsively, my gaze dropping from his. How many times had I felt responsible for Bill's drinking? Why, ultimately, had I refused to leave him?

"I'm tired," I told him unable to meet his look. "Good

night, Alex." Hugging my arms around my body, I turned from him, and retreated across the room.

"Mary."

I paused and glanced back. He looked like a beaten warrior, alone and weary.

"Now that you know, are you sorry?"

"Sorry about what?"

He shrugged his shoulders. "That you married me."

I offered a wan smile, and stepped toward him, wanting to ease his pain, longing to wrap my arms around him.

"You didn't marry a very pleasant man, I'm afraid," he said and turned away from me.

Rebuffed, I turned away myself and withdrew through the door, wondering about the many ghosts that haunted my husband's life.

CHAPTER FIVE

The next afternoon, I took back some control in my life. I called Gail and invited her over.

"Hey, this place is awesome."

My friend stood in the open doorway, the June sunlight pooling on the white tile floor.

"Come in," I urged, and then noticed she wasn't alone.

A plaintive meow came from within a small pet carrier.

"You brought Munster!"

"Yeah. This guy was quite insistent about coming." Gail scooted the heavy cat and carrier inside the front door. "I have the rest of his luggage in the car."

Gail had brought it all—Munster's purple carpeted cat condo, hooded litter pan, gallon jug of litter, bowls and bag of dry food. Retrieving it from the trunk, we lugged the cat and his gear up Alex's plush red staircase.

"I didn't realize this place was so imposing," Gail said between huffs.

"You've never been here?"

"No. Allison never got around to inviting me." She paused at the landing to look back at the medieval entry below. "Those must be the tapestries Allison told me about."

"They look quite old."

"Old? Some of them, maybe, but Allison made three of them."

"She did? Which ones?"

"I'm not sure. She mentioned doing one with flowers in it, and something about fighting knights and a castle."

I shifted the carrier into my left hand as I admired the intricate work of all the wallhangings, overwhelmed by the testimony of a woman's love for her husband.

Shuddering because of a sudden foreboding, I swung around, Munster's unwieldy cage bumping against my leg, and hobbled to my room. Gail followed. Once inside, we shut the door when we let out the offending cat. Heaven forbid that he would get in Mrs. Garrity's way.

"Jrrrrr." The big cat purred and twirled around my legs, glad to see me. I scooped him up and hugged his gray silk body. Munster felt so warm and solid and real. I squeezed him one more time and then dropped him on my bed. He hopped off the other side and disappeared under the bedskirt.

"Where do you want his pan?" Gail asked.

"In the bathroom."

We spent the next few minutes settling the new arrival into his home. Satisfied at last, we checked on Elizabeth, and leaving Mrs. Garrity in charge, escaped Alex's estate in Gail's Ford Taurus.

"You've been quiet. Having a bad hair day?" my friend asked as we turned onto the main highway.

Although my hair was knotted as usual precisely at the nape of my neck, I knew her question was more about my feelings than about my choice of hair style. I glanced her way and considered my response. Gail was my age, single and resigned to it. Considering herself overweight, she dieted and jogged to no avail. Blunt cut brown hair and a fair, but far-from-perfect complexion gave her a certain schoolgirl charm. Her soft brown eyes were always able to penetrate into my soul.

"You might say that," I answered, carefully avoiding her darting appraisal.

"The children miss you." Her tone became conversational. "And the dragon lady keeps bitching because you resigned."

The 'dragon lady,' our name for Kinder Day's owner, needed a little shaking up, and I wasn't sorry to be the one to do it to her. I was just sorry Gail had to face her ugly tongue, and I was sorry to leave the classroom of five year-olds.

"Munster didn't like being left alone," Gail reported.

"Believe me, it wasn't in my plans."

"Yeah. You know what they say about the best laid plans." Gail's knowing look took up where her words left off.

"What's that supposed to mean?"

"Far be it for me to say 'I told you so.'"

I frowned. "Right."

"Really, Mary. You look terrible."

"Thanks." Gail was always direct.

"So taking care of a three-month-old isn't what it's cracked up to be?" she wanted to know as we approached the outskirts of Louisville.

Taking a deep breath, I released it slowly. "That's part of it, but Elizabeth's a really good baby. She sleeps much of the night already."

"I see."

I knew Gail expected more. What could I tell her? We had always shared secrets. In the bright light of the new day, my suspicions about Alex's servants seemed silly and petty, my dreams pure make-believe.

"I'm not sleeping well," I finally admitted.

"I could tell."

I bristled at her sarcastic tone. "Look, Gail. Let's don't play games with each other. You didn't want me to marry your cousin's husband, but I did. I'm trying to make the best of a difficult situation. I need your support, not your badgering."

"You're right." Gail's gaze flickered over my face. "I'm sorry, Mary." She bit her lip and then sighed. "I just don't want to see you hurt."

"You've made that clear."

"But you are being hurt, and I don't know why. It's sorta *déjà vu*. I saw the same thing happening to Allison, but was unable to stop it."

"What do you mean?" My heart tap danced in my chest.

"Well, whenever I saw Allison, she was kinda haunted looking, unhappy." We stopped at a traffic light. Gail's thumbs thumped on the steering wheel. I watched her face as she gathered her thoughts. "For the first years of her marriage, she spent all her time cooped up in that house making those wallhangings hoping he'd approve of her then."

"What?" I thought Alex loved Allison.

"Finally, I guess Allison gave up trying to please him, and started to go out more. I told her not to keep to herself, and she did start going to church and to the park. I think she had some friends she'd eat dinner with. She started to look happier, but Alex became jealous and she stopped going out. Allison got pregnant soon after that, and before her relationship with Alex improved, she got cancer and died quickly."

I frowned at Gail's rambling dissertation. "Being pregnant had nothing to do with her cancer. Alex told me so."

"He told you that?" Gail shrugged and stepped on the gas. "I suppose he should know. All I'm trying to say is that I don't want you to keep to yourself. That house is not a jail. Your husband is not a jailer. Don't lose yourself just to please Alex Dominican."

"I'm not trying to please Alex."

"You married him instead of just signing on as a nanny."

"He wanted it that way."

She raised a dark eyebrow, and I realized she'd set a trap for me.

"He paid those horrible debts Bill's death surprised me with." I wanted her to see things my way.

"You could have paid them back eventually," she pointed out.

"But Bill had ruined our credit. I couldn't stand owing all those people."

"So now you owe Dr. Dominican."

Gail's words drilled ominous holes into my heart. I glanced away from her at the passing shops and houses. I was caught in the snare of my own making. Unwittingly, to be sure, but no less caught. I closed my eyes to the sun that slapped the car window with its heat and brilliance. The warmth on my face was honest. A person couldn't hide from its radiance—just as I couldn't hide now from my dilemma.

"Okay," I said, straightening up and opening my

eyes. "I've made my bed, so to speak, and I've got to lie in it. Elizabeth needs me."

"Elizabeth needs someone to care for her, not necessarily you."

Maybe I need her, my heart cried out in silent protest. I swallowed my innermost confession and went on as if Gail hadn't spoken, "So I'll promise you, I won't change my life. I'll include Elizabeth. I won't lose you or my other friends because of this marriage."

"That's a girl." My friend nodded in approval.

I immediately made good on my word. After Gail dropped me off at my apartment, I gathered together some of my things and packed them in my car. On the way back to Marchbrook Manor, I stopped at the mall and bought a car seat and a stroller so I could take Elizabeth with me when I left the house.

At home I hauled my luggage and boxes into the entry hall and piled them on the clear, white floor. For the second time that day, I dragged another load up the red staircase and bumped down the hallway. Reaching Elizabeth's door, I balanced the box with the car seat in it on my knee, turned the knob and used my hip to push open the door, causing me to back into her mouse-covered room.

"Mary? Can I help?"

Alex's splendid voice made me pause. Hugging the box to me, I pivoted slowly and peered at him over the top. "No thanks. I've got it."

I walked into the room and with a whoosh of air, dropped the box to the floor. Settled in the rocking chair, his angular face softened as he watched his child—Alex held Elizabeth in the crook of his arm. She greedily took her bottle, making slurping sounds as she stared into her father's eyes.

"What are you doing home so early?" I subconsciously tucked a stray strand of hair behind an ear. His physical presence was as shocking as a slap to the face.

"Easy day," he explained. "Helena said you were out, so I thought I'd do the honors. What do you have there?"

I plopped down cross-legged behind the box. "Car seat."

"Good idea. Now you'll have one for your car."

I paused in my attempt at extracting the staples from the box top and glanced up at him. "You've already got one?"

"You can't leave the hospital without one."

"I see." I felt inexperienced, ill-informed, an outsider.

His gaze held a hopeful quality that was hard for me to comprehend. Our gazes encountered each other in silent contest as we gauged the depths of our emotions. In the charged atmosphere, a heightened awareness sizzled between us. His jaw moved, but his gaze never faltered, seeming to strip me bare with the sensuality of it.

"Let me help you." His offer was like a kiss.

"No, that's okay."

"Here, you take Elizabeth. She needs to be burped, and I'm never good at that anyway."

I raised up on my knees and held out my hands to accept the infant. Our fingers, our bodies touched as he shifted her into my arms and I lifted her to my shoulder. Sitting back on my heels, I patted her back.

"This is a man's job after all," he commented reaching down to rip off the top of the box.

"You're just saying that to hear me protest."

His grin was devilish. "Maybe so, but I got the top off, didn't I?"

"Brute strength," I murmured disdainfully.

"Brawn but no brains you're trying to say?" His eyes lit at the game.

"If the shoe fits, as they say." At that, Elizabeth let out her burp.

"Touché."

We smiled at each other as he lifted the car seat from the box.

"Dinosaurs?" His eyebrow quirked in question.

"They're all the rage," I said looking at the car seat covered in a colorful dinosaur-patterned fabric.

With my left arm and hand steadying the baby, I reached into the box and brought out the installation manual and advertising literature. While Alex scanned the manual, I read from the colored flyer, "The Super 9000 has a five-point harness system, three position up front recline adjustment, seat saver base and a front belt adjuster for quick changes."

"Great, but does it work?" Alex quipped.

"It's supposed to be the Cadillac of car seats. Look, it even has a lumbar support for infants five to forty-three pounds."

I stretched over to show him the picture, and inadvertently brushed his trousers with my arm. In the depths of my body, a flame raged into fire. Alex knelt beside me. I sensed he felt the fire as well. He reached for Elizabeth and took her from me.

"Let's see how she likes it." His voice was muffled.

He laid her in the sloping seat and fumbled with the straps. It took a while for him to get the hang of it, but eventually he secured her into the seat as I stared at his rumpled white dress shirt and strong, broad back.

"Now all I've got to do is figure out how to put the seat in the car," I told him, my own voice strained with suppressed emotion.

"Don't worry. I'll put it in for you." He stood up and turned to face me, his eyes now hooded, his body tense.

"Thank you."

I wondered if I would faint because of my sudden desire for this man. I resisted. I chastised myself. I longed for escape from the directness of his gaze. The room was too hot, my face too flushed. Then Munster was there between us, his silky body like a whisper of relief as it lightly touched my thigh and whipped around Alex's ankle.

"Munster!"

"Ah, your dreaded cat," Alex said with a feigned grimace, the tension broken. "You better not let Mrs. Garrity catch him in here."

I scooped up the offending animal and climbed to my feet. "He was in my room. I don't know how he got out."

Alex shrugged as if to say don't worry. "He's a pretty cat."

"Thanks." We measured each other briefly, and then I broke away, stepping around the empty box. "I'll go put him back in my room."

"Hurry back."

I paused at the door, and scanned his face once more. "I've got to bring my things upstairs. They're down in the hall." I felt weak, like a little girl asking permission. He did that to me, making my knees wobble and my heartbeat race.

"I'll get those for you. You just take care of Elizabeth."

My gaze strayed to the infant still strapped in the seat. Quite content, she waved her little hands in front of her eyes. "Okay, thanks."

Carrying my cat across the hall, I shoved him through the crack in the door and shut it. When I turned, I found Alex leaning against the opposite door jamb, his face shadowed by the murky hall lights, his eyes hidden and unreadable.

"I'll just put your things right inside the door, so your cat won't get out again."

"Sounds good," I murmured, lowering my gaze. I stepped closer to him, intending to pass him and slip back into Elizabeth's room.

He stopped me with his presence. I raised my lashes to meet his now forthright gaze.

"You're a good and gentle woman, Mary," he said softly. "I know we will be happy."

At a loss for words, I tipped my chin upward and challenged him with my look. The tension was back. The pull of the hidden rope drew me to him, but I held myself steady. Finally I whispered a choking "thanks" and fled around him to the safety of his now sleeping daughter.

As I picked up Elizabeth, I heard him walk down the hall. The baby sighed in my arms. I supported her head and carried her to her crib where I changed her diaper. She barely stirred, the sucking noises she made the only sound in the room. Oddly, I felt content. The banter we had exchanged reassured me. Maybe things would turn out okay after all. I smiled to myself.

Reaching down, I gently covered Elizabeth with a blanket. As I touched her soft face, I recognized the sudden shrill wail that had preceded my other waking dreams. *No!* I fought it. Grasping the rails of the crib, my palms moist, I sparred with the overwhelming dizziness. But I couldn't stop the crescendo reverberating around me. The wooziness increased as well, causing me to slowly sink to the floor, my sweaty hands sliding down the wooden bars of the crib. As my vision blurred, powerful colors like the banners on a battlefield conquered my consciousness. My world quaked...

****

"Stop it, my lord!" the yellow-clad figure commanded. She was laughing at some ridiculous joke he had told and her sides hurt. "Pray, for the sake of the child!"

Immediately, he quit his play, and took her hand, stroking it tenderly. "Forgive me, my lady. But I do so like to see you laugh."

"I laugh when I'm happy," Mary said, "and I am happy with you, my lord."

"You are such a dear child," he said, stroking her face with his large hand.

She leaned into his palm, savoring the warmth of his touch. "I'm a woman full grown. Woman enough to bear your child." She knew the pride in her voice was evident.

The black-cloaked man smiled. "You have pleased me. In the time since our marriage, I've never been more content."

A small victory. One to cherish forever....

The scene shifted amid a foggy haze. The solar room was dark when, so strong and powerful, he came to her. He touched her reverently with experienced hands, drawing a response from her which clawed at her inner being. She writhed with the pain of desire. When he filled her, she screamed in welcome. When he tentatively moved, she moaned. He kissed her, a hot and full kiss of passion and she rose to meet his demands. Her inmost core broke first, suffusing her with a hot blaze of triumph. He exploded within her, spending himself in his efforts, to fall exhausted beside her, his hand clutching her swelling belly.

And then the scene changed abruptly.

"My lord!" she cried out, the sweet aftermath of lust suddenly taking on a strange and violent pattern. Pangs of fear soaked her with sweat. Pain, so strong that it rocked her whole being, caused her to scream again. The black-cloaked man hovered over her undulating form. The grasp of his fingers on hers was warm and comforting.

"Her time is at hand," the blue-clad woman spoke somewhere in the haze. "This is women's work, my lord. Get you gone and send for the midwife."

His hand disappeared. Where was he? The cramp struck her again, taking her breath. She twisted and turned to ease herself. Something was wrong. She needed him. He was gone. "My lord!"

"Hush, child. 'Tis just the labor pains," the soft voice of Gellis reached the recesses of her mind...

****

The vision ended as swiftly as it had come. I awoke to find myself cowered on the floor, one hand still clutching the bar of the crib, the other pressed against my midriff where I still felt the ebb of passion tingling in my inner core. Suddenly, pain devastated my abdomen. I shook. Salty perspiration and tears toppled down my face into the crevices of my mouth. Weak with the violence of my reaction, I let go of the crib and brushed my hand across my eyes.

I couldn't let Alex find me here. Not like this. Not so out of control. Staggering to my feet, I glanced at Elizabeth. Her pale lashes touched her cheeks, and her little mouth made nursing motions as she slept. I backed away from her innocence, her beauty. At the door I paused to listen for his approach. When he didn't come, I opened the door and ventured across the hall. My own door was shut, so I assumed Alex had finished moving my things. I prayed for it to be true.

Inside my room, I turned the lock. Just as he had promised, luggage and boxes were piled by the door. I spotted Munster curled into a ball on my pillow. I was alone. Alone with my confusion, and my very physical pain. My stomach cramped. I fought waves of nausea. Sweat laced my upper lip and dripped between my breasts. I barely reached the bathroom in time before I got sick.

Hugging the toilet bowl like a life preserver, I retched until there was nothing left. I was thoroughly demoralized, a whipped victim of my unwanted visions. Silent moments passed. Finally I was able to rise. Bracing myself against the cold basin, I scooped water over my face and then brushed my teeth. Feeling halfway human, I went into my bedroom. I had to redo my hair and repair my face before I could encounter anyone else, let alone myself.

But there was something wrong. Allison's brush was gone. My jewelry lay mangled in a pile on the dresser-top as if someone had just turned my jewelry box upside down and ravished it. Buff-colored liquid foundation dribbled on the polished wood. My eyebrow pencil was broken into pieces.

My spine tingled. I gulped the suddenly fetid smelling air. Who was doing this? Why was this happening?

I received part of my answer as I looked at myself in the mirror. "Get out!" was written across the sparkling surface of the glass in the blood red of my lipstick.

CHAPTER SIX

I touched the slick, cold glass of the mirror. Drawing my fingers across the sinister warning, I smeared the lipstick into two thin trails. An icy fear welled up in my heart as I fought for control.

Who was doing this? I remembered the door to my room had been opened a crack. That's how Munster had gotten out. Angry, I lay my full palm on the mirror and moved my hand from side to side trying to obliterate the warning. Whoever had done this had entered my room and violated my privacy. He *or she* had no right—no basis for this attack upon me. What had I done? I pulled my hand away from the mirror and stared down at my blood-red palm.

There was no way I could complain to Alex. He had already denied my charge about the slashed suitcase. What would he say if I accused his servants again? Nothing. I deliberately knotted my palm into a fist and squeezed it tightly.

A sharp rap on my bedroom door snapped me out of my reverie. Shaking the fuzzy preoccupation from my mind, I lifted my chin and drew a deep and cleansing breath.

"Who is it?" I crossed the floor to the shut door.

"Mrs. Garrity."

Great. With my clean hand, I brushed my hair back from my face, and then seized the doorknob. Hiding my red-stained hand behind my back, I wrenched open the door.

65

"Yes?"

Her unfriendly gaze invaded me, piercing the bland mask I had drawn up for protection. I stiffened.

"Dr. Dominican requests the pleasure of your company tonight at dinner." The tone of her voice was sickly sweet.

The housekeeper raised a dark brow at the puzzled look that must have crossed my face. She didn't suppress an unkind smirk. "Dr. and Mrs. Dominican always dined formally at night when he was home," she explained as if to answer my silent question.

I took her remarks as spiteful and so bristled. "Why tonight? Why now?"

Her eyes narrowed. "He said something about never having a true honeymoon dinner. But I don't see why that would matter to him. You know, it's not as if you two have a real marriage—like the one he had with Allison."

She spoke the truth, of course. Alex and I had no true marriage, but I refused to let Mrs. Garrity know the effect her observation had on me and kept my face impassive. Dragging a breath from far within me, I reminded myself Alex and I were married, legally—and in the eyes of the church. This woman was just a paid employee, and no matter how high Alex held her in esteem, I still was his wife.

"Tell Alex I'll be glad to dine with him. In the dining room, I suppose?"

She nodded. As I started to close the door, she smarted off again. "Don't forget to dress properly. What you've got on now won't do."

I flung the door open. This woman certainly had her nerve.

Instead of defending myself, for of course I knew what it meant to "dine formally," I hurled a harsh question at her. "Were you just in my room?"

"Of course not—especially since you brought that beast into the house."

"It's just a cat, and someone let him out." I studied her sharp features.

"Well, I certainly don't want your cat roaming the house. Why would I let it out?" She leaned closer and threatened me. "I hope you don't go running to the doctor again with your hallucinations. He has enough on his mind without you making up lies about his staff."

How did she know I'd talked to Alex about her and Rufus? Had Alex told her? Why did she term my accusation against them "hallucinations"? Could she know about my dreams? Now furious, I realized not even my own fantasies were mine. However horrible, however they upset me, I somehow felt linked to the young Mary of long ago. That this dreadful housekeeper could possibly know about the young girl made my mind tumble. I pulled a protective drape of silence around me and willfully closed the door in Mrs. Garrity's strangely familiar face.

I felt drained, numb. Going to the bathroom, I scrubbed my palm clean. As the tepid water sloughed over my hands, I wavered as if in a daze. In just three days time, I had experienced four visions of another time. Unable to contain these wayward dreams was one thing. Now I was now unable to stop someone from tormenting me. I was out of control again and I hated the feeling.

Returning to my bedroom, I scoured the surface of the dresser with a bath towel, dropping the broken eyebrow pencil and used lipstick into the trash. I righted my jewelry box and straightened it. Finally, I wiped off the mirror, polishing it clean with quick, decisive strokes.

I still wasn't satisfied with the innocence of Mrs. Garrity. And Rufus? What did I know about him? Crossing over to the canopied bed, I plopped down, hardly disturbing my contented gray cat who opened one almond-shaped eye in protest. I sat mute, unmoving, wondering about my problem. Was Alex somehow involved? The suspicion skittered away like a nervous horse. But it was there in the background of my mind, a niggling sensation that wouldn't quite go away.

When it was time to dress for dinner, I took special care, showering, redoing my makeup, and sweeping my dark blond hair up into a dramatic chignon. Luckily, I had an equally dramatic dress to wear. Bill and I had gone to his company's Christmas dance in December, and I had bought a striking black sheath dress, perfect for any time of year. The silk fabric clung to all my womanly curves, and I smiled at myself in the mirror as I contemplated the effect it might have on my new husband. I wasn't immune to the age-old feminine ploys, and the thought tickled me. Even in this supposedly liberated age, it still felt good to dress for a man.

He waited for me at the foot of the red staircase, cocking a black eyebrow when he saw me at the top of the stairs. My gaze caught his as I began my descent. Gripping the glossy banister with my cold fingers, I realized there was a twist in my stomach I couldn't analyze. His swept-backed hair, finely chiseled features, and slightly dimpled chin enticed me. I felt a blush mount in my cheeks. His gaze never faltered. It stripped me naked. I lifted my chin in response, my breath catching in anticipation.

Alex took my cold hand into his warm one. "You look beautiful, Mary."

"Thank you. You're quite handsome yourself."

He grinned, and drew me down the last step, tucking my captured hand under his arm to lay it on top of his sleeve. The rough fabric of his black suit coat and the bulge of his forearm underneath felt good to my touch. Alex exuded a warmth and spiciness that drew me to him, just as his hand held me hostage near his side.

"This afternoon I suddenly remembered we'd never celebrated our wedding."

We walked across the glass-like floor of the entrance hall, passed the steady suits of armor and Allison's spectacular tapestries. *I am a trespasser in another woman's house.* The incessant thought almost brought me up short, but I cast it aside and kept going.

"Ours is not the typical marriage," I offered in quiet explanation for the oversight.

He tilted his head in acknowledgement. "However, I like to think we have something in common."

"Elizabeth?" I asked in hushed voice.

"Elizabeth," Alex countered with a pleasant look on his face. As he ushered me into the door of the dining room, he continued, "That's why I selected you, you know."

I glanced up at him in confusion.

"Your extreme beauty was a decided plus, of course." His eyes lightened in a playful mood. "But your reputation for working with children is what really made up my mind."

This time I did draw up. Alex must have thought his comment flattering, but to me it was another rude reminder of our awkward marriage. I disliked the calculated way he had gone about selecting a wife. Had he chosen Allison that way? Of course not. He loved Allison. Maybe Gail had been right. Although she knew I could never again have children, she had once called me a broodmare. Granted, she knew ours was a marriage of convenience. I wouldn't sleep with him. But she thought I was selling my services to Alex. Maybe even my soul.

Right now I expected Alex to lift my lips and inspect my teeth or run his hands down my legs to see if he'd purchased a sound investment.

The idea of Alex running a hand down one of my legs caused my palms to moisten. As if he could read my mind, I swallowed self-consciously, growing warm and wet in a vital, throbbing place.

Breaking away from his hold, I walked ahead of Alex into the dining room. I wanted him again. In the way a woman wants a man. I wanted a true marriage with Alex. Not a sham. My desire and longing brought out the frustration and anger that had simmered so near the surface of my emotions for three days.

"You make it sound as if I were a good business investment." I whirled to face him, encountering Alex with an irate lilt in my voice. "So now I know why I was chosen. Now I know why you picked poor Mary Adams when you could have selected from many other eager females. After all, you're quite handsome and rich. You had your pick of women."

His head tilted and his eyes narrowed. "I'm sorry, Mary. I knew it wouldn't be easy for you. You told me you were willing to marry me, and I did want someone good with Elizabeth." He raked a hand through his black hair.

I bit my lip. Alex sounded like there was absolutely nothing wrong with what he said. Had he apologized because I expected him to?

"I understand what I got myself into, Alex. It's just that it's been so hard." I hated the pout in my small voice.

His eyes darkened, and I fretted he would

misunderstand. He hadn't believed me about the suitcase, so how could I tell him about the newest warning? And about my dreams. They were too personal and unbelievable even for me to understand.

Hurrying on to explain myself, I said, "Elizabeth is a joy, but Mrs. Garrity is so efficient with her. She makes me feel like I don't belong, like I don't know anything about children." Here I was complaining about Mrs. Garrity after I had vowed not to. I cringed inwardly as I watched Alex's shifting expressions.

"Helena is just doing her job."

"She does it so well. Why do you need me?" There. I'd said it.

His eyes hardened. "Because Elizabeth needs a mother."

His words tethered me to him. I couldn't explain why I was drawn to him at that moment. Elizabeth needed a mother. Her own mother was dead. Out of all people, Alex had wanted me to take Allison's place.

The winds of his emotions blew across his face, barely dying down before stirring again. I saw within Alex's eyes a vulnerability that I hadn't expected, that he tried to cover up.

"I know this whole thing is selfish of me," he said softly.

I shrugged. "Me too, I guess. You paid a lot of money to get me out of debt." *Make the best of it. You got yourself into this.* I looked away, unable to meet his gaze.

Alex stepped nearer. I could feel his presence like a child sensed the arrival of Santa Claus. He touched my upper arms, encircling them, crushing the silk fabric of my dress, pulling me toward him.

"Mary, I knew you were right for this job." Alex paused as if struggling for words. "That isn't quite the way to put it, calling our marriage a 'job,' but I knew you were right."

I glanced up at him, finally meeting his gray gaze. There was something in the depths of his eyes that tugged me to him. I trembled at his touch.

"When I saw you at Allison's funeral with her cousin, I felt some sort of attraction," he confessed. "It's as if I'd known you before."

70

I swallowed. "You helped me through my miscarriage, remember?"

His gaze shifted away from my face, and then back again, as if he were considering what I'd just said. "Yes, I guess that's it, but I still can't shake the feeling that I'd known you from some place else."

I lowered my gaze from his refined features and tempting mouth. The soft shadow of an afternoon growth of beard fascinated me. How would it feel to my touch? How would it feel to kiss those full lips and gently brush the tip of his nose and the shape of his brows with my own lips?

"You were so kind to me then, Alex. I never forgot. That's why I agreed to marry you. It wasn't just the money."

His fingers on my arms tightened. "Good. I'm glad there was something more to it. Maybe we have something to build on."

I looked up again, scrutinizing his face, trying to read the implication of his words. "What are you saying?" I asked, my voice frail and fluttery.

"Maybe we have something to form the basis of a good marriage. Maybe time will tell. I'm willing to wait and see."

Alex smiled then, his eyes clearing as if a storm had just blown through. He reached over and kissed my forehead, his lips blistering my skin where they touched. I shook in reaction.

"Now, let's eat. I'm starving, and Rufus has prepared his best meal. This is a celebration, after all."

Alex released my arms then, but offered me his hand. Taking mine in his firm grip, my wedding band pressing into the flesh of my fingers, he led me into Marchbrook Manor's stately dining room. The spell broken between us, I fought to readjust my thinking and share in his suddenly lighthearted mood.

"Does Rufus do much of your cooking?" I asked, trying to take up my end of the conversation.

"Only on special occasions. I told him to outdo himself tonight."

Rufus was waiting for us at the end of the room. He was dressed in a black tuxedo, looking incongruous with his stooped shoulders and bulbous nose. Standing proudly with his hand on the back of my chair, he bowed before us when we approached, his bald head dipping low, and with the sweep of the other hand, showed me to my place. He helped me push in my seat, and then poured ice water into a crystal goblet. Alex sat to my left.

The tables were arranged suspiciously like a medieval banquet hall, the head table raised upon a dais with a complete view of the room. In my previous glimpse into this room, I had failed to notice the similarity, and so stared in surprise down the length of the empty dining hall so different from the crowded and congenial one of my dream. The raucous banter of castle folk was missing. Gone also were the pungent smells—the stench of sour rushes and wet dogs, the odor of unwashed bodies packed too tightly together, the aroma of roasting meat. I missed the scent of my husband who always comfortably smelled of Bordeaux wine and mustard.

Troubled, I cut off these oddly recurring thoughts. That stuff of my dreams wasn't real. Bill had been my only husband until now and he had never smelled like wine and mustard—more like stale beer, cigarette smoke and mouthwash. Chiding myself, I lifted the delicate glass from the table and drank deeply of the icy water.

"Rufus could be a head chef somewhere," Alex remarked.

Struggling to return my attention to the moment, I glanced at Alex as I set down the goblet.

"He chooses to work for me instead and I'm honored." His comments were meant to praise the small man, and I noticed Alex had touched his servant's sleeve so that Rufus turned to read his lips.

Drawing a line with my fingertip up the stem of the water glass to its fog-clouded rim, I thought about the loyalty Alex inspired in his servants.

The food was delicious—a mixture of salads and vegetables, brisket, chicken breasts and barbecued ribs. Rufus even provided bowls of Kentucky burgoo, a veal, pork and vegetable stew-like dish popular during Kentucky Derby time. Although just hours before I had been sick, I ate hungrily.

"My goodness, Rufus. Everything is so wonderful. I'm

afraid I can't eat it all," I said as he placed another flaky roll on my bread plate. Then I remembered he couldn't hear, so turned his way and repeated myself.

He smiled at me, and for the first time I really looked him in the eyes. They were clear green and so gentle and kind. There was an all-knowing quality about them that seemed to draw me right into his confidence. I had the conviction I'd seen those eyes before—somewhere, just beyond the recesses of my memory.

I lowered my gaze, unsure of how to respond to his look. As he flitted away to serve Alex, I realized Rufus couldn't be the person who had cut my suitcase or written a horrible warning on my mirror. He didn't want me to leave. In fact, I thought the little man liked me.

We took our after-dinner coffee in Alex's library. "It's too bad it's summer. A fire would be nice," Alex said as he offered me a dainty china cup.

"Yes," I answered, taking the cup and saucer from him and turning to stare at the cold hearth. "It would be romantic."

"You haven't had much romance in your life, have you Mary?"

Alex's question startled me. How much did he know about my life? I slowly turned to face him, and self-conscious about answering, bought time by sipping some coffee. I gazed at him over the rim of the cup. He returned my look with a steady, penetrating gaze.

"I suppose not." My reply was muted. "I mistook puppy love for true love, and by the time I realized my mistake, it was too late." Shrugging, I set down the cup and saucer.

"Your husband died so tragically."

Moving away from him, I crossed to his heavy desk. Turning back to face him, I gripped the edge of the desk to bolster my courage, for I knew Alex was asking for more information.

"Bill drank heavily but refused to get help. I was afraid he'd die like he did. I hadn't counted on it happening so soon. Bill was too young to die. Just thirty. I felt regret when he died, but not sadness." How could I admit that Bill's death had lifted a great burden from my shoulders? That is, until I discovered his extensive gambling debts.

We had come full circle again, Alex and I, back to our earlier conversation about the reason for our marriage. I wanted to lay it to rest. I didn't want to talk about Bill. But I did want to learn more about Allison.

"Gail told me Allison handcrafted some of those beautiful tapestries in the entrance hall," I said, changing the subject.

It was his chance to turn away. His gaze dropped from mine. Warming his coffee, Alex murmured, "Yes, she did. The rest are antique."

When he didn't continue, I probed, "Did Allison decorate your house? There's so much that's medieval about it."

"Actually, no. As I told you, it was my father's idea. He's been collecting for years."

His father. The elusive father-in-law I had not yet seen. "When can I meet him?"

I noticed his jaw muscle jerk. "I'm not sure that's a good idea. He's pretty feeble, as I told you, and not quite aware of his surroundings. He wouldn't know you. Most of the time he doesn't even know me."

"I see."

He came toward me then, his eyes sparking with anticipation. "Let's not talk about that. Come here." Alex drew me with him away from his desk over to the library window. After drawing back the heavy drape, he opened what I now realized were French doors and pulled me onto a small balcony.

The sun had already settled, leaving a hazy half-light of the ending day. Oppressive, the outside air hung heavily around us like a sauna. He laid a palm on my shoulder, his fingers grazing the soft skin of my neck as well as the fabric of my dress.

"I know you used to ride horses," he said in a deep-throated voice.

Surprised at his knowledge, I glanced up at him.

"Beyond the rose garden and down a short path is my stable."

"You have a stable here?"

"Yes, and you're welcome to ride my horse."

"Just one horse? Didn't Allison have one?" I asked.

"I'm afraid Allison and I didn't share the same interests in many things."

For a moment, his fingertips bit deeper into the delicate flesh of my shoulder. I glanced at his hard, gray eyes that stared far away past the rose garden into a world I suddenly was afraid I'd never share with him. Alex looked down at me. His gaze grew tender.

"Knight Fox is sometimes a handful, but I bet you're up to it." His smile touched his eyes.

My throat constricted. I hadn't ridden since I was eighteen years old. My pregnancy and marriage had been so unforgivable to my mother that she had sold my show horse and then disowned me.

"Thanks," I breathed. "I'd love to!" I had missed the thrill of riding, and his offer excited me.

"You look so pretty when your eyes sparkle like that," he whispered.

"I do? I mean, they are?" I'd never thought of my eyes sparkling.

Alex's hold on my shoulder tightened. He grasped my other shoulder and pulled me around to face him. The feel of his hands fascinated me. A faint quirk of his eyebrow dazed me. His eyes shimmered with unnameable emotion. Meeting his gaze steadily was an effort. He wanted to kiss me. I hesitated. This was a business arrangement, after all. I fought to withstand the onslaught of his passionate look. It was as if I had no will of my own. What could one little kiss hurt? His gaze became beseeching and tugged at my resolve. Alex tilted his head, lowering it to mine. His lips, his eyes, the sweetness of his breath, so close to me.

"Dr. Dominican."

We sprang apart like guilty teenagers caught in the back seat of a parked car. Just inside the doorway, Mrs. Garrity stood like a tin soldier, a clearly disapproving look upon her face.

"Your father has asked to see you," she said in that drill sergeant voice.

"Yes, thank you, Helena. I'll be right there."

Mrs. Garrity left the library, and we came back inside, closing the door on the balcony as well as the tender mood of the moment.

"I'm sorry." He turned to glance my way. "Guy must be having a lucid period. When he wants to see me, I must go to him."

"Go on." I nodded, urging him to leave. "I understand."

"What will you do? Check on Elizabeth?"

"I peeked into her room before I came down, and she was sleeping soundly. I haven't heard her, so I suspect she's fine." I wandered away from him, suddenly shy. My hand drifted over his history book, still opened face down on the end table. "If I might, I'd like to read some of your book."

Alex grinned. "I thought you didn't like history."

"I can't seem to avoid it in this house," I said referring to all the shining knights.

"It won't put you to sleep?"

"Not a chance."

"See you tomorrow then." He paused at the door.

"Tomorrow."

"Sleep tight, Mary."

And don't let the bed bugs bite, I mutely finished for him as he left the library. What a shame. That horrible Mrs. Garrity certainly had the worst timing. I settled down into Alex's chair and stretched out my legs, tugging the hem of my black dress toward my knees for modesty.

Today had been interesting. I felt as if our relationship had finally started to form. Maybe I wasn't caught up in such a dilemma after all. Marriage to Alex might just turn out okay.

I picked up the thick book, wondering if there was something in it about my Mary and her handsome lord. I didn't even know the lord's name, I mused as I stifled a yawn, hoping the dry history text wouldn't put me to sleep.

****

The vision opened on a happier time.

He found her in the castle garden amid the roses, lilies, heliotropes, violets and poppies. He came to her laughing, and she joined him, happier than she could expect. They sat by the fish pond and talked of small matters—the day's hawking, the baking of bread. When he laid his hand on her enormous belly, the child kicked and his father smiled proudly.

"Our child will be strong, my lord," she told him, vain in her knowledge that she carried an active babe. He had to be the expected heir. His robust disposition in the womb already foretold it.

"He will be a comely lad," his father said as if he too dreamed dreams of things to come. He turned to Mary, holding her hand with reverence. "You, my lady, have brought me this happiness."

She lowered her lashes, her pleasure dimmed because she so selfishly wanted more. Yet it was enough to have his approval she reminded herself, touching her distorted figure. She would have that forever because of the child she had conceived and now carried.

The setting changed swiftly.

Heavy curtains draped the bed to block the dangerous night air. He was with her, melding his tall hard body against her back. There wasn't much else he could do in her unwieldy condition.

"I wish I could ease you, my lord," she whispered in the gloom.

"Precious wife, I worry about you as well. You've turned into a little witch for wanting it." There was laughter in his voice.

"You shame me." She let him hear the pout in her voice.

"Never! You honor me, an old man, with your desire." He kissed the nape of her neck through the weight of her hair.

"You're not old, my lord. Just five and thirty," she asserted. "Stop it! You'll drive me mad for wanting you."

But he kept kissing her, rising on his elbow to touch her ear and cheek with feathery traces of his longing. She needed him so badly that she thought she'd split with the wanting. She moaned, and turned to meet his lips. They managed somehow over her extended belly, and when he climaxed, his cry of triumph was long and loud. Mary was exultant as well, smugly satisfied with her overwhelming power to turn a dangerous warlord into a humble supplicant.

And then the pain began again—great unending rolls of pain. The birthing bed. Ever the focus of the ghostly visions.

She screamed with each wave of pain, wanting him with her, knowing something was wrong.

"Quiet!" The mother-in-law's voice was harsh. She stood stiff like a soldier, a clearly disapproving look upon her face. "Childbirth is ordained to be painful. Hold your tongue and bear what you must."

"Don't talk to milady that way," Gellis protested. "She's just a babe herself."

She's just a babe herself.

Mary floated amid a fog of pain and sweat. A great white mist blotted out her sight and subdued her senses. She moaned now—low and deep in her throat.

CHAPTER SEVEN

"Mary?"

Amid the maelstrom of my mind, my senses ordered themselves, drawing me forward in time. I catapulted awake.

"Mary? Are you okay?"

Sitting upright, I adjusted my eyes. Alex stood beside the chair. Encircling Elizabeth in his arms, he held her upright against his broad shoulder. In one hand, he carried a bottle of formula. Her head bobbed as she gazed wide-eyed at the bright lights of the room.

"You were moaning in your sleep. Are you okay?"

"Yes," I said breathlessly.

The cramp in my abdomen frightened me, but I couldn't let him know. Unyielding in its fierceness, the pain was very real.

"You look pale," he observed, kneeling down beside me.

I held out my hands for Elizabeth and avoided his gaze. "I'm okay."

Elizabeth settled into my arms like a puzzle piece fitted into its correct spot. Alex handed me the bottle, and I silently began to feed the child. Strangely, the insufferable pain began to ease.

"I heard Elizabeth," he began to explain, his eyes full of worry, "and when I realized you hadn't come upstairs, instead of giving her the bottle, we came looking for you."

"Thanks." My gaze shuffled over his face. I felt self-conscious, bemused. Alex had awakened me from one of

79

my dreams. What would have happened if the dream had continued? "You were right about the book. I couldn't keep awake," I offered my excuse with a wan smile.

He lifted a hand as if to feel my brow, but something stayed it. His gaze left mine. "I'm glad that's all. You looked very uncomfortable, pained."

"You'd look pained too if you'd fallen asleep like this," I said, referring to my previous pretzel-like position.

He seemed satisfied and stood, picking up the dropped history text. "I must put this book by my bed if it's such a good sedative."

Smiling at his joke, I wanted him to hold me, but at the same time I wanted him to go away and leave me alone. My contradictory mood troubled me. I glanced down at Elizabeth's pug nose and wide blue eyes that stared up into my own as she nursed.

"I changed her diaper."

"Thanks." I looked back at Alex. "I love a man who changes a dirty diaper."

My remark had been offhanded. I tensed as Alex's gaze strafed my face and then soared past my head to the highest corner of the room. Why wouldn't his eyes meet mine? We both acted strained. I, because of a stupid comment and another mysterious dream I needed time to digest. But Alex seemed oddly uncomfortable as well. He had taken a step back from me in more ways than one. It was as if something had changed about the fledgling relationship we had started to form.

"If you have everything under control, I'll go to bed." His gaze darted back to mine.

"Sure, we're fine."

"Good night again."

"Good night, Alex."

I watched him go, a slow sadness creeping into my heart. The library door shut behind him. Silence. A clock ticked somewhere. Elizabeth made nursing noises. I breathed in and out, the breath squeezing into my lungs. For the first time in the mixed up, stressful three days of my marriage, a lump clogged my throat and a slow tear fell. I bent my head to the hand that held the bottle and wiped my eye dry on my wrist.

All right. Let's consider this logically. I had

80

experienced five dreams or visions or whatever you wanted to call them in three days. They had something to do with the time of King Edward III of England, for the actors in this drama had talked about their king. What did it all mean? Why me?

Elizabeth had emptied the bottle, so I set it down and lifted her to my shoulder. Gently, I patted her back.

None of these dreams had happened until I married Alex. There must be a connection. His medieval decorations, sure. I'd thought about them. But my first visions occurred before I had even stepped foot into my new home of Marchbrook Manor. The young girl of the visions had been married to an older lord for a very specific purpose. Conception. It was a marriage of convenience. Much like my own. Was that the reason I dreamed the dreams? Is that why some of them ended in childbirth—as if the medieval woman was reliving her life while in childbirth. But why did I experience the horrible pain too? I had more questions than answers, and it frustrated me.

"Do you feel better now?" I asked Elizabeth. Drawing her down from my shoulder, I rested my elbows on my knees so I could talk to her and see her face.

"My, aren't you a pretty baby," I said in that silly, motherly way. "Look at your big blue eyes. Bright eyes. You're such a beauty."

Elizabeth responded with her whole body to my nonsensical prattle. Her eyes moved, watching my facial expressions, my lips, my smile. She laughed, and puckered her lips in silent imitation. I ran a fingertip over her soft brow and the edge of her flat ear, across her chubby cheek to the tip of her nose.

"You're as cute as a button, little one. You'll have the boys flocking after you one day."

Elizabeth squirmed as if in anticipation. I pulled her into a standing position on my lap and she put weight on her feet.

"You know I love you, sweet one." Alex had already started the adoption process. In a few months, I would be Elizabeth's legal mother. Although I had known this child for such a short time, I was already attached to her by other, deeper, uncanny bindings.

Jan Scarbrough

"You know your daddy loves you a whole big bunch."
I gave her a hug.

*What about your real mother? She would have loved
you, too.*

As if afraid my errant thought would call Allison
back, I cuddled Elizabeth close to my breast. Unable to
stay still, I climbed to my feet and strolled the quiet
library.

"This is a library. It's where your daddy keeps books.
I'll read books to you some day," I promised.

I squeezed Elizabeth to my heart. She was so warm
and smelled of baby shampoo and formula. Drawing her
warmth to me, I shut my eyes a moment. But Elizabeth
wouldn't let me delay her guided tour. She wiggled in my
arms. Opening my eyes, I began to walk again.

"Here's a book on England in the Middle Ages. This
one's about English kings and queens." I pretended
Elizabeth could understand and described the books I saw
on the shelves. "Here's one about castles and another
about heraldry."

Examining the scores of books, we circled the room.
Wide awake, Elizabeth loved the trip. She loved my voice
and the steady motion.

"Women in the Middle Ages," I read the title of
another text. "Elizabeth, this entire library contains
nothing but books about medieval history."

Drawing a deep, sharp breath, I paused to survey the
whole room. Fear slithered through me like a snake. This
room was a shrine to a time long dead. With no other
subject visible, there was something obsessive about it.
Was there also something obsessive about my father-in-
law who had assembled the books?

I recoiled within myself. The recurring visions of the
young wife and her lord were visions of this distant time.
What did all of this have to do with me? Again I had no
answer, but I sensed something cold and sinister. Was my
marriage to Alex somehow connected?

Clutching Elizabeth, I left the library, not bothering
to turn off the lamps or shut the door. The resulting shaft
of yellow light illuminated the icy floor of the vast foyer,
causing it to glow like some sinister yellow brick road. I
rushed past the stalwart knights and kept my eyes on the

floor so I wouldn't see Allison's multicolor tapestries. I hurried up the sweeping, red-carpeted staircase. As I turned down the long darkened hall, a viperish silence confronted me.

I stopped. My heart careened in my chest. Someone was watching me. I felt its presence just as I felt Elizabeth's vital body in my arms. My cold fingers fumbled for the light switch, but I couldn't find it. The dead-black hallway vibrated with menace. My fear made me crazy and drove me to action. Running, stumbling, I reached Elizabeth's nursery and groped for the doorknob. The door wouldn't yield. I tried again, this time forcing my shoulder in to it until I fell into the room because of my momentum. Catching myself before the baby and I tumbled headlong onto the floor, I twisted around and hit the light switch. The welcoming lights blazed forth to show me Elizabeth's very normal room overflowing with cheerful Mickey Mouse cartoons. I slammed the door shut and locked it.

For a long moment, I remained by the door trembling. My life had become a world of shifting dread. From the visions of far-off times to the malicious threats in my room, I was afraid. Now this new menace, silent and unseen. What was I to do? My only link to sanity was this child. I glanced down at Elizabeth. Her bright blue eyes, wide and alert, looked up at mine. Maybe I had nothing to fear. Maybe it was just my silly imagination.

"You're not a bit sleepy, are you?" Elizabeth grinned in reaction to my question. At least I thought it was a grin. I smiled back. "Come on. I'll rock you."

Flicking on the night light, I turned off the overhead lights. The darkness was cut by a simple prick of illumination. I suppressed my fear and settled into the rocking chair. The ceaseless motion comforted both of us. Back and forth. Back and forth. In the shadows, I watched her small face and she watched mine until the even movement caused her eyelashes to flutter. Elizabeth didn't give up easily, but soon her eyes shut softly. She nursed a phantom nipple as I continued to rock. Once, in her sleep, she stretched her mouth into another smile.

****

I slept in fits and starts, awakening tired and

grumpy. Alex had already left for work by the time I finally arrived at the kitchen dressed in blue jeans and a yellow camp shirt, my hair pulled back in its familiar bun.

"Dr. Dominican told me to tell you he won't be home for supper." Mrs. Garrity's ramrod stiff back expressed her disapproval of me.

"Oh, thanks," I answered, the sound of my voice raspy.

She always made me feel at a disadvantage, like a school girl without her homework. I shook myself mentally and crossed the kitchen floor. At the counter, I poured a cup of steaming coffee. Nearby, I noticed a plate of blueberry muffins and selected one. Full from last night's dinner, I thought one muffin would be plenty for breakfast.

"Those aren't yours. They're for Mr. Dominican," Mrs. Garrity said, her back still turned.

So Alex's father ate after all, I thought scornfully. The mystery surrounding the infirm, old man was a little much for me to endure right now.

"Oh, sorry," I said.

When I started to put the muffin back, she relented. "Go ahead. You can have one. Next time, ask first."

I thought about snapping to attention and saluting. Instead, I gathered my coffee cup and pilfered muffin and retreated to the table.

"Elizabeth was wide-awake last night," I remarked as I tried to carry on a civil conversation. Not receiving an answer, I bit into the muffin and chewed slowly. The quiet room reflected the palpable tension between us.

"I have some shopping to do today," the housekeeper said. She finished rinsing the final pan, and turned to face me, drying her hands on a towel. "I'll be gone most of the morning and into the afternoon."

"All right."

"Put your dishes in the dish washer."

I bit back a caustic retort and took a sip of coffee. The black liquid tasted as bitter as the acrid thoughts in my head. When she left the room without further comment, I couldn't help myself. I stuck out my tongue at the shut door.

Tangled Memories

Feeling childish, I shoved my chair back from the table, and like a good girl, put my cup and saucer into the dish washer. For the rest of the morning, I busied myself with some housekeeping chores. Munster's litter pan needed emptying. After gathering up some of Elizabeth's laundry into the hamper, I assembled the towels, shampoo, soap, and clean clothes I needed for her bath. Because Elizabeth was much too small for the full-sized bathtub, and because I didn't have one of those small plastic tubs for infants, I used the bathroom sink, being cautious not to hit her head against the hard faucet.

"Shooey, what a smelly baby," I cooed to Elizabeth as I undressed her on a towel I'd spread out on the sink top.

Her chubby legs kicked out in response. The rolls of infant fat made her knees and elbows pucker. Elizabeth's baby-soft skin felt like satin to my touch.

And then I saw the red welts on her body—ugly, bruising sores on her legs—as if she'd been pinched. Hadn't Mrs. Garrity seen them?

Fortunately Elizabeth didn't seem affected by the bruises, for she looked up at me with her wide-eyed gaze and seemed to smile. Raw fury ripped my heart as I looked down at her. Threatening me was one thing. What kind of scum would harm an innocent child?

"Let me warm the water," I said, trying to remain calm and turning on the hot water with my left hand while I held her wiggly body with my right.

After letting it flow a few seconds, I plugged the drain. It was warm but not hot. Carefully supporting Elizabeth's head, I lifted her and moved her toward the sink.

Something caused me to stop before lowering her into the water. Was it the rising steam or the swift stab in my gut that made me pause? I laid Elizabeth back down on the towel again, and with my left hand, tested the steady stream of water.

"Ouch!" I snatched my hand back. "Damn, that's hot."

The water was scalding. I quickly turned down the flow and twisted on the cold water. Minutes later, I satisfied myself that it wasn't hot by dipping my left elbow into the pool of water.

"Doing this one-handed is hard," I told Elizabeth.

"My mother always said to test the baby's bath water with your elbow first. Of course, I never had any brothers or sisters, but we often kept my little cousins overnight."

I spoke casually, more to ease my trepidation than anything else. "And Goldilocks said, this is just right," I drawled out the last two words.

I didn't understand. The hot water tap had only been turned on a few seconds. I had done this before, letting the water warm, and then adding the cold to create the right temperature. This time, the water heated too quickly. Elizabeth could have been hurt again.

A fresh chill crawled up my back. I knew someone had turned up the hot water heater. Why? To harm me? Elizabeth? As I softly scrubbed the child's body, I wondered if Mrs. Garrity had done it. If Elizabeth's injury was considered my fault, she could discredit me with Alex. Maybe force me to leave. There was something deadly logical about the thought. I scowled, remembering the cold hostility of the woman. She was out to get me, and I couldn't prove a thing.

But I could find out if the hot water heater had been tampered with. As quickly as possible, I finished the bath routine, fed Elizabeth her bottle and tucked her in for a nap. Leaving the bathroom a mess, I hurried down the dusky hallway, down the flight of stairs and across the immense great hall. In the kitchen, the door to the basement stood open.

Someone had been down there. I flipped on the light switch. Could he—or she—still be there? Stifling the pang of fear that rose in my chest, I scuttled down the wooden steps where the workings of the house were contained. In one corner, the clothes dryer filled with bath towels spun and whirled. The washing machine was motionless, its top open. Somewhere in the vast labyrinth I knew the computer-controlled heating, air conditioning, security, music and intercom systems were located. Somewhere there was a wine cellar. Behind a folding door left ajar, I found the gas water heater. I knelt beside it. The switch pointed to "high" not the customary "energy saver." I was right. The sweet sense of justification coursed through my mind. Now all I had to do was show this to Alex.

As I stood up and backed away from the heater, I

heard footsteps above me at the door. Just as I glanced upward, the lights blanked out and the door slammed shut, throwing the whole basement into blackness.

Alone, frightened, angry, I stumbled my way toward the stairs.

"Ouch!" I struck a shin against the edge of the bottom step.

Gritting my teeth, I rubbed my bruised leg. Who was doing this? I grasped the rough, wooden handrail and inched my way up the stairs. The door was locked. With frigid fingers, I groped once again for the light switch only to remember it was on the kitchen wall, not inside the basement. I grabbed the doorknob once again and shook it, hoping beyond reasonable hope that the door would give.

That's when I heard breathing. Resting my ear against the door panel, I heard a distinct in and out rasping. He was still there. My tormenter. With my heart caught in my throat, I steadied my own breathing. What did he want? Why was he doing this? Snatches of horror movies and real-life tales of terror flashed through my mind. Would I end up in a pool of blood on the basement floor? After all, I was alone in the house except for Elizabeth, Rufus and Alex's father.

Elizabeth! Whoever it was had tried to hurt her earlier today. Would he try again?

"You let me out of here!" Defiant, I pounded the door and tried to keep hysteria out of my voice.

He walked away. Taking slow, hesitating steps, the person who had locked me in the basement went away. I heard the kitchen door bump shut. The silence was deathlike. Slowly, I eased down on the second step, limp with relief for myself, but painfully afraid for Elizabeth.

I don't know how long I remained there, thinking, trying to make some sense of the senseless. Mrs. Garrity wasn't the perpetrator. Even if, as I had thought, she had turned up the water heater, she couldn't have slammed and locked the door. She wasn't even home now. Was she? And what about Guy? Alex's father? He was a shut-in. How could he be the one? That left Rufus. My mind balked at the thought. The little man who had entertained me so graciously last night couldn't be the one. It was all so frustrating, so overwhelmingly bizarre.

Hunkering down, I rested my arm on the top step and put my head on my arm. I felt like a helpless fish on a fisherman's line. Control of my life gone, I could only flop helplessly in the water to rid myself of the hook. Life had played too many unkind tricks on me. I succumbed to a swollen dose of self-pity.

"Mary!"

Alex's strong voice permeated my consciousness.

"Alex!" I struggled to my feet and touched the shut door with my spread palms. "In the basement!"

The door flew open, and I tumbled into Alex's arms. The steady beat of his heart and his warm, muscular embrace eased my anxiety.

"Mary, what were you doing down there?" Alex grasped my upper arms and pulled me away from him to gaze accusingly into my eyes. "Why did you leaving Elizabeth unattended?"

"I didn't mean to," I said, panting, my own gaze seeking his understanding. "I left her asleep and went downstairs to the basement. Someone locked me in and turned off the lights. Alex, someone turned the water heater up to scald Elizabeth."

His black lashes lowered over his gray eyes. I felt the strong bite of his fingers into my flesh. "Mary, what are you talking about?"

"I just told you. Someone intentionally turned up the hot water heater, hoping I'd put Elizabeth into her bath without testing it." I couldn't muster looking at him, his gaze intense, so I glanced over his shoulder. Rufus stood behind him, Elizabeth safely tucked into his arms. I shifted my gaze to the floor. "Whoever he is wanted to hurt Elizabeth."

"That doesn't make sense. Who would harm Elizabeth?"

"I don't know," I said, lifting my eyes to meet his steady gaze. "Who would slash my suitcase?" And write "Get Out" on my mirror and spy on me in the hallway? I thought.

"Well, certainly not anyone here in this house."

Pulling away from his too encircling grip, I paced a few steps from him. "Maybe it was one of your horrid old knights come back to life," I suggested sarcastically.

"Oh, Mary." I heard annoyance in his voice.

"You don't believe me, do you?" I whipped around to denounce him. "Well, just go downstairs and look."

He sized me up with his gaze, and I lifted my chin. Without a word, he turned, flipped on the light switch, and disappeared down the basement steps. I glanced at Rufus, who favored me with a sympathetic stare. Did he think me a liar too? I gulped in a calming breath and released it slowly.

"The water heater is set at 'energy saver' just as always," Alex reported when he returned.

"It can't be! I just saw it on high." What was going on? An arrow of dread pierced my heart. Had someone else been downstairs with me? *But I'd heard footsteps upstairs.*

"You must be mistaken," he said.

"Just like I was mistaken about my slashed suitcase? Really, Alex." I balled my hands into a fist from sheer anger and frustration.

"I know what I saw, Mary."

"And I know what I saw!"

A frown on his face, he wheeled away from our confrontation. With four steps he put distance between us and halted behind the kitchen table. He gripped the back of the chair, his knuckles blanching white.

"I don't like yelling." His voice was deceptively calm.

I pinned him with my gaze. "Neither do I."

"As I see it, the problem is that Elizabeth was left alone. Mrs. Garrity is apparently out of the house. If Rufus hadn't called me, I'd never have known something was wrong. I'd have never come home in the middle of my afternoon schedule, leaving twelve patients waiting."

"Are you blaming me?" I grew incredulous. "I was the one locked in the basement. Explain *that*, will you? And while you're at it, explain how Rufus called you."

"Perhaps you locked yourself down there." His jaw muscles moved. "As for Rufus, we're very sophisticated now. I pay a special service. Rufus types his message into the computer upstairs, and the operator reads it and repeats it verbally to my office staff. Rufus never calls unless something is very wrong."

I vaguely heard his explanation about Rufus, but I was still bothered by his stupid accusation.

I drew the focus back to the locked door. "Now why would I lock myself in the basement?"

"How do I know? How do I know anything about you, Mary? After all, it's not as if we've known each other for a long time." His voice was taunting.

"What's that supposed to mean?" I couldn't believe the turn the argument had taken. "Don't you believe I have Elizabeth's best interests at heart? Why would I agree to this stupid marriage, that's not a real marriage, if I didn't care about your child?"

"Money. Position in the community." He shrugged his shoulders. "There are many reasons people marry."

"And yours was to have a mother for your child. Very noble," I spat out.

"So we both had ulterior motives. We knew that going into this marriage of convenience."

"Right. Why are we arguing about it now?" I asked, as I watched the shifting emotions on his face. "Last night you said something about building a relationship. Why the switch? What have I done that's so terrible?"

My reminder and questions took the barb from his anger. His gaze dropped to the table top. "I told you once, Mary, that I'm often not easy to live with. Now, perhaps, you'll believe me."

"I don't know what to believe," I replied, not wanting to give in, my own anger and frustration not ebbing.

That's when Rufus came between us. He handed me Elizabeth and made motions toward her diaper. I assume it was soiled. He crossed the floor to Alex, and patted his shoulder to get his attention. Alex glanced at him, his mind seeming a thousand miles away. Rufus touched his wrist watch and tipped his oversized head toward the door.

"Rufus tells me it's time to return to work," he said quietly. "I'm glad you're okay now."

"Yes, thank you." I didn't give in, my voice remaining icy.

"As I told Helena, I won't be home for dinner."

"I know."

His gaze landed on my face. It seemed sad. I

straightened my shoulders, not giving an inch. What was going on with him? I longed to probe the depths of his sudden depression, his swift change of emotion.

"Take more care."

"I will."

Alex turned from me, passing an errant hand through his black hair. I didn't want him to go. Not like this. Not after last night.

"Alex!"

He stopped and cast a look over his shoulder.

"Should I wait up?" I asked, lacking the nerve to summon him back and tell him I didn't want him to leave.

He faced me and offered a wan smile. "No, I may be late."

"Okay."

He smiled again as if to apologize and walked out of the kitchen, Rufus behind him. I bit my lower lip and worried it side to side. What had I gotten myself into? For the first time, I took seriously Gail's warnings. Maybe she had been right. Maybe I shouldn't have married Alexander Dominican. Then Elizabeth stirred in my arms. I looked down at her trusting blue eyes, and I remembered the red marks on her legs, the proof I had needed to convince Alex someone was trying to harm Elizabeth. I frowned. Had Rufus been trying to remind me about the red welts? Was that why he had brought Elizabeth to me?

Quickly I unwrapped her blanket only to discover her chubby legs unmarked—the welts faded. I swallowed hard, unable to straighten out the confusion in my mind. All I knew was that I had to put up with my marriage to Alex. For Elizabeth. For *my child*.

Jan Scarbrough

CHAPTER EIGHT

Unable to stay cooped up in the vast confines of Marchbrook Manor, I collected Elizabeth, strapped her into her car seat, and went for a ride. We barreled along the tree-lined private drive and turned onto Highway 42 toward Louisville. The rolling Kentucky countryside loomed lush and verdant in the late June sunshine. Soon it would be July. The heavy heat and humidity of summer would pervade the Ohio Valley, bringing with it an oppressive lethargy. I already felt sluggish, like a child without a playmate on a rainy day.

We stopped first at Gail's house, but didn't find her home. Next we ate an early supper at a small but trendy St. Matthews eatery. Secure in her infant seat, Elizabeth behaved quite well for what I assumed to be her first time in a restaurant. I thought her father would have been proud. I wished Alex had been with us. We should have been together as a family. With my hands curled around a hot cup of after-dinner coffee, I sighed as I watched steam rise from the dark liquid. My thoughts made me feel dejected, so I resolved not to think. I needed some activity to distract me. After paying the bill, I drove Elizabeth to Seneca Park for an evening stroll.

I had bought the "Cadillac" of baby strollers. Elizabeth's arms stroked the air as I put her inside the reclining seat, strapped her in, and lightly draped a blanket over her. I slipped into my walking shoes, and then we crossed the busy street. Countless other people had the same idea, crowding the paved one mile track that circled the park. Blade skaters dodged couples holding hands. A gray-haired woman passed me walking fast and pumping her arms. A sweaty jogger trotted by. Mixing with automobile traffic, bikers, their butts in the air, pedaled streamline racing machines.

"Elizabeth, you'll love it here when you're a bit older," I told the contented and sleepy baby.

There was so much to see. Inside the grassy oval, high-school girls hit balls with their field hockey sticks. Three lean boys tossed frisbees. Dusty women contested a game of softball. A man raced his dog. Coming around the packed tennis courts, I saw the children's playground jammed with toddling "twos" and watchful parents. I stopped a moment to observe the active children and dream of the future.

With a sigh, I pushed the stroller onward. Up ahead to the right was Rock Creek Riding Club, the place where, as a child, I had ridden American Saddlebred horses. As I hurried past, I remembered the days when my mother had stabled Royal Tiara there. Horseback riding had been her way of keeping my thoughts away from my father, who had divorced her so cruelly. It hadn't worked. I longed for him for two years before finally realizing he'd never return. Then as she had wanted, I had turned my attention to riding and showing, winning blue and red ribbons with regularity. All until Bill Adams stormed into my life, changing it forever.

Swallowing hard, I fought back the tears now pooling in my eyes. The day after I had told my mother about my marriage and pregnancy, she had sold my chestnut mare. I recalled my fear and shame. Missing my horse, I also missed my mother. Our estrangement still bothered me. Jutting my chin out and walking faster, I decided not to dwell on it. That part of my life was over and done with. No one received a second chance.

"How do you do, Mrs. Dominican?"

Startled, I glanced at the puffing jogger who had just passed me, made a U-turn and was now keeping time by my side.

"Dr. Hilliard?" I quickly wiped my eyes.

"The one and only, sweetheart."

I flinched at his rude endearment. In eight years as

my gynecologist, he'd never called me sweetheart. Maybe marrying his partner instantly gave him the right. Out of instinct, I straightened my shoulders and placed a polite, but plastic, smile on my face. He took his pulse and continued to huff and puff by my side.

"Do you jog often?" I asked to be cordial.

"Every chance I get. That can't be Lizzy, can it?" he wanted to know, bending low to look down at Alex's child.

"Elizabeth," I corrected, pausing to glare at him.

"No, no, don't stop. Can't cool off too fast. Keep walking."

I paced onward, glad to keep moving. Alex's medical partner was his complete opposite. About a head shorter, he was chunkier, his hairy legs bulging from a pair of skimpy nylon shorts. Some women would have thought him attractive, for he had a pleasant enough face, blond hair, and a quick twinkle in his blue eyes. Yet there was a childishness about him, an irreverence for life. In my mind, he didn't compare to my husband.

"Haven't seen little Liz since she was born. Looks a lot like her mother."

Though innocent, his comment hauled me back into reality. Back into the untenable position I had gotten myself into.

"Did you know the first Mrs. Dominican?"

"Allison? Of course. Beautiful woman. Beautiful woman." Dr. Hilliard checked his pulse again and slowed his pace.

"Her death was such a tragedy," I murmured. It was the appropriate thing to say.

He nodded in agreement. "Happened so fast it shocked everyone. Alex felt guilty. Nothing he could do, of course."

"That's what he told me. He seems very hurt by it."

"Sure, quite a blow to the ol' ego." There was a biting edge to his voice.

"I'm sure if you lost your wife, Dr. Hilliard, you'd feel some sort of sorrow." I stiffened as I paused to glare at him.

He looked me in the eyes and smiled. "Call me John, will you?"

"John," I said, trying to understand what was going

on beyond the man's pleasant smile. "You make it sound as if Alex didn't care for his wife."

He shrugged and looked away. We started to stroll again. "Sure, he cared for her in his own way, I guess."

"So why did you say Allison's death was a blow to his ego? What does that mean?"

"His professional ego, sweetheart. Alex, if you don't know, is first and foremost a physician."

"I know he is dedicated to his practice."

"To the point of being obsessive," John remarked as he shoved a hand through his blond hair. He paused and turned to me. "Listen, Mary. All the bluster aside. Don't let this guy hurt you like he did Allison."

"What do you mean?" As if I'd run a mile, a painful stitch crawled up my side.

"Alex is a wonderful doctor. Competent, conscientious. Although we've had our differences, I'm glad he's my partner." The deep blue of his eyes sharpened as he gazed at me. "His work is the first thing in his life. Allison found that out the hard way."

I didn't want to hear more. To cover my confusion, I bent over the stroller to adjust Elizabeth's blanket. "They seemed to be very happy."

"Things aren't always what they seem."

I stood up and looked at him. We regarded each other evenly for a moment. Uneasy, I walked on. He kept pace.

"You don't look well, Mary. Are you doing okay?" John asked, his shoulder brushing mine ever so faintly.

"Yes, what do you mean?"

"Physically. You've got some dark circles under your eyes that weren't there when I saw you last."

Were my sleepless nights so obvious to a man I hardly knew? "You know, that's really none of your business."

"But I'm your doctor. A good doctor notices these things."

Maybe John was right. A good doctor should be able to recognize pain—a good doctor and a caring husband.

My thoughts trailed into a never-never land that could not be. Alex Dominican was my husband in name only, no matter what I was coming to want from our marriage of convenience.

"I have been bothered by some abdominal pain lately," I admitted, distracted. The sharp pangs caused by my visions were disturbingly real. I wasn't making it up. Whenever I awoke from a dream, the insufferable pains gripped me like the claws of a cat gripping a captured mouse.

"Why don't you come by the office tomorrow about two? I'll work you in."

"Oh, no. I couldn't do that." What if Alex found out about my dreams?

Again John sensed my discomfort. "Remember, I'm your doctor, Mary. I know what's best for you, even if Alex doesn't."

There it was again, that jab at Alex. I cast an uneasy look his way. "John, I don't know."

He stopped me with his hand. Laying it on my arm, his fingers intimate on my skin, he shook his head, and clucked at me like a mother hen, "Mary, Mary. You know you can't tend that beautiful baby if you're ill."

John had me there. He knew what button to push. And I didn't want Alex to know about my medical problems. I glanced away, drawing my arm away from him. "I'll come, but you must not tell Alex. Are you sure it won't be a problem?"

"Sure. The girls are used to working in my patients. No trouble at all." His fingers touched me again like a lover.

"Thank you," I said, finding it hard to breathe. "I'll be there."

"Good." John squeezed my arm, and released me, a grin spreading across his face. "Damn me, but Alex sure knows how to pick 'em. He has quite a taste for lovely wives."

I felt a hot flush surface in my cheeks. I pulled a mantle of dignity around me, straightening my spine. The doctor's attention was hardly appropriate, like the kiss he gave me on my wedding day. I wondered how Alex could keep him as a partner, and how had I missed his rude sexism over the years?

"Thank you again, John, I need to get home."

"Don't worry about Alex. He's at the hospital for the duration."

"You misunderstand. I'm not worried about Alex. It's Elizabeth. It's past her bedtime." I used the baby as my excuse. I should have told John Hilliard that his advances weren't proper, but I was afraid of causing trouble with my husband's partner.

"Well, you take care until then, and we'll just find out what's giving you trouble."

"Yes. I'll see you tomorrow."

He turned and left, striding away from me like a proud lion. I watched him go, the words and emotions of our short conversation churning in my mind. I thought them strange and troubling. When I was Mrs. Bill Adams, Dr. Hilliard never called me "sweetheart" nor claimed I was attractive. I had been the same person then. Or had I? Maybe the four days of my marriage had changed me more profoundly than I realized.

****

"Where have you been?" Mrs. Garrity greeted me at the front door like a sweeping black bird of prey.

"To town," I answered mildly.

She scooped Elizabeth out of my arms and cradled the sleeping child to her chest. "You've disturbed Elizabeth's schedule, exposed her to all sorts of diseases," she snapped.

"Now wait a minute. I haven't done anything wrong." I fought to retain control of myself. "Elizabeth's my responsibility. I wouldn't do anything to hurt her."

"That's your opinion," she said, a vicious sneer on her lips.

Drawing myself up to my full height, I glared down at the black-haired woman. "Elizabeth is not some toy store doll. She's a living child who will some day go to kindergarten and first grade. She can't be kept cooped up in this house all the time."

"That may be so, but she's too young now to go gallivanting around the countryside," Mrs. Garrity answered as she turned her back on me and started up the circular stairs to the second floor.

"I'm her mother," I shouted after her, my empty hands balling into fists. "I'll do what's best for her."

The housekeeper paused on the landing, and leveled a frosty look at me. "Her mother? My poor Allison is this child's mother." Turning, she disappeared down the unlit hall.

Mrs. Garrity's chill words stripped the fight from me. Heavy of heart, I deflated like a day-old balloon. Now the housekeeper would discover the bruises on Elizabeth's legs. Now she'd discredit me with Alex.

What was going on? I had no control over the one thing in this house that was supposed to be mine. Elizabeth. At least the housekeeper's enmity was tangible, something I could see and hear. That was something I couldn't say about the other forces in this strange and frightening house.

Worn out to the bone, a wave of fatigue engulfed me. I settled on the bottom step and dropped my head into my hands. Why had I gotten myself into this mess? My brief respite this afternoon from the mysteries of the Dominican house was over, and I was weak with fear. A grim sense of futility and despair plagued me. Why had Allison been unhappy? Was Alex's career so all-consuming that he had no time for his first wife? But he seemed so sad at her funeral. They had produced a child. Surely, that revealed something about their love for each other?

I glanced at Allison's tapestries. Gail had suggested her cousin hadn't been happy. John had said the same thing. The pieces didn't fit. I shook my head, frustrated.

I had never closely studied Allison's intricate handiwork. In fact, I had avoided it. Now I found myself inexplicably drawn toward the wall hangings, like a helpless shaving of iron was pulled toward a strong magnet. I moved ghost-like toward the nearest one, the startling myriad of colors blurring my vision. Armored knights, beautiful ladies, fanciful griffins and frightful gargoyles swirled together in a mist of blood red, golden yellow, and royal purple. My heart clutched, and emotion twisted into my throat. As if my hand was weighted with lead, I reached upward and grasped the heavy fabric.

"Mountjoy!" I expelled the word with a great rush of breath.

Transfixed, I gazed at the scene Allison had stitched of two jousting knights. One as bright as the sun, the other as dark as night. Behind them, on a high hill stood a castle. I'd seen that castle before. In some other time. And it had been called *Mountjoy*.

How could Allison have known about its sturdy battlements? How could she have seen the rise of Welsh mountains in the distance? Trembling, I released the tapestry and slumped to the cold, white marble floor. How could I have known its name?

A piercing ringing sound clamored loudly in my ears. Slick sweat moistened my palms. The noise grew in intensity, and I raised my hands to cover my ears. No! It was happening again. The vision! Would it be happy this time or would I see the woman writhing in the pain of childbirth? Fear nauseated me. I felt so dizzy—like I was drifting on a cloud of swirling light. My eyes blurred. Suddenly, as the room began to quake, the brilliant shades in the tapestries scattered together into one great kaleidoscope of blinding color...

****

"She hates me!" Mary screamed, twisting out of the hands of Gellis and throwing herself upon the great bed. "My lord's mother hates me."

Tears of frustration and anger soaked the linen pillowcase as Mary vented her emotion.

"Lord Mountjoy's mother has a wicked tongue." Gellis dropped her shaking hand to the top of Mary's head. She paused a moment as if to control her emotions. "Now, it does no good to keen so," she said, trying to soothe the distraught girl. "Think of the child you carry."

The reminder pulled Mary into a sitting position. Her wet fingers clutched the bed sheets. "You'd think she'd be happy I carried my lord's heir," she said with a pout. "After all, it's what she wanted."

The happiness she felt with her husband was bitter gall whenever her mother-in-law was in the room. Mary wiped her eyes with the back of her hand and scooted off the bed. She put her hands on the small of her back and stretched. Her immense belly, distended with the child, jutted forward. Gellis came near and smoothed her skirts.

"Now go back down to the great hall. Hold your head high. You have your lord's heart, and his mother knows it."

"You think so?" Mary asked, her own burdened heart

leaping with hope. She would give thanks if her husband
cared for her, not just the babe she had conceived and
carried.

"The old woman is just jealous," Gellis said,
whispering near her lady's ear.

The soft breath of the servant's words murmured
gently through Mary's heavy heart.

Late that night in the sanctuary of the lord's bed,
Mary cuddled against the firm, naked body of her
husband. She ran lingering fingertips over his strong
thigh and down his hard and hairy leg. She felt him
tense. He rolled over to face her, his long mane of black
hair splaying on the pillow.

"Little witch," he murmured in her ear.

"My lord?"

"You keep me up at night. After a long day and losing
a dog in the hunt, I want nothing but sleep."

"Do you, my lord?"

He pulled her against him, honey blond hair
mingling with coal black locks. His mouth was sweet and
supple against her own. Mary moaned into his lips and
drew her arms around his neck.

"St. Thomas Aquinas must surely be right," he
muttered between kisses.

"Who's that?" Mary asked, and answered his assault
with combat of her own.

"The Dominican priest Pope John canonized a few
years ago," he said pausing for air. Gently he stroked her
high cheek bone, his fingertips traveling along a dusky
brow and down a pert nose. "He theorized that women
were at the peak of their desire during pregnancy."

"How would a priest know?" Mary wondered, her own
hands busy doing teasing things to her husband's midriff.

"Church men have the words of old philosophers as
well as Christian teachings to study." He nipped her
earlobe.

"Not experience?"

"You talk sacrilege, my lady." He traced a pattern of
kisses along her neck.

"Holy marriage is God's will, my lord," she reminded
him as she trailed a fingertip down the hairy line from his
navel.

It was his turn to moan. Squirming with desire, he grasped her hand and placed it around his manhood. "Aquinas's theory is based on the superiority of man," he said, his hot lips again stroking her neck.

"Yes," she gasped.

"The woman, being imperfect, desires conjunction with the perfect man, since the imperfect desires to be perfected," he instructed as his mouth met hers. He plunged his tongue deeply into her softness, capturing her, their mouths twisting together in heated passion. They broke apart, both panting. "Therefore, the greater desire and pleasure belong to the woman," he said, his gray eyes dark with need.

Mary pulled her head back so that she could better see his face. "Sounds like something a witless priest would say." She lowered her heavy eyelashes over the sultry blue of her eyes. "You tell me, my lord, that your pleasure is not as great as mine now." She clutched his manhood, wiggling as close to him as her bulging belly would allow.

He groaned. "In this, my wife, we are equals." He had trouble speaking, his words halting and heated.

As his words left him, Mary joined him in his world of equality. When they became one, their cries of triumph rose together in unison from both their lips.

Until she cried alone. A long, shrill cry of childbirth.
****

My cheek pressed flat against the cold marble floor. In the fetal position, I clutched my abdomen, the sharp pains too much to take. Blinking once, the edges of my lashes rubbing the hard stone, I realized the last of the dream-vision had ended. Alex's massive entry hall dwarfed me. As I stared across its vastness, I felt vulnerable. Alone. By pressing my right hand against the floor, I was able to push myself into a sitting position. I knew I couldn't let anyone find me here, prone and listless. I couldn't give Mrs. Garrity more ammunition. I couldn't admit weakness to Alex. Slowly, my spinning head steadied a bit. But the ache in my gut continued.

I crawled to my feet. Glancing at the tapestry, I realized I had learned two more pieces of the puzzle. I knew the name of the castle of my dreams. *Mountjoy.* I knew its master, *Lord Mountjoy*. And his first name was *Alexander*. The name of my own husband!

Maybe now I could find out if such a place ever existed. Maybe now I could put Alex's curious library to good use. I took a hesitant step. My dizziness persisted. Slowly, I crossed the vacant hall, the armored knights watching me. I grasped the cold knob, opened the door, and flicked on the light. The quiet lay over the room like a sleeping cat.

I went to the nearest bookshelf, my sweaty palms clutching its edge for support. My eyes focused. I took down a heavy, leather-bound text, crossed the short distance to Alex's easy chair, and hunkered down for the duration.

Hours later, I knew much more about English history—how a Norman invader won the battle of Hastings in 1066. Ingloriously called William the Bastard, after that day he had become William the Conqueror. I had learned about Richard the Lion-heart, and his scoundrel brother John of Robin Hood fame. I had read about Thomas Becket, shamefully killed by Henry II's thugs. Yet, in all I had studied, I had gained no clue to my own dilemma. I still didn't understand why I dreamed dreams of medieval men and women, and why Mary and Alexander were so familiar.

CHAPTER NINE

The waiting room for Louisville OB/GYN Associates, Inc. bubbled with activity. Detached, I waited my turn behind a very pregnant woman, and then signed my name on a pad of paper at the reception window.

The white-clad clerk behind the counter read my name. "Have you been here before Mrs. Dominican?" she asked without looking up.

"Yes."

She glanced at me. "Christy" was pinned to her blouse. "Mrs. Dominican?" she queried. "Are you Dr. Dominican's new wife?"

"Yes," I said again, a bit breathless. I felt all the bright and busy eyes in the office turn toward me. "You should find my records under Adams. Mary Adams."

"Congratulations," she murmured. "I hope you and the doctor will be happy."

I watched her leave her chair to search the wall of yellow file folders for my records. *Happy*. What a strange concept. I hardly remembered happiness. Surely, not in the years of my marriage to Bill. His drinking drove a wedge through our marriage, a wedge I had not been able to overcome. Yes, as a child I had known happiness, but not now. I doubted if happiness could exist for me with Alex, not as we were at this moment.

Christy came back to the desk, my folder in her hand. Sitting, she offered me a tentative smile. "You're a patient of Dr. Hilliard," she said, thumbing through my files.

"Yes, and that will remain the same."

She nodded and wrote something down.

"I suppose you'll have to change my address," I suggested, ill-at-ease.

"To Dr. Dominican's address?"

"Yes, Marchbrook Manor. I'm sorry I don't know the route number."

"We have it. What about insurance?"

"Oh, I don't know." I fretted with my purse strap. "I suppose you'll have to ask Alex."

"Fine," she said, gazing up at me. She understood my awkwardness. "Why are you here today? You weren't scheduled."

They all must know about Alex's quick marriage so soon after the death of his first wife. They must wonder, like I, the reason for his insistence, his haste.

"Dr. Hilliard said he'd work me in," I told her.

She noted my comment on the chart, and nodded once more. "Okay. If you'll have a seat, we'll call you soon."

I found a chair in the corner, and picked up a frayed *Parents* magazine. As I slowly flipped through it, my gaze darted from the worn pages to the expectant mothers who filled the stuffy room. A bewildered father balanced on the edge of his chair. They all seemed so young and eager. I felt old and careworn. With my hair enshrouded into its familiar bun, I had tried to cover the tracks of my emotions that rode visibly across my face. My dark circles were concealed by light cover-up, my eye makeup carefully crafted, my lips darkened with red. I dressed in a tailored, navy pantsuit to give myself confidence. Sprinkling lavender cologne along the nape of my neck and on my wrists, I tried to compensate for the jarring, harsh dream-vision of the night before.

But nothing could truly offset my experiences of the last five days. From the afternoon of my marriage to Alex, my life had been turned into a kaleidoscope of stark and frightening images. Sitting here in the crammed waiting room only sharpened those images in my mind. The young Mary, her proud black-haired knight, and his jealous mother. Mrs. Garrity. Jealous herself, and demanding. Rufus, silent but observant. And my husband. A contradiction. Had he loved his first wife? Why then had Allison been unhappy? Why did Alex need me to mother his child?

Alex had not come home last night. With Munster curled at the foot of my solitary bed, I had finally drifted off to sleep. Alex had not been home this morning, and although she had readily agreed to watch Elizabeth, Mrs. Garrity had been her usual un-talkative self. I felt alone—more alone than I had ever been during my marriage to Bill.

"Mrs. Dominican."

Jerking my attention back to the present, I obediently stood up and followed a long-haired nurse into the inner office area. We walked down a narrow hallway, and turned the corner. In a highly lit office, the nurse took my blood pressure and weighed me. Then she led me into a small examining room.

"And why are you here today?"

My hand strayed to my abdomen. "I've had some cramping."

With brisk efficiency, she pulled a white sheet from beneath the examining table. "Please undress from the waist down, and drape this around you. The doctor will see you in a few minutes."

In the steady quiet of the empty room, I took off my suit-coat and pulled off my trousers and panties. Climbing onto the table, I sat on its edge between gleaming, impersonal stirrups, and wrapped the sheet around my waist. Then I waited for what felt like a lifetime until Dr. Hilliard rapped twice and burst into the room like a whirlwind.

"Mary! Good to see you," he said, his enthusiasm overwhelming.

"Thank you, John, for working me in." Nervous, I toyed with the white sheet. I felt more vulnerable in this position than ever before.

The long-haired nurse followed him into the room and shut the door quietly. John washed his hands and then turned toward me, his blue eyes clear and penetrating.

"Now tell me again your symptoms."

My throat was dry. "I have these cramps. Like you'd

have in labor, but although I've been pregnant, I never experienced labor. So I don't really know how labor pains feel." My gaze shifted from his attentive face to the floor. This was absurd. I felt like a child complaining of a stomachache on Monday morning.

"How often do these attacks occur?"

Attacks. An appropriate term for the gut-wrenching pain I had felt. "They started a few days ago. I suppose I've had maybe three or four."

"When, a few days ago?"

His probing was like a blunt knife. I flinched. How could I tell him the truth? That the pain only happened after my dreams. "Saturday. After my wedding."

"I see." John stepped closer. He smelled of aftershave and antiseptic soap. "Do you usually have cramps during your period?"

"No."

He nodded. "Now lie back and we'll just check you out."

His cool hand held mine as he helped me to lie back on the table. I lifted my feet into the stirrups, the cloth draped over me.

"Now scoot your hips all the way down," he said. "Open your knees wide and put your hands by your side."

Unable to see what he was doing, I gazed at the ceiling. I heard the plastic pop as he pulled on sanitary gloves.

"Now, I'm going to give you a pelvic exam." John's bedside manner was well practiced. "I'll insert the speculum, and you should tell me if you have any discomfort."

I glanced toward him. He disappeared behind the sheet. When he touched my inner thigh, my leg twitched.

"Relax. We've done this before." He looked over the top of the sheet, his smile meant to be reassuring.

John straightened and pressed my abdomen, the smile still on his lips, and his gaze biting deeply and intimately into mine.

"I'll go ahead and give you a Pap smear, but I see nothing wrong." He dropped once again out of sight. A moment later, John was finished, peeling off his gloves, and tossing them into the trash. Extending his hand once more, he pulled me up into a sitting position. "Get dressed, Mary, and meet me in my office."

He left and the nurse followed. Slowly, I redressed. I felt unusual, as if I had somehow been transgressed. As if something had transpired between us besides a routine pelvic exam, but I couldn't quite figure out what.

When I opened the door and stepped out into the narrow hallway, I bumped headlong into my husband.

"Alex! I'm sorry. I didn't see you."

His strong hands caught and steadied me. I saw surprise sever the preoccupation on his face. Astonishment turned to annoyance as he realized whom he grasped. "Mary? What are you doing here?" His gray, brooding gaze pierced into my heart like a swift rapier.

"Dr. Hilliard said he'd work me in," I said, my own gaze lifting to clash with his.

"When did you talk to John?" His hard fingers stabbed deeper into the fabric of my suit-coat.

"Yesterday in the park. He was jogging and I had Elizabeth out for a stroll." Things you would have known if you had come home and talked to me like a normal husband talks to his wife, I thought.

"Is there something wrong?" he asked.

Softening a little toward him, I wanted him to understand, to say it would be okay, to hold me. Like a two-year-old who had lost a treasured blanket, I longed for reassurance. A dark strand of his coal black hair flopped casually across his forehead, drawing my attention to his emotion-packed eyes and high cheekbones. My vision blurred. I imagined Alex's noble hand strafing through his hair, disheveling it even more to cause the lock to fall. I imagined his gray-eyed gaze husky with love-wanting, his black lashes dropping seductively to shade the needy look in his eyes. *Alexander would take me then, and draw me into his bear-like embrace.*

"Mary, is there something wrong?" Alex asked again, this time shaking me slightly.

My clouded vision snapped back into focus. A thin spike of dread speared my heart. I had mistaken Alex for the black-hooded lord of my dreams. What was happening to me? Was I going crazy? Unwilling to let him see the

107

turmoil within me, I hauled all my inner strength upward, straightened my spine, squared my shoulders and lifted my chin.

"I've had some cramping," I said matter-of-factly.

"Why didn't you come to me?"

Why? What would you have done? I asked myself, anger a healthy replacement for dread and confusion.

"I told you about the slashed suitcase and hot water incident. You didn't believe me. Why should I come to you with my other problems?"

"Because I'm your husband." The pressure increased on my arms, and I thought he would shake me again.

"Are you sure? Or are you still Allison's widower?"

My caustic remark startled him. "This isn't the place to discuss our personal problems," he said with a hiss.

"Personal problems? As if we have a personal life to have 'personal problems' about." I couldn't keep the mocking tone from my voice, and it only angered Alex more.

A busy nurse excused herself and slipped past, looking askance at us.

"Get in here." Alex shoved me back into the examining room, and closed the door.

"What are you doing?" I retreated until my numb fingers touched the cold edge of the examining table.

"I'm your husband, and I *will* take care of whatever personal problems you have, not Hilliard. Now, tell me about this cramping. When did it start? How severe is it?"

"Dr. Hilliard has already examined me, and I don't intend to get undressed again." My bold taunt served to further cover my fear.

"We'll see about that."

Alex crossed the small space between us and caught my shoulders. In one swift move, he stripped off my suit-coat, letting it fall to the floor.

"Stop it!

"I don't like you seeing Hilliard."

"He's my doctor."

"Not any more."

We parried like two swordsmen. His breath hot upon my face, he gripped the flesh of my upper arms. I stared into his eyes, daring him to carry on this duel, but

knowing full well that my heart risked puncture by his
nearness.

"You're not my lord and master," I taunted again.

The gray in his eyes deepened. I knew I'd gone to far.
In a swift advance, he lowered his lips to mine and
captured them, holding them hostage as he plied them
with an angry assault. I surrendered. My whole body
tingled as I capitulated to his strength and his prowess. I
closed my eyes, and returned kiss for kiss.

"Oh, I'm sorry!"

I opened my eyes to see the face of a startled nurse as
she swiftly shut the door.

As if he'd been stabbed by a blade, Alex dropped his
hands from my arms and backed away from me. He
looked shaken. "I'll see you tonight, and we'll finish this
discussion," he promised, turning on his heels to leave
me.

"Good. I have something to look forward to," I
scorned his broad back, and fought to regain my
composure.

Why had I reacted that way? Why had I invited his
anger? I rubbed my forehead with the icy palm of my
hand. Things had been going so well. For one evening, we
had made a good start. Now as my short marriage
imploded around me, I did nothing to shore it up.

With slow steps, I made my way to John's office and
slumped down in a chair facing his desk. It was a large,
mahogany one with a tiny brass lamp casting a round
yellow glow on its polished surface. Like a silent
spectator, my medical chart lay in the middle of the
desktop.

Dr. Hilliard hurried in and shut the door. Circling
the desk, he sat behind it, opened my file and made some
notations. He leaned forward over my chart, his hands
folded passively, his gaze searching my face.

"As I said in the examining room, I see nothing
physically wrong with you, Mary," he said with easy
familiarity.

"I see," I responded, my gaze flitting from his face to
his hands.

"Now I don't deny your pains, but I believe they may
be more emotional than physical."

Jan Scarbrough

"Are you saying I'm crazy?" I asked, defensive.

"No, not at all. I'm just suggesting you've been under a lot of stress these past few days. Stress can do destructive things to your body. It doesn't mean there's anything psychologically wrong with you."

His voice was soft and beguiling. I glanced up at his handsome face, his eyes inviting friendship. Remembering his intrusive kiss on my wedding day and his brazen attitude toward me yesterday, I struggled to reconcile myself to the professional and caring doctor in front of me.

"Yes, I have been under strain lately." My fingers pinched the strap of my purse.

"Didn't you faint on your wedding day?" John asked, his gaze direct.

"Yes," I said again and looked away. I didn't feel right confiding in him.

"And those cramps have gotten worse since then?"

"No, not worse, I guess," I was uncertain how to answer.

"But you've continued to have them?" he wanted to know.

"Yes."

John sat back in his chair, his hands still clasped. His long index fingers tapped together while he favored me with an unswerving look. "Mary, I've wondered why you married Alex so quickly. You couldn't know him very well."

I shifted uneasily in my seat. Know him well? I felt I didn't know Alex at all.

"It's really none of your business, John," I said.

"Mary, I'm just trying to help you." His tone encouraged trust.

"He paid my debts, the debts my husband left me after he was killed in the car wreck," I said to get him off my back.

John leaned forward again. "I'm sorry, Mary, but that doesn't seem like a viable motivation. You're much too intelligent to marry someone for such a lame reason."

At the barb, I straightened in my chair. "I don't know what you mean." I was tired of everyone telling me I shouldn't have married Alex.

110

"You're a smart woman. Why did you fall for someone like Alexander Dominican? He's using you to take care of that child of his, and your subconscious reactions to the pressure are ruining your health," John declared, his voice stinging.

I swallowed a retort, and gazed directly at my doctor. Maybe he was right. My physical problems had started with my dreams, and the dreams had started with my marriage. My subconscious was playing dirty tricks on me—not to mention the normal tensions of caring for an infant, and the anxiety caused by the malicious threats to Elizabeth and me. I knotted my hands into fists. I was a basket-case. John had put his finger on my problem.

"I don't suppose I fell for Alex as much as I was drawn to him," I confided, my voice hushed.

"Drawn to him?" John's gaze hardened. "Why is everyone 'drawn' to my partner? He's not some sort of magician, is he?"

"No, and sometimes he's not a very understanding man," I said, more to myself than to John. "I can't explain why I married him. It's as if I were compelled for some reason." I finished my inner reverie, realizing I had admitted more to John than I had ever admitted to my best friend Gail, or even myself. I was horrified by what I had done. My first marriage to Bill had robbed me of the ability to trust, but here I had confided in a man, another alcoholic, just like my first husband.

Focusing on his face, I smiled weakly to cover my distress. "So what's to be done? 'Til death us do part, and all," I said.

"Like Allison," he responded, his face harsh with an anger I didn't comprehend.

"But Allison died of cancer. You're not implying Alex had anything to do with it? You already said nothing could be done for the poor woman."

Something flickered across his features, and he stood up and walked to the window. "Yes, you're right. I sometimes wonder though, if she'd been happier, maybe the cancer wouldn't have..." his voice trailed off.

"You said that before, about Allison. Gail said it, too. Why was she unhappy?" I wanted to know. *Were strange things happening to Allison just as they happened to me?*

John turned, shrugging, as if he wanted to cut off my train of thought. "Allison is gone. My concern now is for you." He sat again and scribbled on a pad of paper. "Here, take this," he said, handing me a prescription. "It will help relax you."

"I don't like to take those things."

"Do you like to experience abdominal pain?"

"No."

"Then take it." He shoved the prescription at me. "I'm your doctor. I have your best interests at heart."

"All right," I said, reaching across his desk to take the paper from him. I knew I wouldn't take the medicine John had prescribed. Our fingers touched. I snatched my hand away, and tucked the prescription in my purse. Standing, I regarded John frankly, "I hope you won't discuss any of this with Alex."

"Of course not," he said, "Doctor, patient relationship and all. I'll respect your confidences."

Bristling, I wished he knew nothing of my secrets. I felt vulnerable, as if his knowledge somehow put me at a disadvantage. John came around the desk to usher me out the door, the palm of his hand resting on the small of my back. I felt his touch through my layers of clothing, and I shied like a skittish horse. As we walked down the narrow hallway to the exit, I glimpsed Alex in a far doorway. When our gazes connected, he turned his back, took a chart from a rack, and entered an examining room.

****

I went home to Marchbrook Manor, home to a child I called my own. Elizabeth had just awakened from a nap. I changed her, gave her a bottle, and then brought her with me into Alex's library. Spreading a heavy quilt on the floor, I placed the baby on her back so she could kick and clutch at her toes. Thank goodness Mrs. Garrity would have the evening off.

"I hope you don't mess your life up like I did," I told Elizabeth as I searched the shelves of medieval history books. "Maybe I'll be there for you to talk to. Maybe you'll listen to me. I can give some wonderful advice. Straight from experience."

I pulled a thick volume from a shelf and settled down on the floor next to Elizabeth, my back against the sofa.

Who was I kidding? Teenagers never listened to their mothers. Like I didn't hear mine. I had been too much in love with Bill Adams to think about anything else. Not school, nor my riding. I'd blown the championship that August, failing to qualify for the prestigious final four-rider workout. My mother had been crushed; my riding instructor angry. I remembered all that now with regret. Back then it was as if I had been walking through a thick fog, a thick fog called "true love."

I shut my eyes a moment, tipping my chin up and drawing a cleansing breath. Maybe now that I was remarried, I should try to contact my mother again. Maybe I should make the first move. The futility of her rejection and my father's desertion paralyzed me. Resigned, I opened my eyes. Life had slipped out of my control. I could do nothing to change my parents. Inwardly, I cried at the unfairness of it all.

However, I refused to let myself wallow in self-pity. To ease my present stress, I needed some answers, and they didn't come from a bottle of pills. I had to find them myself. Sitting up straighter and picking up the heavy book, I began to read about the plight of women in the Middle Ages. They were mere objects. In marriage, a woman had no legal existence, and was subject to the wishes of her husband. Feudal society was harsh, but even more so for women who bore their suffering in silence. They had no awareness of themselves as women. Marriages were arranged, but not for love. The more I read, the angrier I got. Women were defective according to the dominant male way of thinking. Even a woman's desire for sex was attributed to her need, being imperfect, to join with a perfect male. I gritted my teeth and slammed the book shut. Now I understood the implications of Alexander's pillow talk with his young wife. No wonder the girl had exalted in her power over her black-cloaked lord, a power that was pure sex.

I selected another book from the shelf. For once I didn't fall asleep, being so caught up in the everyday life of medieval England. Times were cruel. People were cruel. The primitiveness of everyone's existence was beyond belief. Women rarely bathed. When they did, it was in a wooden tub in a garden or before the hall fire.

Even Queen Elizabeth the First of England was ridiculed for bathing once a month. It was hard to imagine those conditions. It was even harder to imagine the city streets of London running with sewage, and the groundwater near a castle teeming with filth. I was so thankful I lived today, for back then I'd have been left with no teeth. I might have even died in childbirth, which was quite common back then.

Rubbing my tired eyes, I put down the book. Little Elizabeth had fallen asleep, her hand tucked under her chin. She made sucking motions with her mouth. I reached down and picked her up, resting her limp body against my shoulder. I climbed to my feet, and left the library, passing through the gleaming entry hall with Allison's eerie tapestries hanging high above me.

"Sleep tight, little one," I whispered after tucking Elizabeth into bed.

She slept so peacefully, her small chest rising and falling in rhythm. I touched her baby-fine blond hair; the love I had come to feel for her heavy in my heart. Sighing, I turned away and went to my room. Now what? Alex would be home soon. Should I dress for dinner again? Undecided, I sat cross-legged in the middle of my bed, disturbing Munster who purred his greeting, and stretched out long and flat for me to stroke his velvety fur.

The telephone rang, but I didn't answer it. Over the intercom Mrs. Garrity's curt voice barked, "Mary, it's for you."

I reached across my bed to the phone on my night stand. "Hello."

"Where have you been?" Gail's tone held rebuke and excitement.

"Where have you been, yourself? Elizabeth and I came by your house yesterday, and you weren't home."

"I was out with Anthony," she said, an air of mystery in her voice.

"Anthony? Who's Anthony?"

"My new friend."

"Friend?" I echoed, bemused.

"Yes, and he's just gorgeous. I met him at the singles' class at Sunday School. He's taken me out almost every day this week, and he's just marvelous. I think I'm in love." Gail announced almost in a swoon.

My warning antennae went up. What was going on here? Gail, my solid and steady friend, always had her head on straight. Now she was falling in love on the spur of the moment?

"I hope you know what you're doing," I said, unable to keep the hesitancy out of my voice.

"Of course, I don't know what I'm doing. I'm just reacting to a sexy man who turns me on," Gail admitted with a laugh. "I'm having more fun than I've had in years. Anthony says we're good with each other. He even says we'll be married some day."

"To each other?"

"Of course, to each other, silly."

The tables were turned, and I didn't like it. Gail had always been the warning bell in my life, little that I had heeded it. Now I wrestled with a way to slow her headlong rush into a relationship. Good or bad, I had no way of knowing, because I didn't know this Anthony. I just heard in Gail's voice a careless excitement that had been in my own eight years ago when I had met Bill Adams.

"Shouldn't you be taking this a little slower?" I suggested.

"Look who's talking. 'Miss I'm Gonna Marry Alex Right Now,'"Gail tossed back at me.

I deserved it. Still I hated to see her make the same mistake. "I had my reasons," I said coldly. "I'm just hearing you talk like I did when I met Bill, and it scares me."

She sobered. "But Anthony's not like Bill."

"How do you know? You've only just met him. With Bill, I didn't give myself time to find out. Before I knew it, I was pregnant."

"But it's not like that, Mary," Gail insisted. "I'm older. Anthony's older. We're not teenagers, you know."

"You always think it's different when you're the one in love," I said, rubbing my temple with my free hand. "I see it from an outsider's point of view, just like you've seen me make all those mistakes. You tried to warn me. I'm just trying to do the same."

There was a long pause. "Point taken." I heard her take a breath. "Now, tell me what you've been up to," she said, deliberately changing the subject, her voice sobering.

"I went to see John Hilliard today."

"Whatever for? You're not sick are you? Or pregnant?"

I tensed at her remark. I deserved that too. "No, I'm not pregnant. I've just been having some cramping."

"So, what did he say was wrong?" Gail wanted to know.

"Nothing. Not anything physical anyway. He gave me a prescription for valium, but I'm not going to fill it," I reported, stretching on the bed and staring up at the ceiling of the canopy.

"So if it's not physical, what is it?" At last, I heard the concern in Gail's voice.

"He says it's emotional."

"Emotional?"

"Yeah, you know, the stress of taking care of a newborn baby," I explained.

"But that's nothing you can't handle," Gail said. "Are you sure there's not something else wrong?"

Good 'ol Gail. She read me well. What could I tell her? About my dreams? They were too unbelievable.

"Some strange things have been going on here," I answered.

"Strange things? What do you mean?" Gail probed deeper.

"On my first day here, someone slashed my suitcase. Then, someone turned up the hot water heater, and Elizabeth was almost scalded. When I went down to the basement to see about it, someone shut me in the basement."

"Who is this someone?"

"I don't know."

There was another long pause. "What's Alex doing about it?"

"Nothing, really. He doesn't believe me." I hated to reveal the truth to Gail.

"You've got to be kidding?" She was incredulous. "That guy didn't listen to Allison either. She had symptoms, and he ignored them until it was too late."

"But nothing could be done for Allison. Her disease was too progressive," I said, defending my husband.

"Sure, but at least he could have heard her concerns."

"Yes, I suppose so." I was tired. My head ached.

Gail must have heard the exhaustion in my voice. "Look, Mary, you take care of yourself. And if you have any more problems, you just call me. I'll come out there and stay with you, if I have to."

"Thanks. You're a good friend, Gail," I said.

"Yeah. And I know you. You're so loyal that you'll stick it out there no matter what. Just don't do anything stupid, you hear?"

"I hear."

We said our goodbyes and Gail hung up. I slipped the receiver back on the phone, and turned back to stare at the blurred colors of the canopy over the bed. I shouldn't just lie here. I needed to get ready for dinner, and if I stayed stretched out, I might fall asleep and dream. Reluctantly, I struggled to my feet and went into the bathroom to strip off my clothes and wash my face.

The roller coaster ride of my recent emotions had left my head spinning. Quickly leaving the bathroom, I paused in front of the dresser mirror. I turned left and right, studying my practically naked profile—the long legs, the tiny hips and trim belly. I was pale and blond, my figure almost boyish. Wasn't that a peculiar thing to notice? I wondered as I ran my fingertips down my sides, tickling my bare skin, and gently caressing my flat abdomen. What would it be like to be distended and bloated by pregnancy like the women I had seen today in the doctor's office? I couldn't imagine the changes carrying a child wrought on a woman's body. It all was so mystifying and profound. As I turned toward my wardrobe to dress for dinner, I wondered if I would ever know how it felt.

Ten minutes later, I grasped the slick wood of the banister and paused. The medieval hall beneath me glowed with light. Alex had come home. A chill of anticipation coursed through my body. I wanted to see him again, and dreaded it. Summoning my courage, I took a deep breath. The tapestry on the wall to my right was a riot of color, drawing my attention. Gail had pointed it out as one of Allison's. As I looked at its intricate design, fear stabbed my heart. Allison's handiwork was painstakingly accurate, for I recognized the roses, lilies, heliotropes, violets and poppies that had been growing in my walled garden—mine and Alexander's.

CHAPTER TEN

Alex stood with his back toward me watching the dusky sunset. A lone ray of sunlight cut the horizon like a blade severing a limb. His shoulders slumped forward as if he carried a burden and I noticed the way he gripped the edge of the balcony railing as if to keep erect. What oppressed him so? The sudden death of his first wife? His marriage to me?

Standing in the cool comfort of the library shadows, I quietly considered him. How would he look in a corselet of double-woven mail and an ebony helmet covering his own black hair? Would he wear the Mountjoy arms upon his shield? Would his sword hilt be encrusted with gold and jewels, its blade as sharp as Damascene steel.

I drew myself up short. My mind was slipping again, back into a world I had never known. It frightened me, just as my coming confrontation did. At least my present-day husband was flesh and blood; his anger at me this afternoon, real.

"Good evening, Alex." I spoke low, my voice as dusky as the coming night.

He turned to face me. Slowly, he stepped into the room, the soft light from the one lamp illuminating his dark features and highlighting his hair.

"Good evening to you, Mary," he replied.

Alex shut the French doors and then turned toward me again, advancing deliberately like a cat stalking its prey. I held my ground and searched his unreadable face for understanding.

119

"I hope you're feeling better," he remarked, standing now in front of me, his gaze fastening on mine.

"Yes, I suppose so." My answer was tenuous.

"Have you taken the valium?"

I stiffened. "How did you know about that? Did John say something to you?"

"No. Dr. Hilliard wouldn't answer my questions. He evoked patient, doctor privilege." Alex's gray eyes were hard.

"Then how did you know about the valium?" I asked, growing angry.

"I read your file."

"That's unethical," I snapped, my fingers curling into fists.

"I'm your husband," he said as if that explained his violation of my privacy.

We held each other's gazes, staring at each other, neither of us backing down.

"I'm your husband," he said finally. "I am worried about you."

"Oh." He stripped the wind from my sails. I whirled away from his awesome presence, away from the overpowering scent of spicy aftershave, away from the heady, gray eyes. "So, you think I'm crazy too?" I countered after putting the desk between us.

"No, not crazy. Stressed, perhaps." His voice was soft, thoughtful.

"That's another word for it, isn't it?" I said, my fingers brushing the hard mahogany of the desk.

He didn't answer me, but stabbed me with his piercing gaze. The muscle in his right jaw moved. His lashes lowered, shadowing the gray eyes. Finally, he turned from me, drawing a hand through his black hair as he paced the length of the room. When he returned, he stepped around the desk and stopped in front of me.

"I know marriage to me hasn't been easy," he said. "But why John Hilliard?"

"Please?" I responded, unsure of his question.

"Why take up with my partner?"

"Take up with your partner?" The level of my voice rose remarkably. "What do you mean by that?"

"You were with him last night."

The bluntness of Alex's accusation hit me like a cudgel. "With him? I ran into him at the park. I told you that."

"Our relationship may be unusual, Mary, but I expect loyalty from you just the same." His voice was low and threatening.

"Loyalty? My God, Alex, what are you talking about?" A strange sense of unease washed over me.

"You and John Hilliard. I won't stand for it." Alex took a step forward, his gaze riveting me to the floor.

What could he possibly be thinking? In my eight-year marriage to Bill, I had never been unfaithful. Alex and I had been married only five days, and he was already denouncing me for something that never had crossed my mind. The irony of it punched me in the gut. Here I'd wished for a real relationship with my husband, and he was accusing me of infidelity. I laughed in his face.

"*You* must be the crazy one. You're dreaming something that doesn't exist." My fists curled claw-like because of my anger.

"That's what Allison said when I asked her."

"Allison? I don't know anything about you and Allison. I promised to be a good wife to you, Alex. I have been and will be. It's as simple as that."

Our gazes fought with each other, each vying for supremacy. No one gave. My breathing became shallow in my chest, my mouth dry, my heart pulsing. And then he touched me. Gently. With his forefinger lifting my chin to scour my face once again with his penetrating gaze. It was as if he wanted to delve deeper into my soul, to rake me clean, to probe my innermost self.

"I believe you," he whispered.

"Alex."

I barely spoke before his lips touched mine in supplication.

"Forgive me, Mary," he said into my parting lips. "Forgive me for being so unkind."

My hands opened in submission. Why did he do this to me? What ran through his mind? One minute my accuser, the next a penitent. Was his remorse real? I endeavored to trust him, just as he tried to trust me. His lips made thinking difficult. The pressure of his mouth upon mine, the sweet torment of his tongue, his heady aroma, and strong male presence were dousing my anger, my resistance and my doubt.

"Oh, Alex," I groaned, needing more.

My words stayed him. Pulling himself away, he turned from me. I shook with desire. As on the afternoon of our wedding, I had become wet with wanting. Instead of easing me, Alex retreated leaving me yearning for that which never could be.

"I'm sorry, Mary." The husky sincerity in his voice mollified me. "We shouldn't do this. It *will* drive me crazy. I don't know about you." He turned to face me again, a lopsided smile on his lips and a roguish look in his gray eyes.

Yes, I wanted to shout, *we should kiss*. And you *are* driving me crazy. You and your alter-ego from the past.

"You're right, Alex. We shouldn't toy with each other," I replied, striving to steady my breath and put on the proper demeanor. "We've covered this ground before. We knew what we were getting in to with this marriage."

"And we're two mature adults," he said, his thoughts trailing off.

Then why do I feel two years old? I cried inwardly. I lowered my lashes and felt a disappointment within my breast that seemed centuries old.

At the same time, we both heard Elizabeth's cry of distress over the intercom. He glanced at me.

"I'd better go to the baby," I said softly, my gaze connecting once again with his.

"I'll go with you. Maybe Elizabeth will want to join us for dinner," Alex suggested.

Stepping nearer, he took my hand into his. The pressure of the heavy Dominican wedding ring sliced into my left palm. The ring tied us together like a tether linking a falconer with his bird of prey.

"She'd enjoy that," I acknowledged quietly.

Our anger with each other dissipating like a quick summer storm, Alex smiled and I responded with one of my own. Holding hands, we left the library. Alex's warm presence helped me endure the walk across the marble floor of the foyer, the knights in armor, ghost-like in their attendance on us. With determination, I ignored Allison's disturbing tapestries, concentrating instead on her husband, on his masterful presence by my side, on the strong grip of his hand.

A solitary night light penetrated the dark of Elizabeth's nursery. Alex flicked the main switch as I crossed the floor and light flooded the room. The baby wailed plaintively, her small fists striking the air, her face flushed and wrinkled.

"Hush, hush, sweet one," I cooed in my motherly manner.

Picking up Elizabeth, I pulled her to my breast and rested my cheek on hers.

"Alex! She's burning up!"

Elizabeth's small body radiated fire. I touched my lips to her forehead to confirm what I already knew.

"Let me see her," Alex said, taking his daughter gently from my arms.

Placing her back in the crib, Alex loosened the tight-fitting sleeper.

"I don't think she's vomited, but I'm wondering about diarrhea," he commented to himself as he checked the diaper.

He glanced at me after verifying his hunch. A raw pain gnawed at me as I read the concern in my husband's eyes. Quietly, he began to clean her up with a wet wipe.

"Get me the thermometer. I think Mrs. Garrity keeps it in the top drawer."

Complying with his request, I stood by helplessly as Alex took Elizabeth's temperature with the rectal thermometer.

"She's really sick, isn't she, Alex?" I asked for lack of something else to say.

"Yes." A frown settled on his face. "One hundred and five."

"My gosh. What should we do?"

"You bathe her to cool her off," Alex replied. "I'm going to call Linda Wiley."

"Who's she?"

"Elizabeth's pediatrician," he answered.

"What if she isn't home?"

"She'll be home for me," Alex said firmly.

Unsnapping the sleeper, I glanced at his troubled

face.

"Hurry up," he directed, already leaving the room. "We don't want her to have a seizure."

Seizure? Because of the high fever. Frightened, I rushed to strip Elizabeth, wiping her clean the best I could, and wrapping her in a large blanket. With her hot body tight in my grasp, I carried her into the murky second-floor hallway. Alex's bedroom door stood open, the soft yellow glow from within throwing a square light across the floor. I stumbled, my heart pounding. The last time I had bathed Elizabeth, someone had tried to scald her. Some unseen force had discredited me with my husband. I felt its presence around me in the blackness of the corridor. Its sinister proximity sent sheets of liquid fear through my veins. I froze. The child's cries echoed along the passageway.

I breathed deeply, my concern for Elizabeth's health overtook my dread of the unknown. Tightening my grip on her hot body, I escaped into the bathroom, its brilliant light warm with welcome. Rufus was there before me, like a phantom out of the gloom. My startled gaze locked with his. Eyes mirroring my anxiety, he reached for the baby.

"Rufus, she's sick," I said, but somehow he already knew. Behind him, the tap flowed and the basin already filled with water.

Relinquishing Elizabeth into his arms, this time I tested the water. It was tepid. Not too cold. But I knew it would feel like ice on Elizabeth's feverish skin. Rufus unwrapped her, and together we lowered the naked and screaming infant into the basin. The little man supported her body while I smoothed water over her with a wash cloth.

"She's so hot," I uttered, my voice breathless. "Hush, sweetheart. We're doing this for your own good."

Nothing eased Elizabeth's crying. The cool water shocked her flushed skin, but it had to be done. I bit my lip in concentration.

"How's she doing?" Alex asked.

I hadn't heard him enter. Glancing up, I shook a damp strand of hair out of my eyes. "She hates this, Alex," I replied.

"I know," he said, his voice strained.

For an instant, he rested a palm on my shoulder. To comfort me? I didn't know. But his touch sustained me just the same.

"What more can we do?" I asked. "Do you have any children's acetaminophen drops?"

"Yes, in her room. Dr. Wiley said to treat her symptoms, and bring her into the office first thing tomorrow."

"Not tonight?"

Rufus lifted Elizabeth from the water, and I wrapped her in a clean towel, holding her tightly in my arms.

"No. Since she's not vomiting, we'll keep her from dehydrating, and keep her fever down with acetaminophen and tepid baths. Linda said it might be a virus, and in that case, there's nothing a doctor can do for her."

Alex's voice was tight. I could tell he wasn't pleased with the pediatrician's recommendations, but there was more to it. He was thinking about Allison, and his inability to prevent her death. The parallel was disturbing.

"Shouldn't we insist on taking her to the hospital tonight?" I was unwilling to let the heartache remain for long in Alex's eyes.

"Linda is on call, waiting for the delivery of triplets. She assured me I could handle it. My first childhood illness, and 'I'm a baby doctor,' she said." His gray eyes lit a bit as he poked fun at himself. "But I'm not *that* kind of baby doctor. Once they're delivered, I have nothing more to do with them."

I frowned. "Surely, she understood your concern."

"Yes, but she lectured me about overreacting."

"Overreacting? Elizabeth's got a high fever. We're not overreacting." I didn't like Alex's choice of pediatricians. I didn't know much about little babies, but I felt there had to be something more than take aspirin and call me in the morning.

Alex thrust a frustrated hand through his hair. His suddenly tired eyes were dark now. The lines of his face seemed to have fallen. I wanted to wrap him in my arms as I did Elizabeth. I wanted to take the burden from him.

"Mary, she's right. If it's strep or something

treatable, tomorrow is soon enough. We just need to keep her fever from spiking."

"Well, let's get at it." I glanced around. "Where's Rufus?"

Alex's smile was reflective. "He comes and he goes. Just like a little gnome."

It was a funny choice of words. "He was here when I needed him," I said quietly.

"That's Rufus."

Alex laid a hand once again on my shoulder, and guided me out of the bathroom. This time I felt no evil presence in the hallway. This time my heart seemed to explode within me—deep with concern, but hopeful as well.

Again, Alex took Elizabeth's temperature—one hundred and three degrees. We'd done some good. I diapered her, and dressed her in a loose-fitting gown. Alex administered the acetaminophen drops. Finally, I settled down in the rocking chair to let her nurse the bottle Alex gave me.

"Oral electrolyte maintenance solution," I read the label. "What is this stuff, Alex?"

"It's easier on her than formula, and it restores the fluids and minerals she lost with the diarrhea."

"She seems to be taking it well enough," I said, glancing up at Alex. A funny look in his eyes, he leaned against the door jam watching me.

"You make a good mother, Mary," he said.

A tingle of pleasure surged through me. "Thank you." But Alex wasn't listening. Something distracted him, for his gaze had drifted over my head.

"I don't want to lose her too."

"Please?" What was he talking about?

Alex pushed himself away from the door, and shuffled around the room. He touched a tube of diaper rash medicine. His hand strayed to the stack of disposable diapers. Silently, he picked up a stuffed teddy bear.

"Alex?"

"I don't want to lose her, Mary," he repeated. Turning, his eyes haunted me, like gray tombs of sadness.

"You're not going to lose Elizabeth," I said, trying to be positive. "She's probably not that sick, and we're getting her fever down."

"But I have so little control." His voiced was hushed velvet.

"Alex, you're thinking of Allison. No one could help her. Elizabeth just has a childhood illness." I was alarmed by his lack of response. "Kids get sick all the time," I said repeating the phrases I'd heard the mothers at kindergarten say. Was it in vain that I attempted to reassure him?

He quietly came to me and knelt at my feet, the toy bear still clutched in one hand. His action shocked me. I swallowed, my heart thumping wildly. Hesitantly, he stretched out his free hand and caressed the cap of Elizabeth's hair.

"She's so innocent," he said.

"Yes." My response was a gasp.

"It's hard to believe she's real." His eyes sought mine. "That's why I wanted a mother for her, Mary. I never had one and I want the best for her. What if I can't give it to her? Maybe a mother can."

"Oh, Alex. I'm so sorry all this has happened to you, Allison's tragic death. You must be devastated. I know it's hard to get over losing a loved one." I longed to touch his now bowed head, to comfort his fears and sorrow. I felt so inadequate, unable to find the right words.

Alex lifted his face, his gaze focusing on mine. "Allison? I never loved Allison."

His astonishing revelation clawed away my carefully crafted assumptions. Not love Allison? But the tapestries? Allison had loved him. She had created the delicate depictions of medieval castles and knights. She had carried his child. Was that what he meant about Allison and Dr. Hilliard? Had he dreamed up an affair between them, just as he had concocted the story about me and the good doctor? Had that driven them apart?

"My father wanted me to marry her." He looked away. "I guess because I always felt guilty about my mother's death, I've always done what he wanted. But I never should have listened to Guy this time. It wasn't fair to Allison."

"Alex, what are you talking about?" My tone was sharper than I desired. "You didn't love Allison?"

127

"The only person I've ever loved is Elizabeth."

His eyes sought my understanding. I wanted to understand, but some underpinning of my image had shattered. Alex was not the man I had married. As I struggled to retain my composure, I saw Alex contending with his own battle. He struck a hand through his hair, and set his jaw. Minutes passed and the gulf between us widened.

"I'm sorry. That's all I seem to be saying to you tonight." Alex stood, towering over us. His words were clipped. "You'll watch her a while. I'll come back later." And then he left us.

The room was quiet. Elizabeth slept. Silently, I laid her in her crib, and touched my lips to her forehead. She seemed cooler. I pulled up the railing, and returned to the rocker. Back and forth. Back and forth. The steady clack, clack of the rocker sustained me. Love, love...The sound of the rocker seemed to echo the word.

Although Bill and I had grown apart swiftly and irreversibly, I had loved him once with the same irrational passion that had made Gail love Anthony. I had loved my own parents, and they had left a void within me because of their rejection. I had loved my silly kindergartners. I loved Gail. My mind rebuffed Alex's words. How could he have gone through life without loving? What was that about his father? Why hadn't he loved Allison? Would he ever be able to love me?

Dim hope, at best, but I wanted him to love me. I wanted this to be a marriage, true and fine. I wanted to raise his child with him, and have some of our own. Dreams never came true, for me at least. Allison had loved Alex, hadn't she? Gail said she'd been unhappy. So had Dr. Hilliard. Of course, Allison had been unhappy, married to a man who didn't love her. She had been just as unhappy as I had been when married to Bill. Somehow I had never thought of Allison and me as soul mates. Yet we were connected.

Just as Alex and I were connected.

No way! That's just a fantasy. Something I had dreamed up. There were no mysterious silk threads tying me to Dr. Alexander Dominican. The only thing that tied us together was a scrap of paper, however legal. We were husband and wife in name only. Gail was right. Alex was using me.

I didn't like the truth. It gnawed in my gut like a rat gnawing grain.

What was the truth? Everyone perceived it differently. I longed for absolutes, and found in my life only vague questions. What if I talked to Alex's father? What if I found the mysterious Guy Dominican. He could tell me about his son. Maybe then I could understand.

Love...love...I had always wanted to love and be loved. It was a driving force in my life. It was why I had gone to bed with Bill Adams. It was why I had married Alexander Dominican, I thought bitterly as my eyes shut.

CHAPTER ELEVEN

A shaft of sunlight severed a crack in the draperies and fell fully on my face. Breathing deeply, I turned my head to avoid it, not ready yet to confront the impending day. I couldn't escape it, just as I couldn't escape the jarring, good morning purr by my ear. Opening my eyes, I saw Munster curled into a knot beside my pillow, the fine gray fur of his tail tickling my nose.

"Good morning, silly," I said, stretching a languid arm out of the covers and rubbing Munster between his warm ears.

"Jrrrr," he purred again, his yellow, almond-shaped eyes staring at me.

Letting my arm fall back to the blanket, I shut my own eyes. My body relaxed under the hypnotic presence of the affectionate animal. I was so tired.

Elizabeth! With one swift motion, I sat up, disturbing Munster who slipped quickly off the comforter and scuttled under the bed. I'd forgotten Elizabeth and last night's tense vigil. Alex had promised to call me, but from the looks of the sunshine streaking into my room, the day was far advanced. Had he forgotten? Or just ignored me?

Guilt-ridden, I threw off my lethargy just as I tossed off my covers, and scrambled into jeans, shirt and tennis shoes. Sweeping back my long honey-colored hair, I wrapped it into the familiar knot at the nape of my neck, and rushed out of the room. Across the hallway, I found Elizabeth's door standing ajar. She was gone. The colorful crib empty. Panic tightened in my belly. Had Alex's strange confession actually been a foreboding? Had Elizabeth died?

I ran downstairs. My soft shoes scarcely made noise on the hard foyer floor. Alex's library was cold and dark, so I dashed into the kitchen with its glaring light a bitter welcome.

"Mrs. Garrity!"

The austere housekeeper turned to look at me.

"Elizabeth. Where is she?" I sounded breathless, as much from worry as from my hurry.

Her eyes narrowed. "Dr. Dominican has taken her to the pediatrician," Mrs. Garrity said with rigid rudeness.

"He was supposed to awaken me. I was supposed to go along." I didn't understand. Why had Alex left me?

She shrugged and turned back to her cooking.

Furious, I advanced toward her. "Do you know why Alex didn't get me up?" I asked, trying to keep my voice steady.

"Something about letting you sleep."

I heard her, but her words sank in slowly. Was Alex concerned about my well-being? Is that why he allowed me to sleep late? I sagged into a chair at the kitchen table. Vexed, I pulled at the corner of Allison's blue embroidered place mat, my fingers worrying the tasseled ends while my mind seized on every excuse. Maybe there was more to it. Maybe Alex just didn't want me along because I really wasn't Elizabeth's mother.

"Was she any better this morning?" I asked the stiff back of Mrs. Garrity.

"No, thanks to you," she mumbled beneath her breath.

"Please?" Had I heard her clearly?

"I said, 'No, thanks to you,'" she repeated and whipped around, the blade of her paring knife pointing at me.

"Excuse me?"

"Don't play innocent with me, missy," Mrs. Garrity said, a snarl curling her lip, her black bobbed hair swaying with her anger. "You're the reason Elizabeth got sick. If you hadn't taken her out of this house, none of this would have happened."

"Now, wait a minute. My outing with Elizabeth

didn't cause her illness." I straightened my spine at her insinuation.

"Can you be sure?"

"Well, of course not." My palms grew moist and I lowered them to my lap. "But Elizabeth will some day be a very active child. You're not going to keep her a prisoner in this huge house."

"It wasn't your place to take her out. She's too small. She's just a baby." Mrs. Garrity's gaze tunneled into me.

"Why isn't it my place?" I retorted, my fingers curling into fists. "I'm her mother."

"You're not her mother. Elizabeth's poor mother is dead." The housekeeper's eyes clouded and she turned away.

"Is that why you hate me so much? Because I've taken Allison's place?"

"Taken her place. No one can take my Allison's place," Mrs. Garrity stated bluntly. She faced me once more, her words like acid. "You're no Allison. Dr. Dominican will never love you."

A chill coursed down my back. "He didn't love Allison," I said, my voice hushed, my eyes unfocused on the blue place mat.

"What do you know? You're just a money-grubbing shrew. You have no business in this house. None."

Mrs. Garrity spoke with a savagery that cowed me, but I wouldn't let the horrid woman know how I felt. I stood. "Dr. Dominican thinks I have a reason to be here. That's all that matters."

Turning away from her sharp stare, I retreated, back into the crystal cold foyer with its massive tapestries and aloof suits of armor. Was Mrs. Garrity right? Would Alex ever love me? With a cold hand clutching the slick banister, I hesitated, seeming suspended in the hostile world of Marchbrook Manor. I wavered, my left foot poised on the first step. Allison's most beautiful tapestry suspended above me—the garden at Mountjoy Castle. In my mind, I smelled the heady fragrance of the flowers. Sharp reds and yellows mixed with the blue and black colors of the fabric. The colors swirled in my head, blurring my vision, causing me to sway.

No! I fought it. I was slipping into another waking

vision. Struggling to remain in the here and now, I grasped at the hard banister as my reality. I needed answers. Slowly, pulling myself up the first step and then the next, I reached the landing. And then I ran, fleeing from my hurt feelings and my fears.

When I reached Elizabeth's room, I saw the door to Guy Dominican's wing standing open—oddly inviting. Panting, I halted and stared at it. What was going on? It had never been opened before. As I frowned, my heart took an extra beat. Without a conscious thought, I walked steadily toward the door and passed inside the inner sanctum.

There was a sharp aura in the hallway, crisp and biting. I heard only my breath as I strayed past a long portrait gallery of Dominican family ancestors. The hall was illuminated by spotlights softly aimed at each portrait. The eerie beams cast sullen shadows and created an acrid sensation in my stomach as I focused my eyes on each dead Dominican forbear. Ornate gold frames supported the massive ancient paintings, some dulled with age. Others were of this century: early photographs of prim women in long skirts and fashionable bonnets posing stiffly with somber men in dark suits. I noticed a dainty color cameo of a young woman, her dark hair set in soft 1930's style curls. She wore a simple gray dress with a white lace collar that set off the color of her eyes. They were gray—like Alex's.

Nearby an immense modern portrait of a woman in a satin and lace wedding gown drew my attention. The severe white played stark contrast to the glistening gossamer cascade of her golden hair. I could not tear my gaze away as I recognized Allison—the blue of her eyes and the shape of her face a perfect reflection of Elizabeth's.

A chill coursed the length of my body. Slowly, my left hand closed into a convulsive fist. With the index finger of my right hand, I lightly traced the outline of Allison's oval face. She was so lovely. How could Alex not love her? I felt lanky and dowdy in the presence of her fine features.

"She was beautiful, wasn't she?" A ghostly voice floated in the brisk silence.

I whipped around. In the strange light, I saw a gaunt

man hunched in a wheelchair, his face a road map of years. Oddly, his black hair belied his age, as did his graceful hands whose tapered fingers remained strong and only slightly gnarled, his fingernails clean and square-cut. The old man's eyes were bright and keen.

"Yes," I managed to say, my throat shriveled with fear.

"We'll have to add your picture to our little wall of history," he said as he wheeled his chair around and started down the carpeted corridor.

Realizing he knew me, I followed blindly behind. My stomach churned. Cold perspiration broke out on my forehead. His motorized wheels made soft whirring sounds in the silence.

"I'm so glad you all came to see me, my dear," he said over his shoulder.

"I wanted to see you sooner," I confessed and then wondered why he had gained such an admission from me so easily.

"Yes, Alexander is often protective of me."

"He told me you were an invalid."

"Don't look like one, do I, my dear? Not a complete one, that is." Guy crossed the threshold into a large room banked by a glass wall of windows.

The blazing sunlight startled me, and it took my eyes time to adjust. In contrast to the chilly hallway, the room was sweltering. I stood just inside the door, my gaze tracing the old man's progress into the room. When he reached a small table, he turned the chair again to face me.

"Come in, come in, my dear Mary. I may be an old man, but I certainly do remember my manners." He motioned with a tapered finger. "We'll have tea."

"Oh, no. Don't go to any trouble," I protested.

"No trouble. Not at all," he said and pushed a button within reach of his hand.

Astounded, I came forward to perch precariously on the edge of a Queen Anne chair. With surreptitious glances, I surveyed my host. He appeared fully aware and in control of his senses. Could this be a lucid period Alex mentioned? At other times was he senile and incoherent? It didn't seem possible. Was Alex lying? I worried my lip side to side.

"My little button here turns on a light. I use it to summon Rufus, since he can't hear, don't you know," Guy explained. "Ah, here he is now."

I twisted in my chair to see Rufus approach. When he saw me, he paused, his gaze linking with mine as if in wonder at my presence, but then he continued forward, his head bobbing in subservience to the man who had called him.

"Rufus, don't you know, we'd like some tea. The English kind, Earl Gray. With real cream. But of course, you will know how to do it right. I'll take some wine." Guy shifted his gaze back to me. "I don't have to tell Rufus. He just knows what I want." His piercing glance was meaningful.

I nodded, for I had experienced the same feeling in the little man's presence. "Yes, Rufus certainly knows how to be helpful," I murmured.

After the tea and wine arrived and Rufus withdrew, Guy favored me with a direct look as he sipped from a crystal goblet. "I suppose you think we're an odd bunch here at Marchbrook Manor," he said.

"No, not at all." I sipped the scalding, fragrant liquid from a porcelain cup.

"Come on, my dear. You can be honest with me." He smiled a knowing smile. "We have a sharp-tongued housekeeper and a silent, hunchback dwarf. You can't tell me you don't think it odd."

"Well, yes," I murmured, holding the dainty cup in my hands. What was he getting at?

"And then Alex," Guy acknowledged as he settled his goblet down on the table. "I'm afraid my son can be a bit odd himself, don't you know."

"Odd? No, not odd. Sometimes Alex is aloof, but I'm sure it's because of our strained circumstances." I was quick to defend my husband.

The old man shook his head and clasped his hands together, his index fingers extended and touching each other. "Yes, yes. If his mother had lived, poor boy, I'm sure he would have turned out differently."

"It was horrible misfortune for Alex," I agreed. "That's why he wanted to marry me. He missed not

135

having a mother, and he wants Elizabeth to have one."

Guy wagged his clasped hands and index fingers at me. "I did what I could, don't you know? But I was busy, building my business so I could provide for the boy, and a man just doesn't know." He shook his head again. "Do you know what I'm trying to say, my dear? A man just doesn't know how to nurture a child like a woman."

I shrugged. "That's not a popular view today, Mr. Dominican. Many men stay home and take care of their children."

"Hurumph. That's woman's work. You know it and I know it. You just admitted to me that's why Alex married you. You have much to learn, my dear. Honesty is more becoming than deceit."

I felt my face aflame. "I still maintain what you say is a cliché. I don't mean to be deceitful. It's a fact that a child needs two parents. That's why Alex married me."

"As you say, as you say," he nodded again and turned to pick up the tea pot. "May I?"

"No," I said, declining his offer for more tea and feeling somewhat provoked.

Guy sipped his wine, a quick look tearing into me. I shifted in my seat.

He lowered his goblet, and smiled a soft, magnetic smile. "Well, I want you to know, my dear, I'm glad you are here with us, reasons not withstanding. You make a pleasant addition to our small family."

I sensed a change in approach. "I'm afraid I don't compare in attractiveness to your former daughter-in-law. I am sorry about her death."

"Yes, so tragic, don't you know. Alex feels responsible," the old man said with another shake of his head.

"I tried to tell him it wasn't his fault."

"Hard headed about it? Boy has a mind of his own, never listens," he said. "I should know. I'm his father." Guy's smile was ingratiating.

"On the contrary, Alex seems willing to do what you ask," I remarked.

He lifted his black brows, reminding me of his son. "How so?"

"Allison," I said, measuring his facial responses.

"Alex said he married Allison because you wanted him to."

"Of course, I wanted him to marry her. About time. The boy was thirty years old. High time he got married and carried on for the family. Allison was good for him. She did a lot for the boy's career."

Even in the sultry room, I fought a shiver.

"And I'm sure you'll be good for him too, my dear. Perhaps you'll give him a son."

Did I hear him right? Nerves skittered along my back. "I don't know how that can be, Mr. Dominican. Our marriage is much a marriage of convenience."

He gazed back at me mildly. "I'm confident, my dear, that your charm will convince Alex that it is otherwise."

I could not bring myself to answer him, and so sipped my now tepid tea. I wasn't about to tell him I could no longer have children.

"But, let's not talk about these troublesome things. I want to know about you, my dear Mary." The old man's smile was now engaging, his dark eyes soft.

I drew a steadying breath. In short, choppy sentences I revealed some of my past, my marriage to Bill, my college degree, my love of horses. Guy lured the information out of me, his questions probing but congenial. By the end of half an hour, I found myself relaxing, not as defensive, pulled into the hypnotic web woven by Alex's father.

"You'll have to bring young Elizabeth to see me, my dear," Guy suggested. "I never tire of seeing my granddaughter."

"Yes, I'd like to do that when she's better." I set down my cup and saucer and stood. "I need to be getting back. Perhaps Alex has returned by now, and I want to find out how Elizabeth is doing."

"Yes, yes. Forgive me, my dear, for keeping you." Guy touched the button by his hand. "Just ascribe it to a lonely old man. Ah, here's Rufus to show you out."

I turned to look at the small servant whose eyes narrowed into a squint.

"Don't I get a goodbye kiss?" There was control in Guy Dominican's soft voice.

I glanced back at my father-in-law. He rolled his

137

"Okay," I said, offering a wan smile, and bent toward his offered cheek.

I felt like a dog seeking to please. As I lowered my lips to his cold face, something illogical gripped me. Was it the bothersome smell of mustard and aged wine? Was it the pliant skin, oddly supple for a man his age? Was it the deadly earnest look in his eyes that seemed to see into the window of my soul?

Alex's father touched the back of my hand with one of his graceful fingers. "Don't forget to come see me again."

"As soon as I can."

And then Rufus was at my elbow, ushering me out of the sun-drenched room. He hurried me along the somber corridor past the incessant gazes of the Dominican ancestors. At the door to my own wing, I could swear he shoved me. I pirouetted in astonishment, only to have the door shut in my face. With a loud click, a key turned in the lock.

How was I to assess my visit with Alex's father? The old man seemed genial enough, but there was something more that I couldn't place. Rubbing the dampness from my palms, I walked back to Elizabeth's room. Still empty. Dust motes rode the shafts of light from the window. I strayed toward the sunshine, and let it descend upon my upturned face. To my right, I recognized the bank of windows that belonged to Guy's wing of the house. Its curtains were now drawn, the sharp reflection of the glass casting blades of light in the heavy summer sun.

I let my gaze slip away casually, back to the sun washed nursery. The colors of the Mickey Mouse characters on the wall blurred in my vision. I felt hot and cold, my breath suddenly coming in uneven gulps. A ringing noise swirled around my head, deafening in its sharpness, melodic in its sweetness. No! Against my will, I drifted toward another dream. I struggled to pull myself back. Back. Back to the unusual reality of my life.

****

"Milady!" The voice of Gellis trembled with fear.

Mary looked up from her sewing, instantly mindful of her serving woman's anxiety.

138

"Our lord has injured himself at the hunt. The men are carrying him back and will soon be in the inner bailey."

Eyes wide with fright, Mary stood, her prettily stitched baby garment dropping unnoticed to the floor. "Is he badly hurt?"

"They say not, but he's unable to ride. He was thrown from that new black horse of his."

Mary clutched her heaving breast. Her husband's new destrier was too young to be trusted. The black beast had been bred strong to withstand the shock of combat, but the stallion was also strong-willed. She had warned her husband, but her warning had gone unheeded. Now he was possibly maimed.

Sweeping past her servant, Mary hurried down the stone steps from her solar. Her advanced pregnancy had made her thick and lethargic, but not today as she ran with the speed of her childhood. She had crossed the hall and had made it to the inner bailey by the time the men came bearing her husband between them on a makeshift litter.

"He's alive, milady," her husband's clean-shaven squire greeted her.

"Alive?" Mary read the expression on the young man's face. "What aren't you telling me?"

She spun from the noble servant to crumple over the prone body of her husband. Pale, his imposing features softened in unnatural sleep. Gingerly, Mary pushed back a black lock of hair from his forehead and gasped when she saw an ugly gash, clotted with dried blood. She touched the tiny depression in his chin, and covered his closed lashes with her kisses. Was he dying? Gellis had said not, but he was so motionless. What would she do without him? Mary had come to depend on the great, tall lord she had been forced to wed. What would life be without him? For the first time in her marriage, Mary thought herself in love with her husband.

"Move the child away." Her mother-in-law's voice was shrill.

Powerful hands lifted Mary and pinioned her while her husband's mother inspected her son.

"Take him upstairs. We'll tend to his wound, and he

should be awake soon," she pronounced her verdict swiftly.

"But how can that be?" Mary cried aloud. "He looks so still. We must go for the physician!"

Her mother-in-law hurled Mary a sharp look as piercing as the stare of a gerfalcon. "Control yourself. He's just been rendered unconscious. His color is returning, and his eyes flutter already. My son is strong, and has been hit in the head many times. You have much to learn, madam, if you are to be the wife of a mighty lord."

Incapable of expressing the myriad of emotions tumbling inside herself, Mary simply nodded. Fear tempered the anger she felt toward her mother-in-law, and Mary allowed the older woman to take charge, escorting her back upstairs and ordering the servant women to minister to him. Mary made no move to help, knowing her rebuke to be accurate. She was without any experience in such matters. On other occasions, Mary might have been resentful, for she was the lady of the household, wife to the great lord. But today, sitting fretfully and quietly in the window seat, she was content to defer to her mother-in-law and cast surreptitious glances at the great bed.

"Just as I predicted. His head is too hard to have suffered much damage." There was a note of relief in the voice of her husband's mother. She dropped a bloodied cloth into a bowl of scented water. A serving woman carried it away.

"Mary?"

She sat forward on the window seat. "My lord?"

Quickly crossing the newly laid Spanish carpet, Mary fell on her knees by her lord's side. Her mother-in-law stood taut and firm. Mary ignored the woman's sharp glare. She didn't care. This was her place. He was her husband.

"You're awake, my husband," she said, taking his hand into hers.

"You were right, little one," he told her. "The stallion was not yet ready for the confusion of the hunt. Just as the greyhounds brought the stag to bay, the black devil was startled. Not paying close attention, I lost my balance as he reared and fell. I'm afraid my pride is hurt as badly as my head."

"I am sorry, my lord, but your dignity is something quite easily mended. A smile and a laugh will ease the jesting of your fellows. If you don't appear to care, they won't bother you about it."

He covered her hand with his. "You are as wise as you are beautiful. I am a fortunate man indeed."

Mary leaned forward and caressed his lips with hers.

The scene shifted. It was now August 1, Lammas, the feast of first fruits when bread made from wheat was blessed in church. Mary left the chapel after morning mass, and crossed the courtyard. The day was clear and beautifully bright. She had given thanks for her lord's delivery from danger. She had prayed for him and for their unborn babe who filled her womb. She felt ripe and ready, fresh in her awareness of her newfound love. For the first time since she had come from her father, Mary was truly content.

Again the scene changed, and the pains came, bearing down with the swiftness of a gerfalcon after its prey. She flew with each cramp, rising over the hills of her own anguish. Mary screamed with each new flight. Nothing seemed to assuage her misery, nor her sense of doom.

"She's already been in hard labor twelve hours," Gellis complained to the sweat-stained midwife.

"I know," the ancient woman said as she swiped the back of her hand across her brow.

"What's wrong?" Gellis asked, dipping a cloth in scented water and bathing Mary's face with it.

"The babe is too large. It can't get out," the midwife answered. "My skills are ample, but I have no means to deal with such a difficulty.

"My God," Gellis muttered, and crossed herself quickly.

The talons of the great bird cut deeply into her pale flesh. Mary cried out in her attempt to ease the unending pain.

CHAPTER TWELVE

I cried out, the strange fusion of dream and waking slicing into my soul. Deep within, my pain was profound. My muscles strained with each indrawn breath. Slowly, I turned my eyes to the sunshine that struck through the nursery window and clouted my face with fierce heat. What was happening? I couldn't stop them, these alien visions. I couldn't make the medieval Mary go away.

I shivered from fear. Too much of my life was beyond my control. Too much of it.

"Mary?"

I turned. Amid the lances of light, I could scarcely see his expression.

"Alex?" I moved toward my husband and child. "How is she?"

Secure in the crook of his arm, Elizabeth was muffled in a pink blanket. I touched it, and drew back its edge, revealing her flushed face and soft features. With a quick glance at him, I read the half-concealed worry in his dark gray eyes. His breath, silent and uneven, brushed my upturned face. I paused for a long moment, my gaze locked with his, and then lowered my lips to Elizabeth's forehead.

"Yes, she's still hot," he said in a dispassionate tone.

But he wasn't detached. I sensed it in the tautness of his shoulders and the irregularity of each breath he took. Slanting him an irritated glance, I reached under the bundle he carried, and lifted Elizabeth from him.

"Really, Alex. You said you'd take me with you. At

least tell me what her pediatrician said." I carried the child to the crib and began to change her diaper.

"You startled me. I didn't expect to see you here."

He stood behind me. "Where would you expect me to be?" I asked to conceal my surprise.

I heard his confusion. "It's just with the light behind you, you looked so....different."

My heart thudded slowly. "What do you mean?" I dropped the wet diaper into the covered container.

When I glanced at him again, a subtle smile touched his lips. "Beautiful...like some noble lady."

I fought a silent trepidation. His choice of words reverberated in my mind.

"You still haven't answered my questions about Elizabeth," I grunted to camouflage my own confusion.

He seemed to shake whatever spell that held him. "I'm sorry." His tone lightened. "Part of it's good news. There's no ear infection or strep. No overt reason for her illness. Just a virus."

"Just a virus," I repeated. "That means there's no cure."

"The only treatment is what we did for her last night. We just have to wait and see if her body shakes this thing on its own." Alex's voice caught as he turned away.

Allison again. My lips tightened. Elizabeth began to fuss. Her chubby legs kicked out in protest as her fists struck the air."

"Impatience, miss, is not becoming," I cooed to her and snapped the legs of the terry cloth sleeper.

Alex handed me the bottle of electrolyte solution and Elizabeth and I settled into the rocking chair. Back and forth. Back and forth. Elizabeth gazed at my face while I watched her father put away the things from her diaper bag.

"I often feel out of control," I said, breaking the quiet.

He glanced at me, lifting a black brow.

"Perhaps as she grows, we'll feel like that more and more." I looked into Elizabeth's bright blue eyes. She studied me, too wise for such a little one, and made sucking sounds as she nursed the enhanced water solution. "What will we do when she has her first date?" I asked and went on to speculate, "She'll wear a party dress and he'll present her with red roses in a wrist corsage. You'll drive them to the dance."

A ghost of a smile lit his eyes. It was impossible for me to resist.

"You're wrong. The guy will probably have long hair, wear baggy jeans and an ear ring. By then Elizabeth will have colored her hair green," he said. "They'll go to a rock concert or something, and he'll bring her home late."

"You'll be worried and report them to the police."

"And she'll be grounded for a month."

"I think you've got this child-rearing thing down pat," I said in amusement.

For a moment, we retained a degree of intimacy, and then it was gone. Alex shifted his gaze from me. To cover his uneasiness, he excused himself to check his answering machine. His leaving was like the opening of a fresh wound.

****

The setting sun flooded the sky with flame and washed the mouse-papered nursery with hushed pink shadows. Elizabeth slept in her crib, her tiny restive movements showing her internal struggle to fight off the virus. I moved around the room like a ghost. A melee of thoughts my only company....

I felt unsettled. Time and again during that long day of watching Elizabeth, I had relived the strange visit to my father-in-law. Had I somehow been manipulated by the old man? What lay behind his allusions to my giving Alex a son? I shuddered, for it was too much like my dreams.

Reconstructing those dreams throughout the day, I had fought the fear that resurfaced every time I recalled them. Put together, they told a story. A sad story. I drew a deep breath, and allowed my hand to drift along Elizabeth's feverish brow.

The medieval Mary was dying. I had felt her pain deep within my own being. What would happen to me when I envisioned her death?

The question drew me up short. My heart thudded slowly. I wiped my damp palm on the leg of my jeans as I stared at Elizabeth.

"Dr. Dominican wants to see you."

Whipping around, I found the imperious Mrs. Garrity glaring at me. Our gazes challenged each other. When I didn't speak, she continued, "He said you're to come down to the kitchen for dinner. I'm to stay here."

"Oh, thank you. Elizabeth's asleep."

"I see that." Her tone was sharp.

"Yes, I'm sure you do," I retorted and shouldered past the obnoxious woman.

Inside the safety of my room, I paused to snatch a breath. Slowly I expelled it, trying to quell the anger churning within my stomach. Why did I let Mrs. Garrity get to me? Was I a wimp, or was it this marriage of convenience that was straining my soul and coloring my reactions? I had never let Kinder Day's owner intimidate me in this way. I leaned against the closed door. It was solid beneath my back. My breath laboring, I hardly knew how to answer myself. I hardly knew where I was going, let alone where I had been. With a sluggish stroke, I drew a hand across my shut eyes.

Alex was waiting for me. I shouldn't delay. Reluctantly, I opened my eyes to the murky bedroom. Pushing myself upright, I flicked the light switch on the wall by the door. Nothing happened.

The dark quietness of my room that had been reassuring now seemed to overshadow me. Swallowing defensively, I strode to the window and drew the drapes, hoping to catch the fading light of the day. The weak glow cast fitful shadows across the floor.

"Munster?" My voice trailed away. Where was my cat?

Silence closed in, thick and tangible. With shaky steps, I crossed to my bed. Something was wrong. Something lay under the coverlet. Was it Munster? Grasping it, I tossed the spread back. My pillow had been scored with something sharp. Feathers scattered over the blanket, and a gagging scent of pungent perfume overwhelmed me. It was like a sweet flower garden. Allison's perfume. Stark terror stopped the breath in my throat as I threw the coverlet back over my mutilated pillow.

The swift whisk of my cat's plume-like tail around my legs startled but steadied me. I released my breath.

"Oh, Munster," I moaned and swooped him into my arms, squeezing him hard. Munster let out a plaintive meow. He had been frightened too. Burying my face into his gray, angora fur, I clung to the warm and breathing animal.

What was I to do? Tell Alex? The bed was proof enough to quell his doubts that someone was out to get me, but for some reason, I didn't want to run whining to my husband. I didn't want to be a wimp. Who could have done this? Hateful Mrs. Garrity? She'd had ample opportunity, for I'd spent my day with Elizabeth. Rufus—the small man who I felt to be my friend? What did I really know about him, or about anyone in this house?

I stepped away from the slashed bedclothes, carrying Munster with me. At the window, I peered into the fading gray light of the day. The view from my eastward window showed me the deserted entrance park and circular driveway leading to Marchbrook Manor. I was isolated. Alone, except for my cat who I clutched to my beating heart.

What about Guy Dominican? Could he have somehow entered my room and damaged my bed? But he was in a wheel chair. Surely, I would have heard it pass Elizabeth's door. Then there was Alex. The husband I hardly knew. The husband who drew me to him as if by some enchantment. The man with the gray eyes who loved only one person—his daughter.

Munster had had enough. He growled deep in his throat, and I opened my arms to let him drop. He trotted into the bathroom, his feathery tail carried high above his back. Leaving Munster to his cat pan and bowl of food, I escaped from my room that held no solace for me.

****

I felt light-headed, dizzy. I hadn't eaten since the morning, and the smell of bacon and eggs from the kitchen pulled me. Was Alex cooking breakfast? But it was dinner time. Steeling myself, I stepped through the door of the kitchen. I had forgotten the impact of him. The stately beauty of him. Even with a silly apron around his waist, he carried himself with a masculine grace and bearing, his black hair shimmering from the overhead lights.

"It seems strange to see you standing at the stove," I said, a smile curving my lips and remembering his earlier reaction to seeing me.

"I hope you're hungry." Alex stood with his back toward me.

"Yes, very," I responded and crossed the room wondering about his motives. "May I help?"

"No, just have a seat." He turned to offer me a flicker of a grin, his gray eyes intense and compelling.

"Elizabeth's sleeping," I said, sitting again at Allison's table.

"Any change?" he asked approaching me with a plate of fluffy scrambled eggs. Alex's spicy aftershave blended with the aroma of eggs, fried bacon and potatoes, and brewing coffee. His solid presence was reassuring. His hospitality, charming.

"No, but she's resting quietly."

"Good. We'll be out of the woods before you know it." He leaned near, serving me. "I wasn't sure what you'd like." He tipped his head like a cat watching a bird. "I'm not a very good cook. I'm afraid breakfast is the limit of my abilities."

"It looks wonderful," I said.

He cocked a dark brow. "Wait until you taste it," he replied with half-concealed amusement.

With a kind of fascination, I watched him serve me. As he poured my coffee, I caught his gaze and then let mine drift to my plate.

"As a child, I always enjoyed the pancake suppers my dad made. It was a special time," I reflected.

I felt his gaze upon me. "I'm sorry you miss your parents."

Vaguely, I was aware of his perception. It took me aback. I felt myself give him a queer frown. "Well, that can't be helped." I dug into the eggs, the tines of my fork making scraping sounds in the suddenly quiet room.

For a moment he gazed past me. "At least you have your memories."

"You have your dad," I offered, hoping to soften his shifted mood that seemed so sorrowful.

"My father was more of a taskmaster than a dad," he said, and then quickly changed the subject. "I'm afraid I can't take credit for the blueberry muffins."

"I know. They're Mrs. Garrity's specialty."

Alex settled beside me and began to butter a muffin. He looked like he wanted to say something, but didn't know how.

"Did you go into work today?" I asked instead, and took a sip from my coffee cup.

"No, Hilliard covered for me." He bit into the muffin. "I hope he doesn't screw anything up," he said after a swallow of coffee.

"You don't trust him?" I toyed with my food.

"Not really."

"Why did you hire him then?" I wanted to know

His mouth tightened. "A favor to Allison."

"Allison?"

"They were friends in California." His face contorted.

I wondered at it. "They were friends? When was she in California?"

"Sometime before she returned to Louisville and I met her." Alex shrugged and changed the subject again. "You're not eating your meal. Is it that bad?" He gazed at me with a hypnotic gray intensity.

"Oh, no. It's great." I dug back into my plate of eggs and potatoes. When I looked up, I caught him smiling at me. I felt a flood of warmth and pleasure. "You're making fun of me."

"You may have me there," he said.

The familiarity between us was alive. I could not keep myself from smiling. We ate quietly for a while.

"Mary?" he murmured.

Startled by the use of my name, I glanced up.

"I always wondered why you and your mother don't get along."

My hand tightened on my fork. "I don't know. I disappointed her, I guess."

"When you got pregnant?"

"Yes." We passed another moment of silent reflection. "It's kind of ironic, you see." I lifted my eyes. "For most of my life, I've tried to do the right thing. When I made one mistake, she couldn't accept my imperfection, I guess."

"None of us are perfect."

"But I tried to be, you see. I married Bill before the

miscarriage, and then I stuck with him even through our troubles," I explained with a fervent wave of my hand. "Maybe it had something to do with my father deserting her. I suppose I was my mother's reason for living. Her happiness."

His body was as immobile as a rock. I felt his stillness.

"Did you ever feel something was missing?" he asked in a hoarse whisper. "From your life, I mean? Like a jigsaw puzzle all complete except for one missing piece?"

I lowered my fork. My breathing became rapid. "All my life."

Moments later, the tenseness left his shoulders. His gaze touched my face, his eyes dark and rueful. "We're a pathetic pair, aren't we?"

"Maybe we belong together," I answered impulsively. When I thought about what I said, I felt my face grow warm.

"Eat your dinner." His gaze rested tenderly upon my face.

Squirming in my chair, I returned my concentration to the meal, my lower limbs burning with something more than embarrassment.

"Dr. Dominican!" The sharp voice of the sober-faced housekeeper drew us to our feet. "Elizabeth!"

Together we started forward. Mrs. Garrity held the bundled Elizabeth near her breast.

"What's wrong?" My own voice was barbed with fear.

Throwing an angular shoulder toward me, she turned to exclude me, and offered Elizabeth to her father. "The child's fever has broken."

Alex lifted his daughter into his arms. "Just holding her, I can tell," he said with a pleased look in his eyes.

I felt absurdly out of place. Mrs. Garrity seemed to preen herself, as if her mere presence with Elizabeth had reduced her fever. I raised my chin, indignant at the woman's implication that I had neglected my duties.

"The only problem is some sort of rash," Mrs. Garrity said coming nearer to show the rash on Elizabeth's chest.

"Roseola," Alex said with a nod. "That explains it." He turned to include me.

"A common childhood illness." I was vastly relieved.

Alex's gaze skimmed over Mrs. Garrity's black head to lock with mine in a meaningful glance. Only I knew his anxiety had been so great.

****

Later that night, I felt cold and sick inside as I entered my bedroom. Expecting it to be dark, I was surprised when the light flicked on brightly. My heart thudded. I paused for a long moment, and then walked forward to my bed. Someone had cleaned it. The shredded pillow was gone; the sheets clean. Only a faint residue of Allison's perfume remained. So it hadn't been a dream.

The tart odor caused my throat to close in fear. Who had ripped my pillow? Who had tidied up my bed? A chill like an ice-clotted winter glove on my face gripped me. I felt cold and then hot, pellets of icy sweat beading on my brow. The overhead light grew too bright. Its winter whiteness shattered into the hues of the spectrum. A honed-edge sharpness pierced my ears. Cupping my hands to my ears, I fought to block out the sounds. I swayed. I tried to control it. I tried to resist. Until I felt myself falling, falling into the shroud that was my bed.

****

Alexander lounged languidly in the cool shade of the castle garden. His mother and wife had insisted on his rest. After the witless fall from his black charger, he had been woozy for a few days, and even now, welcomed the respite from daily activities. Toying with the well-worn queen of his chess set, he reclined against his elbow and stretched his long torso out into the grass. The rustle of feminine skirts caused him to look up in time to watch his very pregnant wife waddle toward him. She was the one who needed to rest, he thought with a twang of guilt. Pregnancy had removed the innocence of her own childhood from her face. As she had increased in weight, Mary had gained an appearance of maturity which suited her well. She bloomed from good health and often sang as she went through the day. He hoped she was happy. For some reason, her happiness was becoming important to him.

Mary was smiling now, gazing at him with something akin to love in her eyes. Alex felt his own heart lurch with delight just as another part of his anatomy swelled with wanting.

"Come sit with me, milady," he said, patting the soft turf by his side.

"Oh, I'm afraid I can't possibly sit down in the grass, and if I did, I wouldn't be able to stand up." She said with a grin as she explained her own awkwardness.

He reached up and caught her pale hands, pulling her forward so that she stood just above him. As he gazed into her indigo eyes, he thought about her reluctance to wed him, and how she had made the best of a difficult arrangement. He remembered their wedding night, and his own decision to give her the opportunity to learn his body and his ways. His patience had been repaid by many nights of lovemaking. He grew warmer with need as he thought about his wife's own savage responses.

Mary must have seen his need, for he knew it bulged quite readily under his hose. Cocking her head, she lowered her lashes seductively, making the blood rush even faster throughout Alex's body.

"Don't do that to me, Mary." He hauled her down on top of him, his body absorbing the shock of her fall.

"You'll regret this, my lord," she asserted with a warning of her own.

"Not as much as you will for trifling with me." Alex nipped her ear lobe and nuzzled her neck.

"Stop it. The servants will see us."

"Let them."

He rolled her over in the grass, and plied her mouth with his until she surrendered, kissing him back with a passion of her own. He felt her nipples harden under his touch, and pushed himself as close to her as her condition would allow. When the babe kicked in protest, he backed off, awestruck over the miracle they had created between themselves.

"Are you happy?"

Mary nodded in reply, gently fingering his soft black gipon.

"I know you were once promised to another. Do you mind now being married to me?" Alex touched her where the child had just moved.

"No, my lord," she said quietly. "A knight's life is often violent, and Richard died at a tournament, doing something he loved. It's the way of the world that many people die young, but life continues. I've come to accept my fate. Do you mind me not being your first wife? I know you and she were childhood sweethearts."

"Ah, puppy love." He gazed mutely at her. "That attraction ended soon after our marriage—the many miscarriages and her anger at her fate."

He didn't have to say more, for Mary had heard about his first wife's bitterness. For a moment, she gloated in her own success, but then a stab of anguish pierced her heart. Would Alex have been as happy with her if she hadn't gotten pregnant so readily? Would she have been as happy with herself? Why couldn't their love be simple? She despaired of ever knowing the truth just as pain pierced her abdomen.

She cried out in her agony but was too exhausted to twist away from it. She was wet with her own sweat, her naked body covered only by a plain sheet. Cool cloths barely soothed her brow, but Gellis was steady in her attention to her. Even in her suffering, Mary was still able to comprehend that nothing more could be done for her. The stressed look on the midwife's face spoke the fact quite well. Silently, between contractions, she lifted up a prayer, shutting her eyes against the all-consuming torment.

An eternity later, the space between her legs felt damp. Weakly, Mary opened her eyes, and reached up to grasp the sleeve of her servant. Did the woman's ashen face match her own? Gellis slowly lifted the sheet. Her face paled even more, a low, gut-wrenching moan escaping her lips.

The blood was red, a bright, virulent red. It was warm and Mary was cold. The critical liquid oozed out of her body, just as another spasm shook her to her very core.

"My God! Push, child, push!" Gellis yelled.

The midwife elbowed the serving woman aside, quickly regaining her composure and taking charge. "She hasn't the strength. But, lordy, there's the crown of the head!"

Excited now, the midwife pushed down upon Mary's afflicted belly as the pain pounded in relentless waves.

And the blood dripped like raindrops...great globs of life-sustaining fluid...bright and red.

CHAPTER THIRTEEN

I awoke with my scream echoing through the silent, light-flooded bedroom. Lying lengthwise across the bed, I drew my knees to my stomach, the pain within me intense and horrifying. I felt strangely disembodied, and wrapped my arms around my body as if to keep myself intact. What was I to do? How could I stop these dreadful dreams? Dreams twisted with happiness and pain, love and hate? A slow tear trailed down my cheek and dropped onto the coverlet.

The woman of my dreams was dying—her life passing before her eyes. Would I die too? I hugged myself harder drawing upon whatever reserve was left within myself and praying that my ordeal would end soon, but nothing helped. The intense pain remained. My eyelashes drifted shut to block out the light.

When I awoke again, Munster had pressed himself against my legs. I stretched and he moved, indignant that I had disturbed him. It was morning. Another day. Struggling to sit up, I gazed around the boundary of my room. It held no warmth for me. It was still Allison's. My lips tightened at the thought.

Elizabeth was better. She smiled and responded with baby coos and gurgles when I talked to her. She ate heartily and slept peacefully. I tended her that morning with little enthusiasm. I was too much within myself, struggling with the depth of my dreams and the uncertainty of my welcome here at Marchbrook Manor. About noon, Mrs. Garrity relieved me, telling me with a vexing hurumph that Alex wanted to see me at the stable.

I had never been to the stable. Although Alex had suggested I ride his horse, I had never found time. After discovering the path from the inner garden, I had no trouble finding Marchbrook Manor's impressive, though compact, barn.

Opening the heavy oaken door with hesitation, I pushed it inward upon its hinges. Inside, all was cool and quiet, smelling like cedar shavings in a thousand hamster cages, and of manure and leather. I had almost forgotten that horsy, barn smell. It was welcome.

Entering the dimly lit aisle, I went from stall to stall, looking inside only to find each one empty. Where was Alex? He was supposed to meet me here.

At the end of the aisle, I heard shuffling sounds of a horse, and for the first time I saw Alex's horse. He was a powerful black gelding, huge, standing over sixteen hands. He was massive with a big chest and a wide back. His legs were fine but sturdy. Tossing his head, he flared his nostrils at me, knowing me a stranger.

The bottom half of the stall door was oak. The top half was made of metal bars, allowing me to see the animal clearly. Almost immediately I recognized him as an American Saddlebred. I could identify his breed by the way his long neck came out of his withers, and by the fine shape of his head and point of his ears. Intelligence burned in his eyes as he snorted at my nearness and struck an objecting hoof against the wall.

Suddenly, horror, as deep and permeating as a dreary day long rain in December, clutched at my heart. I had seen this horse before. I had seen the look in his fiery eyes, the insolent toss of his ebony mane. Digging my fingernails into the palm of my sweaty hand, I backed a step. My throat grew dry. This horse—Knight Fox— seemed large enough to carry an armored knight into combat.

But what did it mean? Why did I feel such an overpowering link of familiarity to an animal I had never seen? Was he a ghost horse? Was this the black stallion from my dreams? I retreated another step, wanting to scream out of frustration for all I had felt and seen since I had come to Marchbrook Manor. With a tremble of fear, I bit my lip to keep another scream from taking shape and escaping once more from my lips.

Did Alex really ride this vicious animal? He'd known of my love for the Saddlebred, but never mentioned his own knowledge of the breed. I realized again how little I knew about the man I had married. I realized how little I knew about what was happening to me.

Withdrawing across the aisle as the giant gelding protested my nearness with an angry snort, I felt a warm swirl of breath on the back of my neck and pivoted to find another horse gazing at me. Much smaller, this chestnut mare's snort was one of welcome. Tia? She was like my old mare Royal Tiara, but Tia had a blaze shaped like a backward question mark on her face. This mare's face was not marked. I glanced quickly at the nameplate on the door of the stall.

"My Lady," I read aloud.

"For you, my lady," Alex said, stepping from the shadows and sweeping me a courtly bow.

I met his approach with dead silence. Only the steady beat of my heart sounded loud in my ears. The man, who came to me in the dimness, seemed a specter.

"Mary? Are you okay?" He looked at me in bewilderment.

Gathering my scattered wits, I nodded my head, but I still could not speak.

Alex touched me. He held the soft flesh of my bare upper arm, the grip of his fingertips subtle. I fought an absurd desire to pull away.

"Did I scare you?" he asked, concern in his voice.

"Yes," I managed to say, lowering my eyes, unable to look at his classically drawn features and dark, hooded eyes.

"I'm sorry. I wanted to surprise you."

I lifted my gaze to meet his. "You did."

"Did you see her?" Alex was suddenly like a kid with a new toy. He lifted a nearby nylon lead, and pulled back the door to My Lady's stall. "Isn't she superb?"

I watched as Alex threaded the chain through the mare's halter, over her nose, and hooked it on the other side. He led the fine horse out of the stall, out of the barn, and into the sunshine. I followed down the aisle as if in a trance.

Alex lifted the mare's head and touched her front legs with his booted toe to move them forward. "Out," he commanded.

My Lady stretched out, distributing her weight evenly on all four legs. This gave her a long, lean line, showing off her arched, well-flexed neck, her defined withers, deep and sloping shoulders and her strong back. In spite of my earlier fright, My Lady's beauty beguiled me. I came closer. The horse's wide-set eyes were expressive, her ears graceful and alertly pointed forward.

"Like her?" Alex cast a sideways glance at me while keeping his attention on the mare.

"She's beautiful," I said a bit breathless.

"The trainer I brought her from said she's had a limited show career. They were going to breed her, but thought she'd make a good pleasure horse instead."

I felt My Lady's shoulder and her skin twitched, sensitive to my touch. I looked up at Alex. The sunlight played on the side of his face and his hair. There was a phantom of a smile in his eyes that seemed silver in the brightness.

"She's yours," he said. "A belated wedding gift."

I was speechless. A thrill, deep and abiding, grabbed at my heart. Silently, fighting tears, I moved forward and slipped my arms around Alex's neck.

He was warm. His breathing was deep but a bit erratic. The downy fuzz at the nape of his neck smelled like spicy aftershave.

"You have me at a disadvantage." His lips were soft against my neck. "I can't hug you properly while holding the mare."

Alex's words hauled me back into reality. I stepped back, breaking the link of intimacy, and swiped my eyes with the back of a hand. I felt like a clumsy schoolgirl. He sensed my awkwardness, I knew, because he touched my cheek with a free fingertip.

"Put your jodhpurs and boots on. We'll go for a ride together."

"Okay."

"Hurry up. I'll saddle the horses."

With a backward glance, I ran down the path to the

massive gray house. Overwhelmed with surprise and delight, I let the garden door bang shut and twisted my way through the garden path. To my left, the bank of windows on Guy's wing of the house threw back the sunshine with violent energy, causing me to squint. A curtain dropped against a glazed window, but I was too happy to care that I was being watched. Inside, I approached the vast coolness of the foyer from an unfamiliar direction. For once it held no threat. Even Mrs. Garrity, who stood on the balcony with Elizabeth in her arms, didn't intimidate me. Catching the banister and swinging around, I swooped up the steps.

"Where are you going?" she asked in her most hostile tone.

"Alex is taking me riding."

"What about Elizabeth?"

"Oh, you'll watch her for me, won't you? It's just for a little while. He bought me a horse." I felt flushed and flattered, totally willing to give up the steady control of my emotions I tried to maintain. Rushing onward, I left Mrs. Garrity dumbfounded in my wake.

"Munster, I'm going riding!" I spoke to my sleeping cat as I whirled into my bedroom.

Like a teenager late for a date, I scrambled into my gray Kentucky jodhpurs and black, ankle-length, riding boots. Somewhere in the back of my drawer, I found my leather gloves. At the dresser, I pinned my hair, catching the stray blond strands and pushing them back into place.

"Munster, kitty," I murmured, going to his purple, carpeted cat condo sitting near the window. "Maybe things are starting to work out."

Sunlight pooled on the sleeping animal. Expecting a jarring purr in welcome and a lift of a head in acknowledgment, I moved closer and touched his velvet gray fur. His body was as still as stone. I breathed rapidly, unable to control the absolute panic that tensed my body.

"Munster?" I repeated in a hoarse whisper.

The cat's body lay flat on the top of the condo. I saw the puddle of blood beneath him. Stark terror stopped the breath in my throat and froze my heart with horror.

"No, not Munster. *Not Munster!*"

I was sick with it. I couldn't comprehend the evil that had taken the life of a cat. *My cat.* And then all rationality ceased for me. There was no explanation I could accept. Nothing to satisfy the revulsion I felt. I wanted to get away from this strange, cruel place.

Shrieking in pain and anguish, I started to run blindly, pulling at my hair and clenching my teeth. Somehow I found myself out of the house, fleeing through the twisted garden path. Hysterical sobbing tightened my chest and clouded my vision.

"Mary? What's wrong?"

I shook off Alex's restraining hand. He held Lady's reins in his other one.

"I can never go back in there!" I cried out.

"Why not?" Alex wanted to know, a smile tentative upon his lips.

"Someone killed my cat."

The humor evaporated from his face. "Killed your cat? The gray one?"

"Yes." I dropped my gaze. "Someone killed him and left him lying on his cat condo."

Alex tensed as if someone had struck him a blow. "Who would do something like that?"

"I don't know." I lifted my eyes to him, trying hard to control my emotions. "Who would trash my things, write warnings on my mirror in red lipstick, and try to scald Elizabeth? You told me your servants wouldn't do things like that."

Alex's lips tightened, and he grabbed my shoulders, his fingers biting into my flesh. "I'm right. They couldn't be involved."

"Well, who then? Guy?"

"Don't be ridiculous." Although his voice was like punishment, he averted his gaze from mine.

"*Someone* killed my cat. Suppose Elizabeth is next?"

"What are you talking about? Are you crazy?"

Now I had caught his attention. Alex's gaze raked over me.

"Elizabeth is small and helpless," I told him. "Just like a cat. I know it sounds unbelievable, but so many strange things have happened to me in your house, things you don't or won't believe."

Alex's eyes were shaded, his body stiff "You have to admit, Mary, your story about the scalding water was unfounded."

"The hot water heater *was* turned up. I saw it," I snapped.

"But I didn't see it. There was nothing unusual in the basement."

I shook out of his grip and stepped back with a toss of my head. "Go up and see Munster's body, then. That should be enough proof for you."

Tight-lipped and tense, we climbed the red staircase to the second floor. I refused to go into my room. Alex glanced skeptically at me before he stepped across the threshold.

"There's nothing on the cat condo," he called a moment later.

"His body was there. I saw it."

"You seem to see many things." Alex's weary comment unnerved me.

With reluctance, I entered the room and went to stand next to him. Looking down, I saw a stream of sunlight bathing the two-story kitty condo. It was bare. No body. No blood. Stricken, I searched Alex's face only to see pity written in his eyes.

"I know what I saw!" Anger surged in my chest. "Where is he then? Where is my cat?" I turned from him and ran to the bed, stooping to look underneath. "Kitty. Munster, kitty."

"Mary." Alex came to me and clutched my upper arm, pulling me upright. "Don't. Maybe your cat left the room. Maybe he's just lost."

"No, he isn't, Alex. He's dead. My Munster is dead." I snatched my fist to my mouth, but the sob came anyway—and then the tears came, tumbling on their own like rain in the spring.

"We'll find him."

Alex put his hand out to touch me. I shook it off and frantically searched the room with my wild gaze. "I've got to get away," I mumbled.

"You'll be okay, Mary. You just need rest." Alex reached for me again.

"No!"

Turning, I fled once more from the room. I ran this time as much from my husband and his disbelief as from what I had witnessed moments earlier. Mrs. Garrity's disapproving stare followed me down the red velvet staircase. I felt the heat of her censure as I ran from the house—from the nightmare that had become my existence.

"Mary, wait!"

Reaching the stable, I ran inside to find My Lady standing patiently in her stall. I flung the reins over the horse's neck and led her outside. Lady pranced nervously to the side as I gathered the reins into my balled fist. Steadying myself, I stuck my left foot into the stirrup.

Alex approached at a jog. "What are you doing?" He grabbed for me.

"Get away! You've never believed me!" I pulled myself into the saddle as the animal sidled sideways, and kicked out with my booted foot, striking his hands.

"Mary, wait!" Once again Alex's words tolled like a warning bell striking fear straight into my soul.

I glanced down to see him watching me, and still terrified, gave the horse her head. Lady responded by springing into an animated trot. Delirious, I urged the animal forward by pressing with my legs, and we broke into a canter, swiftly leaving the stable behind. Uncertain where to go, I threw caution aside and allowed the horse to choose her way. Lifting myself from the saddle, I placed my weight into my stirrups and leaned over Lady's neck like a racehorse jockey. Her red mane hit my face. Wind whipped through my unrestricted hair, blowing it back in a long banner of flight.

As if all my worst nightmares stalked me, a black figure astride a black horse raced after me. I swallowed my fear. We galloped blindly down the side of a hill, across a small meadow, and plunged into the Kentucky woodland. Somehow my horse knew the way. An animal path trampled through the underbrush and scrub trees provided our avenue of escape. Again I crouched low over the mare's neck, while I dodged painful brambles and briars. Together we jumped a fallen log, hardly breaking stride. But as fast as we raced, the black fiend raced faster. With its longer strides, the black gelding rapidly closed the distance. I heard the sounds of pursuit behind me—the snapping of tree limbs, the thud of pounding hooves. Just as I started to fret about the slowness of our flight, we broke out of the woods onto another stretch of grass. Digging my heels into the mare's sides, we sprinted recklessly into the wind.

"Mary! Stop!" Alex's panic-filled words were blown away.

Crazed, I defied his command.

"Mary!"

Suddenly the mare skidded to a halt, sliding back on her haunches and throwing me up on her neck. Immediately, I jolted backwards. Struggling to remain in the saddle, I fought for control. When I righted myself, I stared over the edge of a craggy limestone cliff. Eyes wide with fright, I saw far below me the gray line of the Ohio River. Except for the instinct of the animal beneath me, I would have been killed. In silent homage, I laid my gloved hand on My Lady's neck. It trembled beneath me. A measure of sanity returned.

"Mary, what's gotten into you? You almost killed yourself."

I whirled the mare around to glare at my husband. Clad in black on his powerful black horse, he looked like some ghost from another era. Panting, I raised my chin in fear and defiance. A muscle in my jaw twitched.

"I'm aware of that." The mare beneath me pranced in uneasy rhythm.

"What are you running from?" Alex asked.

"You have no control over me." My reply sliced through the spring air. "I'm not your slave, and I'm not some medieval woman whose only purpose in life is to do your bidding. I will go home. You can't stop me!"

"Mary, what are you talking about?"

I jerked the reins to my left and squeezed the mare's sides with my legs. Lady bounded forward, astonished by the severity of my signals. Alex and the great black gelding stopped our retreat.

"Get out of my way!" My hair tumbled around me.

He tried to grab my reins. "Not until you calm down. Talk to me, Mary."

"Why? You won't believe anything I tell you." I was

frantic with my lack of control. I saw nothing but black shapes in front of me, blocking my path, confronting me. In blind rage, I rode forward.

"Stop!"

As Alex pulled his giant black horse upward, the animal threatened the air with his heavily shod hooves. Thwarted, I reined Lady to the right only to meet again my black-clad tormentor and his warlike horse. Whichever way I turned, he blocked my way. I screamed with frustration and fright. I wouldn't let this man get the best of me. When I pivoted again to the left, the black horse was a jump ahead of me. Again the animal reared. My brave mare shuddered beneath my legs.

"I hate you Alexander Dominican!" I shrieked through tears.

Alex's horse turned in an agitated circle. "No you don't."

"Yes, I do! This marriage is damned! I want to get away from you." I started forward once more.

Slowly, like the view from a slow motion camera, the black gelding reared again. Just as slowly, Alex toppled off. Already unbalanced, the horse fell on his side amid a wild thrashing of hooves. In seconds, the black animal regained his feet, yet Alex remained silent and still on the ground. Lady stood immobile beneath me. My palms were wet inside my gloves.

Dizzy waves washed through me. Like so many other things, this had happened to me sometime in the past. Not in this particular way, not in this same manner, but it had happened. My heart trembled with remembering. My body ached with a longing and an anxiety retained from some previous time. Some unfathomable force pulled me toward Alex in a way I couldn't control. I fought it. A fierce battle raged within my mind and spirit. I convulsed with it. I opposed the certainty growing strongly within my being that I could not leave without knowing if my husband was alive or dead. After all, he was my reason for existence.

Still I fought the strange pull. I urged my horse forward, past the prone body of my husband and away from the insanity surrounding this whole episode of my life. The chestnut pranced a few steps, her head bobbing.

Instead of the peace I craved, a quiet cloud of anguish descended upon my heart. I glanced back. I stopped. Tears spilled down my cheeks. Without a conscious decision, I dropped my reins and glided from the saddle. Without thinking, I ran back to the fallen form of Alexander Dominican.

Dropping to my knees in the grass, I lifted his head and cradled it in my lap. The curtains of his lashes hid his eyes, but his breathing was strangely regular, giving me hope that whatever Alex's injury, it was not serious. Heart in my throat, I frantically touched the rich blackness of his hair, only to find that slices of afternoon sun had come before me, grazing the dark strands with gold and making it feel warm to my fingertips. His hair was both heavy and soft, and I found myself lost in its texture as I brushed it away from his forehead searching for some wound.

"Oh, Alex," I said, aware of how breathless I sounded. "I need to go for a doctor."

Instead of the ugly gash I had expected, I was surprised to find his skin unblemished. Only the natural marks made by the puckering of his eyebrows marred his olive complexion. I stared at Alex as if he were some dream unfulfilled. With both my hands, starting at the center of his forehead, I smoothed the tracks of his brow, tracing my way until I reached his temples. Slowly, I pursued the line of his cheekbones, migrating downward with my feather-light touch, skimming over the beard-like roughness of his face, and ending my journey in the valley that was the cleft of his chin. In awe of the very beauty of his masculine face, I was also stunned by its immobility. My heart hammered. My breath came in gasps. Beneath my outward trance-like movements, my insides were growing warm with a yearning so timeless that it was hard for me to comprehend. Why at a time like this, should I desire him?

Aching, I lifted one finger, and gently caressed his still lips, so full and passionate, yet at the same time susceptible. I trailed the very edges of his mouth, and returned to the center, my fingertip burning where it touched him. Compelled by something I could not suppress, I lowered my head, my blond hair falling around us both like a blessed veil. When my lips touched his in a prayer of absolution, charged pulses electrified my body, sprinting from one extremity to the next and ending like an unholy explosion somewhere near the pit of my stomach.

"My lady," Alex murmured against my mouth.

Jolted by his sudden address, I was further shaken by the way his tongue captured mine, answering my entreaty with a demand of his own. He was ruthless in his gentle assault upon my senses. I begged for mercy, lost in a sweet kiss that ravished me and left me wanting more.

"You're beautiful," he said, his words lingering on my own lips.

Somehow, he was able to reach up and grasp the nape of my neck, hiding his hands in my hair, and pulling me down quite awkwardly. For a moment, I was on top of him, and then we were rolling together in the fragrant bluegrass of the meadow. His fingers were all over me, kneading and probing and doing glorious things to my body and my soul.

"I knew you wouldn't leave me," he whispered and playfully nipped my ear lobe.

I jerked and tried to sit up. Alex hauled me back into the long grass and covered me with a heavy right leg.

"Get off me."

"Why?"

"You tricked me! You didn't fall off your horse." My accusation struck a glancing blow into the wind.

He kissed my left eyebrow and dribbled tiny kisses down my tear-streaked cheek. "I know. I did it on purpose to make you stop."

I tried shoving him with my hands, all the while willing my body to stop its heathen dance of fire. This time, my mind was losing the battle, and as Alex began unbuttoning the first two buttons of my sleeveless shirt, I felt myself defeated. My mind shut out the horror I had just witnessed, my grief, everything but the man beside me.

"You didn't know I would come back."

"I trusted." He nuzzled my neck.

"Trusted what? My gullibility?" I tried to be angry. I

knew I should be, but I found my throat to be so sensitive to his tickling that I couldn't sustain my argument.

At my question, he stopped his pleasing aggression. Propping himself up on one elbow, Alex looked at me, his gray eyes so muted and distant that I thought I would misplace myself in their depths. Tenderly, he brushed a long blond tendril of hair away from my eyes, his fingers upon my forehead exciting.

"I don't know what I trusted," he said, revealing his own uncertainty. "I just know this is meant to be."

He searched my eyes for a hushed moment. Hypnotized, I returned his gaze. When he lowered his lips to meet mine again, I perceived his words to be true. For whatever reason, we belonged together now—at this time and at this place. Acceptance brought me peace, and as my heart soared, throbbing relentlessly in my chest, my mind succumbed in silence.

We began to court each other. Alex continued his methodical unbuttoning as I agonized over his slowness. Finally, he reached the top of my jodhpurs, and without remorse, pulled the hem of my shirt out of my pants, and spread open the soft fabric. For a moment, a soothing wind caressed me above my breasts, cooling my hot flesh, until he bowed his black head to cover my bareness, and began to stroke me with his tongue. I clutched at his heavy locks, holding on as if my life depended upon it. The wet onslaught made me squirm as raw desire flamed within my very being. When he unsnapped the front hook of my bra, exposing me even more to his keen gaze, I moaned in response, so full of sublime pain that I found it hard to cope.

"Mary," he murmured, and conquered the tip of my breast.

When he looked at me again, his eyes bespoke a profound longing. I released the grip I had on his hair, and let my fingers again explore the contours of his face. I could tell my very touch was a turn-on to him, and I found my own desire erupting within me like sheets of fire.

"I want to love you," he said softly, and clasped my hand to his lips, opening my palm to entice it.

I answered by spreading my other palm against his jawline. I couldn't speak. I couldn't find the words, for my heart was so full. I wanted to love him too somehow knowing it was the right thing to do to find a measure of comfort—to make me feel alive once more.

Slowly, he lowered himself again to ravish my mouth while I began to unbutton his night-black shirt, revealing the curly, coal-colored hairs on his chest. As his tongue rummaged aimlessly, causing its own chaos, I removed his shirt from his shoulders, despairing that I couldn't do more. Alex helped me, taking it off and tossing it carelessly aside while he still held possession of my mouth.

I reveled in the strength of his shoulders and the way the muscles of his chest rippled beneath the coarse texture of his hair. Closing my eyes, I savored the feel and taste of him. My breasts rose and fell to the rhythm of my laboring breath. My senses were overcharged. When my roving hands touched the waistband of his trousers, I felt a shudder go throughout his body. Alex groaned, his lips still against mine. He swallowed, and lifted his head. I opened my eyes. We were so close, but I needed to be closer. Just as I read the same plea in his eyes, I loosened the reluctant hook and tugged on the zipper.

"Oh, Mary."

I was too slow and awkward for his wishes. He helped me again, leaving me a moment to strip away the rest of his clothes and shoes. I watched him standing over me, his muscular calves covered with hair, his thighs strong, his manhood ready.

"Alex," I whispered, my outstretched hand beckoning.

He knelt beside me, daring only to touch me with his gaze. I saw the muscles in his temples move, the look in his eyes intense. Reverently, he extended his hand, and parted my jodhpurs in one swift gesture. I laughed as he tried to pull them down, for my jodhpurs hugged my hips like a lover. I wiggled here and there, and finally, we were successful. Working together, we disposed of my thin panties, and then he hovered over me to deprive me of my shirt, my last civilized barrier. Now unrestrained, I lay naked before him, feeling very much the wanton woman I wanted to be with him.

"Love me, my lady."

With torturing slowness, Alex lowered his body to

cover mine. I grabbed his shoulders, urging him to hurry. The smile that lit his eyes and touched his lips was sultry. I felt taut, like a wound spring, and seeking release, lifted my hips to meet him. I was wet with wanting.

He prolonged my agony by plying me again with his tongue until I could stand it no more. Pulling up my legs and entwining them around his hips, I brought us closer. He ceased his torment then, and succumbed against my lips, drawing my breath away with his ardor. Gently, he entered, and held himself still within me as if he were afraid.

He raised his head and gazed at me. "This seems so right." His voice touched me like a summer breeze.

"Yes!" I gasped, offering him my lips again which he took with devotion.

For a moment, I savored his familiar fullness, but coerced by a blind instinct as old as time, I began to move, slowly at first and then faster as I struggled to unite with his soul.

In a quiet torrent of sensation, I came with his name upon my lips and in the wind. Alex answered me by calling my name, the surge of his manhood leaving him exhausted at my side.

Afterwards, neither one of us could speak, and so he pulled me against him, cradling my head upon his shoulder. I hooked my arm over his damp chest and relaxed my leg across his hips that were sticky from our lovemaking.

As we lay together, the white heat of the sun soothing us, I sensed an intimacy with this man that I couldn't explain—as if we had done this private thing many times before.

CHAPTER FOURTEEN

The push-pull of my emotions rubbed the raw edges of my soul. Part of me sensed completion, a circle come together. Another part, the thinking part, questioned it. Our lovemaking was proper because we were married, but I was his wife under certain circumstances. We had an agreement. I had been bought and paid for, so to speak. Business partners didn't make love.

Alex's warm fingertips pressed into my shoulder blade as he walked me home from the stable. He guided me along the twisted garden path, the heady scent of early roses wafting in the breeze. My heart thudded, sending hot pulses of blood flushing throughout my veins. I fought flashes of fantasy, the aroma of the flowers causing me to remember.

Remember what? Something that had never happened? Something my mind had conjured? The only reality was the fact of my husband's passionate fingers caressing the nape of my neck and sending thrills of yearning through me. Nothing else existed. Not a medieval woman heavy with child, nor her black lord and master. I had made them up. They had nothing to do with Alex and me. Nothing to do with my own wild predicament. *Nothing to do with my dead cat.*

Heartsick, I stumbled. Alex steadied me.

What paths were we now to take, Alex and I? Could we be a true couple? The desire was there. The exquisite tension of sex. Where was the love? Alex said the only person he loved was his daughter. Elizabeth. Our reason for coming together.

"Change your clothes. I want to take you out to eat," Alex said as we passed into the cool corridor near the great medieval-styled foyer.

He turned me toward him, holding both my shoulders now, his gaze stroking my features. My chest burned as I looked at him.

"It's a celebration, you know," he murmured, his eyelashes dropping over gray eyes, seductive in their intensity.

"Of what?" With thoughts of Munster still devastating me, I found it hard to speak.

"Of us."

Us. The word had such a definitive ring to it. As right as sunshine in June and a winter storm in January. I blinked up at him, my whole mind suddenly beguiled by the man who held me an arm's length away.

"Can we take Elizabeth with us?" I asked on a whim.

"Elizabeth?"

"Yes, like a real family."

He considered my request, his head tilting to one side. "Being a real family would make me very happy."

I felt my face grow hot as he continued to gaze at me.

"I like your hair down like that. It was too severe pinned up," he said softly.

I reached up to my face, touching the long strands of honey hair that ran wild about it. For the first time, I realized what a mess I must be. Grass stain. Dirt. A scratched elbow.

"It's much too long to hang down."

"Why don't you cut it?" His query was kind.

"Because it's a part of me. I've always had long hair."

But why was I standing here, talking about the way I wore my hair, when Munster lay dead upstairs? My heart hammered, and my eyes pooled with tears. I shook with unrestrained grief. Nothing had changed by our lovemaking.

"What's wrong, Mary?"

I straightened my shoulders, pulling myself a little away from him although he still held me. "Munster," I answered simply. "I can no longer stay in that bedroom."

"My lady." Alex hauled me against his chest, holding

me, soothing me. "You won't have to stay in this room. We'll move your things into my room. You'll sleep with me from now on," he said, breathing quietly against the top of my bowed head.

When I didn't answer, he muttered, "You need some rest before we go out."

I was hardly aware that he led me up the stairs and into his masculine bedroom. I hardly knew that he pulled back his sheets, removed my boots and tucked me into his bed. But I realized when he left me, for his leaving felt like death.

When he returned, he sat on the side of the bed. "We won't be able to go out after all. Mrs. Garrity will bring you some tea, and maybe a bit of soup. Rest. I'll be back in a little while."

I seized his hand. "Where are you going?"

"There's an emergency. My answering service just called and said it's serious. I'm sorry I have to go, but it won't be for long." He patted my closed hand as a father would comfort a child.

My fingers lost their grip, slowly, one by one. And then his hand left mine. My fingers remained cramped and curled, my arm outstretched in a silent, but unanswered plea. With a shudder, I shut my eyes in vain hope I could block out the insanity that still swirled around me.

****

The medieval Mary laughed in spite of herself, for Alexander, her lord and husband, had procured a troop of entertainers for her enjoyment. She could barely move, her confinement upon her, and so found his kindness delightful. They had just finished their mid-day dinner. With the last course of newly harvested fruits, aged cheese and spiced wine upon the table, Mary found herself too stuffed to partake. Besides, the antics of the small band were by far too diverting. There was a gap-toothed woman who balanced on the tips of swords. Mary wondered how she managed that painful feat. Her companion led forth a scraggly looking bear cub, and made the animal do tricks with a ball. Another played upon a pipe while another beat a drum, adding a tone of enthusiasm that was not really needed. Mary's favorite by

171

far was a dwarf in a short, red gown and jagged hood with a tassel on the top. He juggled balls and then the lord's best silver goblets. Next he turned somersaults and cartwheels and danced a little jig to the accompaniment of the musicians.

Alexander leaned toward Mary and covered her hand with his big one. "Happy?" he asked, the familiar scents of mustard and wine upon his breath creating a stab of longing in her lower extremities.

"Yes, my dear husband." She lifted an eyebrow with request, a provocative look in her eyes.

"Nay," he replied with a laugh, as if knowing full well what she meant. "You're far too along for that." He inclined his black head toward the entertainers. "You see, I've brought you something else for your amusement."

Mary pulled a frown and felt the gentle squeeze of his hand. Returning her gaze to the acrobats, she longed for the birth of their child. Then they could set about making another child, and another. The thought made her smile a little. It wasn't so bad being married to her lord. He had turned out to be a kind and loving husband. Again, the nagging sadness jolted Mary's contentment. She had been selected solely to bear the long-awaited heir. After that happened, what would become of Alexander's devotion? Would it evaporate just as the little gnome had made a ball disappear before her very eyes? She sighed then, knowing it was God's will to keep the future from her.

Yet some perverse need to know made Mary turn to her husband. "What if the child is not a son, my lord?" she asked him with quiet dignity.

Alexander scowled, and she felt the pressure on her hand increase. "Our daughter will be beautiful like her mother. We will teach her to be chaste and dutiful, and she will grow in wisdom. When she is ready, she will make a magnificent marriage to a great lord and make her parents proud."

"You won't mind if she isn't a son?"

"We can always try again." With a gleam in his eyes, he shrugged his shoulders. "You worry too much. Watch the jugglers."

Mary returned to observing the merriment, aware

that a man could not understand a woman's concerns. Ever honest with herself, she also realized she had not spoken her true worry. Would Alexander love her, child or no child? Would he ever love her for herself? Mary shuddered in her mind and bit her lip.

The little gnome pranced toward them, cocking his head, his tassels bobbing crazily, a quizzical look in his eyes. The tall man who had led the bear followed respectfully behind, his gaze lowered. "He'll read your palm, milady," the second man explained. "Rufus has the gift. He can see into the future."

Mary looked down at the wizened little man who held such an appearance of deference in his scrutiny of her. Her heart thumping in her breast, she felt her palms grow damp, and wiped them self-consciously on her gown. Did she want to know the future? Unfortunately, Alexander took the decision from her, motioning the little man forward and pulling back Mary's chair from the trestle table.

"He doesn't speak, milady," the taller man said.

"Why, how shall I know what he reads?" Maybe this was her way out.

"He motions with his hands, and I can tell you."

"Of course." She felt her spirits sink.

Rufus knelt at her feet, the hem of her yellow gown touching his bare knees. Mary extended her right hand, and he took it with reverence. He grasped her palm with his hard and callused hands, engulfing her own fingers and scratching them roughly. Mary marveled that for such a small man he had such huge hands. He turned her tiny one over and over, examining all the marks and running his fingertips along hers. Once he sharply glanced up at Mary. Their gazes held, and she thought she saw fear in his eyes. Grinning at her, as if to make her at ease, he looked back at his partner and began to motion with his right hand, as he continued to hold her palm with his left one.

"The child will be a boy."

All around, the gasps of surprise were followed by remarks of gratitude. Mary peeked up at Alexander who stood behind her. She felt his reassuring hand on her shoulder. As his fingers stiffened, she knew he was glad.

"He will grow up to be a strong warrior like his father." More nods of approval. "He will own many lands, even beyond those of his father. That is all Rufus sees," the man with the bear explained.

As a gentle applause rang in Mary's ears, she studied the face of the little gnome. He lowered his eyes, and let go of her hand. In her heart, she understood he knew more and for some reason he refused to tell. When he looked at her again with a gaze so painful and tender, he nodded ever so slightly to acknowledge her comprehension. What could it be? What did he know about her future?

The little man reached out and patted Mary's hand to comfort her. He seemed to be trying to tell her all would be well. Some day. Everything would right itself.

****

Rufus was the link. I awoke with that thought, and with a very startling recognition. *Mary de Mandeville, the woman of my dreams, and I were the same person.* Swift spikes of dread catapulted through my veins. My heart pulsed harder. I grew cold. *How can that be? Had my dreams really happened?*

What was Rufus doing in the present as well as the past? With half-fused eyes, I gazed from under Alex's navy and forest plaid sheets. The darkened room felt inhospitable. Although my most recent dream must have been meant to bring me solace, I felt no peace. Things weren't right. I wondered about my sanity. How could I remember something that took place in a time so long ago?

Propping myself up on my elbow, I reached the telephone by the bedside and dialed Gail. She wasn't there. Only her hollow voice on her answering machine.

"Gail, this is Mary. Please call me as soon as you get home. No, call me tomorrow morning. Early. I need your help," I whispered and then returned the receiver.

With a sigh, I sank back into the warm sheets and pulled them under my chin, as if their closeness would block my mind from anxiety.

"So you've talked your way into Dr. Dominican's bed," Mrs. Garrity said, snapping on the overhead lights and walking into the room without a single knock.

I had no answer for the hateful woman. She placed a tray of food on a nearby table.

"Allison's room wasn't good enough for you?" She stood over my bed, her sly glare raking me.

Still I refused to be baited, and held my lips tightly pursed together.

"What's the matter? Cat got your tongue?" she asked with a malicious grin.

"Get out of here! Get out of my room!" I struggled to sit up, my hair wild and my face hot with anger.

"You mean Dr. Dominican's room." Mrs. Garrity's voice was sickly sweet.

"You killed my cat, you hateful woman. I know you did!"

"My, my. I must warn the doctor about you. You're losing your composure. You're paranoid, seeing things that don't exist."

Crude terror cut through my mind. Did she suspect something? Did she know about my dreams?

"He can't leave his daughter with someone like you," she continued, tipping her black bobbed head in my direction. "When he understands, he'll get rid of you."

Each indrawn breath ripped my chest apart. "You may be wrong, Mrs. Garrity," I said with control. "You may find yourself out of a job, not me."

"Try it, missy. Just try it," she threatened, a sneer on her lips.

"Get out," I said between clenched teeth.

Her leaving was a blessing, but I didn't stay in bed long enough to give thanks. Throwing back the sheets, I sat up, slung my legs over the side, and pulled on my short, black boots. If Rufus was with me in the present, could someone else from the past be here too? The idea was troubling. Lord Mountjoy, Alexander, my husband in the past—could he be Alex, my husband now? What about Gellis, my servant? Or Lady Mountjoy, my jealous mother-in-law? A snakelike fear crawled into my stomach. Mrs. Garrity. She hated me because of Allison. Was she my mother-in-law from the past?

I drew a deep breath. This line of thinking was absurd. Going to Alex's dresser, I raked agitated fingers through my tangled hair, and stared at my reflection in the mirror. Smudges beneath my eyes gave my face a sallow look. With my fingertips, I tried to smooth out fine crows-feet near the corners of my eyes. I pressed upward on my temples and then stroked downward along my cheeks. Wavering, my body numb with reaction, I struggled with my outrageous thoughts. Was I considering the possibility of reincarnation?

Alex had put my purse on the dresser. Taking a hairbrush from it, I pulled the brush through the lengthy strands of hair. The bristles dug into my scalp, stimulating it. The act of brushing my hair was reassurance like a time-honored tradition. No wonder I had always kept my hair long and straight. I'd never before understood my compulsion.

Gail had always complained about my hair. "Good grief, Mary. You need something quick and casual, not an ancient style that makes you look like your grandmother," she would scold me.

I smiled at the remembrance, for it was not my grandmother that was in question. Evidently, my subconscious had tried to replicate a hairstyle from my past—a very distant one at that. This time though I didn't re-pin my hair, but wrapped a band around it to pull it back from my face.

I needed to go to Alex. Would he know about us? When I told him about my dreams, would he remember? I shivered. Would he even care? Alexander, Lord Mountjoy and Mary de Mandeville had lived, but had they loved? I bit my lip until it hurt. The palms of my hands were damp as I laid down the brush. I needed to resolve this predicament or I would go crazy. If I wasn't already....

With cold determination, I grabbed my purse, and escaped the confines of Alex's room and the restrictions of his mausoleum-like mansion.

CHAPTER FIFTEEN

As day dissolved into night, thunder clouds subdued the summer sunshine. The lowering gray clouds matched my mood, for I had little hope. When I told my story to Alex, would he believe me? Or would he remember? A vague chill of anticipation slithered down my spine. There had to be some reason these dreams started with my marriage. Was Alex involved? Was he Lord Mountjoy?

Silence filled the inky black waiting room of Louisville OB/GYN Associates. Gone was the bubbling activity of my last visit. Behind the reception window, Christy's seat was vacant. The bank of yellow file folders, illuminated by a lone security light, stood like a legion of soldiers. My throat felt swollen. My heart kindled with misgiving. By admitting my dreams to Alex, I was taking a chance. One that would change my life forever.

A nurse in the emergency room had suggested I try Alex's office, because he had come and gone. Luckily, I had spotted a night watchman, who had let me inside. Now, as I stood in the quiet darkness, I wondered if I had made a mistake. Maybe Alex had started home instead of coming back to his office.

"Damn it to hell!"

A bright shattering of glass followed the outcry from within the office complex. The sound pulsed through my body. I startled like a bird.

"Alex? Are you there?"

With a rush of fear, I opened the door to the inner offices, and ventured into the unlit corridor. At the end of the hall, a slash of light stabbed the floor from an open doorway.

"Alex?" I called again. My boots made soft footfalls on the carpet.

"How fitting you should attend my wake, Mrs. Dominican." Dr. Hilliard appeared in the hall, the light from the doorway throwing stark shadows across his pale face. "Isn't it interesting how life is made up of chance? Or maybe you'd like to call it destiny?"

"Where's Alex?" I demanded, my breathing short and deep.

"What? No welcome for me? Your own physician?" His voice held a twinge of sarcasm.

"I'm looking for my husband," I replied, stiff with indignation.

"Ah, yes, the good doctor." John turned and went into his office. I followed him to the threshold, and clutched the edge of the door with a cold hand.

"Sure I can't be of service, sweetheart?"

"My name is Mary. And no, you can't help me unless you know where Alex is," I said stepping into the office.

John put a paperweight into a simple brown box. The light from his brass lamp pooled on the surface of the desk, casting subtle shadows of dread around the room. On the side opposite the desk, I noticed a shattered bottle on the carpet, and wine stains dripping like blood down the mauve wallpaper.

"I suppose your dear husband is in surgery assisting Dr. Miles," John said, his gaze following mine to the splattered wall. "I'm sorry I can't offer you anything to drink, sweetheart. As you see, my bottle met with a little accident."

"You're drunk," I snapped, anger crawling through my veins. I had seen his kind too often.

He laughed. "You're not the first to accuse me of intoxication this evening, madam." He swept me a formal bow, the glitter in his blue eyes mocking me.

"How can you behave like this? You're a doctor. You have responsibilities!"

"Like husband, like wife," he said with another smirk.

"What do you mean?" I advanced toward his desk.

"Dominican said the same things only moments ago. He also mentioned that nasty little word 'alcoholic.'"

"Well, it's true. You are." My fingers curled into fists.

"Ah, a matter of opinion, my sweet Mary. I don't miss my appointments. I perform my duties. An alcoholic doesn't do that. I may be a little high, as you see me standing here, but I'm not a falling down drunk. Not like my father and my brother." His words drifted off into solitary musing.

"Alex is concerned about you," I said, my gaze playing over his sagging features.

"Alex is only concerned about himself." John looked up at me, his eyes brittle.

"You must admit, drinking can't be good for you or your practice."

"I don't have to admit a thing," he said. "Besides, it's not *my* practice."

"What do you mean?"

"Your loving husband fired me. Told me to get the hell out. So you see, sweetheart, I could care less about his *concern*."

I was afraid. I backed up a step. John noticed, but went on with his packing.

"Maybe he'll reconsider," I said, my gaze following his long tapered fingers as he picked objects up from the desk and put them in his box.

"Not likely." He paused and favored me with a sympathetic look. "You don't know your husband very well, do you?"

"I don't know what you mean."

"You and Allison."

"What's Allison got to do with this?"

"She didn't know him either. She didn't know the ultimate professional. The perfectionist. There's no room for screw ups in Dr. Dominican's view of things." His harsh voice filled the small office space with anger.

"There's nothing wrong with that."

"Tell that to Allison."

"Allison is dead."

"Perceptive. So perceptive." His voice became like silk as he came around the desk.

I moved back a step until my legs touched the edge of

a chair. "I understand you knew Allison in California," I said, watching the shifting light in the doctor's blue eyes.

"She was beautiful then, so happy and carefree." John's gaze swept above me as if he were remembering.

"I've seen her wedding picture. She was beautiful." My thoughts veered to the gossamer-haired woman I had seen in Guy's family gallery. I was so sorry she had died without once holding her own child, a pleasure I had taken.

John must have read the reflection in my eyes for his own look softened toward me. "I'm sorry for you, Mary," he said, his voice for once without mockery. "You're innocent like Allison. He tricked her into believing he was something he was not. She didn't know he was a cold and unloving man."

I gazed into John's blue eyes, captured by their intensity. "Alex loves his daughter," I whispered.

"That's mighty big of him." The derision returned. "If I had been lucky enough to have Allison's devotion, I would have cherished it. I would have never let her go unloved. Dominican did. He made my Allison miserable."

My lashes lowered at the anger and sadness in his remark. What did John mean? Had he been in love with Allison?

"And now you, Mary. He's making you miserable."

I flinched as his warm fingers touched my chin. He lifted it gently, my gaze catching his and holding. My breathing came in labored spurts. I felt my pulse quicken with dread.

"Look at your eyes," he murmured. "They're so troubled. The dark circles make you seem haunted. Are you haunted, Mary? Has this man tormented you like he tormented Allison?"

"I don't know what you're talking about." I was barely breathing.

"After Allison met him, she never wanted me again. She lived for that man. She tried to please him, but nothing satisfied him. And then there was that manipulative father of his. Maybe if she'd been lucky enough to conceive earlier in the marriage, but she had trouble, and then she was dead. Dominican killed her with sadness as sure as the cancer."

John's eyes shifted as he read the emotions that must have shadowed my face. He held me with more than with his fingertips touching my chin. He held me spellbound by feelings I could not comprehend.

"You shouldn't love the man so much, Mary," he warned. "Your past is not perfect either."

"No," I answered, my lips hardly moving.

"Allison was far from perfect. She miscarried like you. She had a hard life trying to make it in California. She wasn't pure enough for him. Neither are you, Mary." John's warning sounded hollow in my ears.

He took my face into the palms of his hands. With soft strokes, he moved his thumbs over my cheekbones. I couldn't stir. I couldn't turn away. And then he lowered his lips to mine. Deep within me, I wanted to fight him. I wanted to pull away and rip his hands from my face. But I held still and let him kiss me. I let the comfortable scents of garlic and good Bordeaux wine tempt my senses. I let his heavy lips mold to mine, and his tongue bayonet my mouth with passion as old as time.

Standing there in his grasp, allowing him to rape my mouth with his tongue, my mind became a black vortex of confusion. Lord Mountjoy? John's scent was so familiar to me. So much like my husband in the past. Had I mistaken Alex for my former lover because of his name and his resemblance? If so, what was I to do? And what did it matter? Alexander, Lord Mountjoy didn't love me. Neither did Alex Dominican.

Swaying, my body tingling, I pressed my hands to my ears as John's kiss deepened and lengthened. The heavy scent of garlic and wine oppressed me. It nauseated me. The sound around me soared to a crescendo of discord. Part of me knew I was blacking out. I was sinking once again into the oblivion of the past. Another part of me resisted the hot and sticky pursuit of my soul.

"Stop it!" I twisted my mouth away, and struggled to escape his grasp.

"What are you doing here, Hilliard?"

Alex rudely ripped John away from me and tossed him aside like a toy. I was terrified, because of the fury in Alex's eyes. My lips were raw, just like my soul. Lowering my hands from my ears, I wrapped my arms around my body, numb with familiar grief. Alex glanced scornfully at me once, his eyes bright orbs of anger.

"Keep your hands off of me," John said with a snarl. He shook himself like a dog to rid himself of Alex's touch. He put distance between himself and Alex, stepping behind the desk to continue his packing.

"Really, Hilliard, you amaze me." Alex tipped his head, a black shock of hair dipping over his forehead. "I told you to remove your things. Instead, I find you kissing my wife."

John glanced up at his accuser, a glitter in his eyes. "And it was a great pleasure."

My legs couldn't hold me. I dropped to the chair that touched the back of my legs. My limbs were paralyzed, my breathing forced. The tension in the silent room was suffocating.

"Any interest in Mrs. Bowman?" Alex asked, breaking the silence. "You almost killed her. I would have expected some concern from you."

"You have enough concern for both of us, Dominican," John slurred as he picked up his box and shouldered past Alex. "Really, I'm glad to be leaving this hick town that calls itself a city. Hasn't been the same since Allison died." At the doorway, he paused and glared at us. "You lead a charmed life, Dominican. I don't know how. You don't deserve the things you've been given."

And then he was gone, leaving some deep void in my heart and an even deeper question. A faint scent of garlic remained on my face where he had touched me. My mouth tasted of aged wine. Dizziness clouded my mind, numbing my spirit so that I had little care for the anger in Alex's eyes as he stood over me.

"What are you doing here, Mary?"

"I came looking for you." With effort, I lifted my gaze to meet his. My heart twisted with longing.

"Why were you kissing Hilliard?" The gray in his eyes deepened angrily.

"He was kissing me," I replied with remoteness, my gaze slipping from Alex's face.

"But you let him."

Alex's accusation was like a blade in my back. I made no denial, but hugged my arms around me even tighter.

When I didn't respond, Alex lowered his shield of anger. His shoulders seemed to sag from pent-up tension and he moved away from me. Stooping, he began to pick up the shattered glass against the wall. Thunder rolled in the distance.

"I hope I didn't let the guy off the hook too easily," he muttered. "The practice may be sued because of this."

"How's the woman?" I asked in a hushed voice.

"Well, she didn't die," Alex said. "Although Hilliard's neglect almost caused her death."

"What happened?"

Alex stood and turned to the desk, laying the broken glass on top. "Mrs. Bowman came in with abdominal pain. Hilliard diagnosed an ectopic pregnancy, and went in to remove it laparascopically. What he found was a bleeding right ovary and a belly full of blood. He underestimated the blood loss, and although the patient initially did well after surgery, by the time I was called, her hemoglobin had dropped to seven point nine. She'd already received plenty of blood transfusions, so we knew we were in trouble."

The talk of blood parched my mouth. My heart rose to choke off the breath in my throat. Instead of the sterile surroundings of a hospital operating room, I saw the dark and dank solar of a medieval castle and the struggling body of a woman with her lifeblood dripping from her.

My husband ransacked his black hair with a wayward hand. He began to pace the tiny room. "Dr. Miles performed the surgery. We cut her open, Mary, and found five units of blood in her abdomen. She was bleeding to death right in front of our eyes. Fortunately, we packed off her pelvis and checked for other bleeding sites, and found nothing wrong. It was D.I.C., something any medical school intern knows to check for."

"What's that?" I asked with suppressed emotion.

"Disseminated Intravascular Coagulation. In other words, she'd bled so much that she'd lost her clotting factors."

"Will she be okay?" My voice sounded like it came from far away.

"Yes, but she's very lucky to be alive. I thought we'd lose her. Mrs. Bowman has a very strong will to live."

When Alex uttered those words, something started in my mind. 'A strong will to live.' *In another time and another place, I had experienced a strong will to live.* Alex came around the side of the desk, and once more stood over me. I labored to look him in the eyes.

"If Hilliard hadn't been drunk, maybe he would have picked up on her symptoms." As Alex considered me, his mood shifted and he smiled. "I did something today I should have done a long time ago," he murmured.

"What?"

His eyelashes shadowed his gray eyes. "Fired Hilliard...and made love to you."

Alex's large hands reached toward me, gripping my bare upper arms and pulling me up. With an endearing fingertip, he brushed a strand of hair from my face. His breathing was slow. He smelled of spicy aftershave and antiseptic handwash. I blinked up at him, and licked my roughened lips.

"Let's go home, Mary," he whispered. "We have another crisis to solve there."

I felt stupid, lost. I was suspended in a state of blank bewilderment. "What's that?" I asked, for I couldn't think. I couldn't remember.

"We have to find your cat."

"My cat?" What was Alex talking about? I frowned, concentrating, and then I jerked with memory. "My cat is dead!"

His grip tightened. "I know that's what you think, but he isn't, Mary. Your cat has just gotten loose in that big house, and we'll find him."

"No!" I shook myself free. "You don't believe me! No!"

"Mary! Get a hold of yourself. Is there something wrong with you?" Alex grabbed me again, and his hands were like shackles. I shuddered at his touch.

"That's right," I said boldly and with care. "There's something wrong with me. I'm not perfect. You can't expect me to be. I'm human, Alex. Human."

As I rambled, I knew I echoed John. But I couldn't stop what left my lips. I couldn't overcome the feeling of chaos in my mind. I needed relief. I needed some sort of peace.

"Mary, maybe I should get you something for your

nerves."

"You know I don't take that stuff!" Some part of me saw the concern written in agony on Alex's face, but the confused part of me just dug myself in deeper.

"Come on. Let's go home. I'll put you to bed."

"No! I want to go to Gail's. She'll understand. I don't want to go back to Marchbrook Manor." Pleading with my gaze, I lifted my hands to his beard-rough face. The familiarity of that movement ached within me and deepened my torment. "Alex, don't you see? I need some time to myself, to think."

For once I must have sounded sensible. "Think about what, Mary?"

"About us. About our arrangement. Is it what I want? Is it right for me, given all the circumstances?" For a moment the responsible, staid part of myself surfaced, and I was able to explain a little of my problem.

Alex's gaze lingered on me almost with a loving examination. If he had told me he loved me then, I would have surrendered. I would have returned with him no matter the consequences, but he didn't love me. He had said so that night in Elizabeth's room. The open window of my heart began to shut. For a lifetime, an eternity, I had longed for love. It had been denied me and the lack of it created a chasm in my soul, a void so big that nothing seemed able to fill it.

Our hands dropped from each other's grasp. I was alone. Silently, I found my purse.

"I'll take you to Gail's," he said.

"I have my car." We talked like strangers.

"You're not in any condition to drive. Doctor's orders."

CHAPTER SIXTEEN

"Mary, you look like a drowned rat!" Gail stood at the front door staring at me.

"May I come in?" My question was muffled by the rain that slithered down my cheeks.

"Of course, silly me." She stepped back and threw the door open wide.

I glanced back at Alex's BMW to see it draw away from the curb like a white phantom.

"Who's that?" Gail asked, as she pulled me into her house and shut the door.

"Alex."

"Won't he come in?"

"No, he's going home."

I met the inquiry in Gail's brown eyes as she dropped my hand, and I wrapped my arms around my body. They were scant protection, I knew, but I felt vulnerable even in front of my best friend. How could I explain the chaos of my life? Here I stood in Gail's entry, still wearing my jodhpurs and boots, dripping water and making a puddle on her floor.

"I guess I'm having a bad hair day," I said, lifting one hand to the witch's tangle that was my hair.

"Oh, Mary." I heard the catch in her voice. "You're going to sit down, and I'm going to make you some hot tea. You'll feel better before you know it."

"What is it about hot tea? Does it have some sort of magic healing power?" I laughed a little at the thought.

"Sure. On a dreary night like this, hot Earl Grey tea

has a calming effect." Gail ushered me into her quiet living room.

The cozy room was a jumble, with magazines and newspapers scattered here and there on the floor. Colorful paper cutouts suitable for five-year-olds littered the coffee table. The furniture was old basement and new antique, a collection of comfortable chairs and sofas. One floor lamp burned like a spotlight. For once, I let down my guard, feeling sheltered and safe in Gail's humble home.

"Take a seat. I'll be back in a jiff."

Hunkering down in a corner of the sofa, I let out a big breath. How would I explain myself? What kind of a nut thought about medieval knights and ladies? Why would Gail believe me? *Only that she's your best friend, stupid,* a niggling voice said in my ear. She'd believed me when I told her about the slashed suitcase and the strange happenings. That's more than Alex believed. A profound sadness engulfed me.

"Oh, I didn't know anyone was here," a startled voice boomed across the room.

Startled myself, I glanced up to see a nice-looking, sandy-haired man standing awkwardly in the door to the bedroom. He wore only a white bathrobe.

"I'm sorry." I stood up, red-faced. My hand strayed to my hair.

"It's just Mary," Gail said, coming back into the room with a steaming mug in her hands.

"Mary, this is Anthony." She said his name with a significant drawl and a piercing glance at me.

"Hello, Anthony." I extended my hand.

Embarrassed, Anthony gave my hand one big shake, and then dropped it awkwardly. "Excuse me. I'm going to make myself decent."

I raised a meaningful eyebrow at Gail as she handed me the hot tea.

"Don't say a word. He's just visiting."

"In his bathrobe?"

"Now, don't you start on me, Mary."

I cupped the hot drink between my hands and let the steam warm my face. What did it matter? Gail was a big girl. I wasn't her keeper. Settling into the sofa once more, I sipped the tea.

Jan Scarbrough

"What? I expected a fight." Gail propped herself on the arm of the chair like she was riding a horse.

"No. No fight," I said with a shrug.

"Something must really be eating on you. Have you left Alex?"

I searched Gail's astute eyes. Lowering my mug, I bit my bottom lip and shook my head no.

Anthony reentered the room at that moment, this time dressed in dark pants, a white shirt and conservative tie. He glanced sheepishly at me, coming to stand behind Gail and resting his hand possessively on her shoulder. I flinched at the intimacy of his action.

"There's something wrong, but Mary won't talk about it," Gail began with an accusing tone to her voice.

"Maybe I should leave," Anthony offered.

"Oh, no. I don't want to interrupt." I stood up again, poised for flight like a bird.

"Mary, don't be stubborn." Gail's tone allowed no other option, and I flopped down once more. "Is it about those strange things happening at home?"

Home? Gail meant Marchbrook Manor. With a sweep of my hand, I brushed the strands of honey-colored hair from my face as I fumbled for words. What I had to tell would sound like fiction. I'd sound like an idiot.

"Yes, and there's more," I finally said. "Someone killed Munster."

"Munster?" Gail's voice rose in alarm.

"Who's Munster?" Anthony asked in a quick aside.

"Mary's cat."

My mind roved back to the horrible sight of Munster's slaughter. I fought the rise of bile in my throat. My hands began to shake and I set the mug on the coffee table.

"Who did it? Don't tell me. You don't know." Gail's gaze was direct.

"No, and Alex doesn't believe me because by the time I took him to my room, Munster's body was gone."

"Damn," she muttered under her breath, and then turned troubled eyes to Anthony. "Since Mary moved into her husband's house, someone sliced her suitcase, tried to hurt Alex's baby, and now this. Mary, you're going to have to leave that place."

188

I twisted my hands. There was more. The burden of it was too heavy to carry alone. Words came to me like silent specters. "Gail, there have been dreams."

"Dreams?" Gail started forward until Anthony restrained her. She settled back to hear me out.

"They began when I married Alex. I don't understand them. I've had them while I sleep and while I'm awake. They tell a story, and they frighten me. I'm afraid I may die."

"What kind of story, Mary?" It was Anthony who asked the question.

I looked away. "About people in the Middle Ages. The same people. I think I'm one of them."

My revelation was met by silence. Gail tossed Anthony a significant glance, but pursed her lips together and kept quiet.

"Tell me what happens in the dreams," Anthony urged quietly.

"I've never told anyone this." My eyes shifted self-consciously from one to the other. "There's a woman named Mary. She's young and pregnant. Her husband is a great lord, in England. There's a castle. I've seen it." My voice trailed off, remembering.

"You saw it in your dreams?"

I gazed at Anthony who looked so steady and sincere. Maybe he was a good match for Gail. Maybe she was really very lucky. "I saw the castle in my dreams, and in the tapestry at Alex's house."

"Tapestry?" Gail sat forward again, her brown eyes riveted on me.

"One that Allison made."

"Oh, Mary."

"I know. That's what so bizarre about the whole thing." I cast them a subdued smile. "Alex has a servant named Rufus. He's in the dreams as well."

"Maybe it's a far memory." Anthony's brown eyes were thoughtful.

I glanced quizzically at them.

"Anthony is a psychologist." Gail favored him fondly. "He's hypnotized people who have past lives."

"Reincarnation?" Thin chills of exhilaration coursed like ice through my veins. I was frightened and curious like a cat exploring a new catnip toy.

"Possibly," Anthony hedged.

"But I don't believe in that stuff."

Gail nudged him with a rude elbow. "Go ahead and talk to her about it."

Moving her leg, Gail made room for Anthony to set down in the chair. He leaned forward with his elbows on his knees. With understanding eyes, he gazed at me. "Our concept of the past is sequential. It's possible your past is affecting your present."

"What do you mean? My childhood?"

"No, a far memory—of times long ago."

I frowned. "That's crazy."

"When we've done past life regressions, we've discovered the human can communicate historic data graphically and accurately. The person hypnotized has never been exposed to this historic information."

Worrying my lips, I considered Anthony with growing trepidation.

"Another thing we've also found is that you're probably interacting with many people who were important to you in the past incarnation. People seem to be reborn in another time frame, seek out each other and explore their relationships once more."

"You don't believe that stuff, do you?" My question held a sense of self-doubt.

Anthony sat back and shrugged. "It doesn't matter if I believe it or not."

As he favored me with his quiet, confident look, I shifted uncomfortably. "I don't understand why this is happening to me."

"Because something was left unfinished."

"Unfinished," I grumbled. "There's nothing unfinished. I know how it's going to end. That medieval Mary is going to die. She's going to die in childbirth."

Gail had paled, her breathing shallow. She rested her hand on Anthony's shoulder.

"But there's something left undone. Your dreams are trying to tell you what that is."

"Does the black lord, my husband, love me?" My eyes blurred as my mind cried out with yearning.

"What happened in your past life is like ripples from

a stone tossed into a pond," Anthony said, his voice hushed. "The cause and effects of your past actions ripple through time. You are responsible for everything that happens to you, but only if you have control of yourself."

"I have control of nothing," I said with finality.

"With awareness of your destiny, you will have control."

He sounded so sure of himself. I envied him for it.

"Once you know the past, you will be at peace. You will have inner harmony, and that is the same thing as wisdom. Wisdom, your new knowledge, gives you freedom."

My eyes blurred. I gripped my fingers together, pinching them, hoping to remain focused. "How can I get this peace?"

"I can stimulate your far memory."

"But she's dying. What if..."

"No, it can't go that far," Anthony assured me. "With hypnosis, we set aside your conscious mind, narrowing your attention span so you can focus on this thing from the past. The suggestions I give you can't make you do anything against your morals or religion. There's no way you can die doing this."

I glanced at Gail. She seemed to be willing me to put myself in Anthony's care.

"But I don't know who the black lord is, in the present," I whispered.

"Surely, it's Alex," Gail spoke up.

"I thought so too, but just this evening I had this feeling it was John Hilliard."

"One of Alex's partners?"

I looked at Gail. "His ex-partner."

"All the more reason for you to find out the truth." Anthony's tone allowed no option.

"What do I do?"

"You must be completely relaxed, open to suggestion. Gail, dim the lights, and Mary, stretch out there on the sofa."

"I feel strange doing this."

"How have these visions come to you?" Anthony moved the chair closer to the sofa as I lay down.

"Some are dreams while I sleep. The others start

with a heightened awareness to sight and sound. There's a bright light or an explosion of colors."

"And then your mind succumbs to these visions from the past?"

"Yes."

"Mary, I want you to close your eyes."

"Okay."

"Now listen to me. In your deepest memory, in your subconscious, you hold a memory of everything that has ever happened to you...every thought, deed, and action. You know every waking and sleeping moment of your life, now and in the past. You know about every life you've ever lived."

Anthony's deep voice soothed me like a warm bath. I heard his words, and began to believe.

"Mary, you have the power and the desire to draw upon all this knowledge in your mind. Let this knowledge flow down into your conscious mind now as we work together. If you and your present husband Alex were together in another lifetime...in another time and place, I want you to go backward. I want you to travel to something important that took place in this other period of time, and I want you to tell me about it."

****

Mary's last contraction had ended only moments before. She lay panting, drifting between the pain, her eyes half closed against the light, because suddenly everything burned around her. They must have lit a thousand candles as if they could drive away the darkness threatening to take her from them.

"Do something for her!" Gellis demanded.

"There's nothing more to be done," the haggard midwife whined. She wiped a dirty hand across her sweaty face and pushed back a strand of greasy hair.

"Then save the child."

Mary heard the stern pronouncement from somewhere in the dark recesses of her solar. The voice was strong and determined. As her mother-in-law stepped forward, her gown blue like the harvest sky. Mary shut her eyes. The torment began again and she lost all awareness of herself, the words coming to her from a distant void.

"I can use a decoction of flaxseed and chickpeas to moisten my hands. With the next contraction, I'll try pulling the baby out."

"Go ahead."

"No! She'll die for sure. You'll rip her apart!" Gellis protested.

"Either way, she's dead," Mary's mother-in-law said. "We must try to save the child."

"That's all he wanted, the whoreson!" Gellis screamed.

Like the raucous echo of the winter wind, the noise of a slap resounded throughout the chamber. Mary heard weeping. *Gellis, my loyal maid. She shouldn't cry for me. This was my destiny.* The little dwarf Rufus had seen it. He had known. Mary opened her eyes just as the current pain subsided, and turned to find the gaze of the midwife riveted on her.

"Do it," she told the woman, barely able to make her wishes known.

The midwife nodded. They understood each other. Noble lady and serf, they were both women who grasped full well the liabilities of their gender.

"No. No, milady." On her knees, Gellis buried her head in her arms. Mary heard soft sobs next to her right ear.

It began again—the flight of the gerfalcon, the wash of the pounding surf, the contractions that rent life from her body. "Alexander!" Mary felt the slick hands of the midwife upon her. "Gellis, I want Alexander."

She suspected Gellis went for him, because she left her side. Unable to wonder about it, Mary was all-consumed with fire.

"I have the babe," the midwife said between her rasping pants. Her great red tongue lolled out of the right side of her mouth, and fleetingly, Mary thought her comical.

The next constriction of her abdominal muscles came immediately upon the last one. The midwife's hands were inside her, and then the urge to bear down overpowered her. Mary pushed with what faint strength she had left. It couldn't have been much help, for her burden didn't ease. She pushed again. Anything. Anything to rid herself of

Jan Scarbrough

the staggering pain.

"Again, milady!"

Like the popping of a cork from a flask of wine, the baby's head spurted out between Mary's legs. Immediately, she relaxed, her head rolling back upon the sweat and blood-soaked mattress. The next contraction and the passing of the shoulders were nothing. All was over. All was done.

The women at the foot of the bed huddled around the slippery newborn. "Look, milady." The midwife turned to the mother-in-law, and preened herself as if she'd conceived the child. "'Tis a boy!"

"Sweet Mother of God," Alexander's mother whispered, crossing herself in a sign of gratitude. "Does he live?"

Mary's eyes drifted shut. The cooing and clucking midwife must have wiped away the mucus from the baby's nose and mouth, and then like from a distance tunnel a thin cry echoed in the room. The child lived. In Mary's open heart, she gave thanks.

"Let me cut and tie the cord, and then we'll wrap the babe. You, milady, can present him to our lord."

The midwife completed her tasks, and as the two women tended the child, Mary heard Alexander enter the room. *My lord, are you happy with me now that I've presented you with a son?* She was too weary to open her eyes. Her lids felt heavy, like weights resting upon the delicate bones of her cheeks. She meshed into the bed, all her senses magnified within her soul. Mary's parched mouth felt like ashes. The solitary drip, drip, drip of her lifeblood as it splashed off the bed onto the new carpet from Castile sounded like a roll of thunder. She smelled the putrid scent of death, and then suddenly it didn't matter. Her body wasn't important—only her love for Alexander, and their child. Serene and full of peace, Mary floated away—oozing. Drifting. It was so easy to die. She took one last gasp.

Then Mary hovered above herself amid a glorious white light. Its brightness blinded her, but because of it, she saw so much more. High in the air, she wafted over her bed, buoyed by some unseen force. There was no pain—only a great awareness.

Hesitating, Alexander stood on the outskirts of the room, a compelling figure with his black hood hiding his face. Chin lifted, his mother marched toward him with outstretched hands, carrying Mary's child. Dramatically, she offered him to his father. With curiosity, the lord took the infant and cradled him in the crook of his arm.

"A boy, my dear son, and the Mountjoy heir." The triumphant gleam in the lady's eyes bespoke so much.

Alexander nodded, acknowledging her declaration. "He's a comely lad. Is he healthy?"

"He appears so," the midwife spoke up.

"But we must still pray," said his mother, crossing herself. "Life for these young ones is so hazardous."

Alexander smiled down upon the child, and tenderly pulled back the tiny one's swaddling clothes. With a great long finger, he pressed the baby's flailing fist. A look of pure love entered his eyes when the infant caught hold of his finger as if he already recognized the man who had given him life.

His gaze softening, Alexander looked up at his own mother. "My son's mother?"

At his words, a long wail resounded throughout the solar. Eyes wide and face pallid, wringing her hands, Gellis had crept unnoticed toward Mary. She had dropped to her knees again and clutched her lady's still hand in a vain attempt to draw her back. Now she moaned, her heart crushed, her anger perceptible in the way her eyes blazed as she glanced up from the bed.

"Little care you, but she's gone," Gellis made bold to speak directly to her lord.

"Gone?" Alexander clutched his son too tightly to his chest.

"Dead." Gellis did not flinch from the harsh word.

As the assertion sank in, Alexander thrust the child from him into his surprised mother's arms. "What say you?" He approached like a wary cat.

Gellis rose, defiant. "She spent her body for you, my lord." With no respect in her voice, Mary's servant dragged out the words "my lord" making them a curse.

Perplexed at the woman's wrath, Alexander glanced down at his wife. "Mary?" As if unwilling to believe, he looked back at the maid who glared at him from across the gulf of the great bridal bed.

"Women die in childbirth, my lord."

"Mary?"

"My God, yes! You heard her screams of pain. Since yester morn she labored for you, sacrificing her young life to make you happy." The words caught in Gellis' lips. "She'd have done anything to please you. But you. You didn't even care. You and your hateful mother. Damn you. Damn you, all."

"Get her out of here," Alexander's mother ordered the other serving women who had entered the birthing chamber and now stood staring at the heartrending scene.

Twisting out of their grasps, Gellis dropped again to the side of the bed, and covered her lady with her embrace. *Gellis, I'm sorry to have failed you.* Mary longed to comfort her maid, to tell her she was all right, that there was no more pain. Reaching out to stroke her maid's bowed head, she couldn't break the barrier of the light so intense was it. She grieved at her inability to communicate. Finally constraining the ever-devoted servant, the other women led her weeping from the room while Mary watched helplessly.

Still Alexander stood paralyzed above his wife's body, never moving a muscle except for the slight twitch in his left jaw.

"Come away, my lord." His mother placed her hand on his sleeve in a gesture of request. "I've sent for a wet nurse, and the servants must prepare the body."

"Stay away from me." His command was as deadly as a snake making ready to strike.

"What?"

"Get out of here! Take the child with you. Leave me with my wife!"

She inclined her head to those still working in the room, in silence ordering them to leave. "It will be as you wish, my lord. We'll await you just outside the door."

Then they were gone—snuffing out the thousand lights, leaving a lone taper to illuminate the bed.

Falling to his knees in the semi-darkness, Alex seized Mary's immobile hand and brought it to his lips. "Oh, Mary. My dear child. Why?" He stroked her palm as if trying to restore its warmth. "We were so happy..." His thoughts trailed off into a void of hushed recriminations as the tears began to seep from the corners of his dark lashes.

Tortured moments passed for him as Mary watched from her peaceful perch of white light. When Alexander jerked back his hood, ran his fingertips through his untamed black mane of hair, and turned his anguished gray gaze up to the ceiling of their once happy chamber, Mary's heart lurched in sorrow.

"I never told you." He raised his fist to strike the air. "I was afraid, and never told you." He lowered his gaze to the prone body, and timidly touched a dark blond strand of hair that had plastered itself to the still forehead. "I love you, Mary de Mandeville. I love you more than the life and breath in my own body. I never thought you would die. Now it's too late. Now I'll never be able to tell you."

Oh, Alexander. Her heart heavy with regret, Mary longed to reach forth and touch the bowed black head, to caress his heavy raven locks, to feel the weight of his body press upon hers. It wasn't meant to be. She had given him his desire, made his fondest wish come true, brought his child into the world—for what? The look in his eyes bespoke a wild torment that rent his soul apart, and Mary could do nothing for him.

"It's all my fault," he muttered. "You were much too inexperienced to wed. I should have left you with your father. You were so young and brave, kind and gracious. Gellis is right. You would have done anything for me, and I failed to tell you the truth. I thought...Never mind. It doesn't matter now. You're gone."

His tears were torrents, running down his face in rivulets of remorse. Mary had never seen him like that—so out of control. Finally, he succumbed upon her body, clutching it in despair. Stretching out her hand, Mary struggled to touch him. Her fingertip lingered above his wild black hair. She strained, almost stroking the rough texture of him.

All too quickly an ethereal white light engulfed her, pulling her backward as she continued to watch her husband. *No!* She fought her fate. *How can I make it right?* Her understanding had come too late. *Why hadn't he spoken sooner?* Knowing he had loved her all the while created an intense sadness within her closed heart. Knowing he wanted her as well as the child induced profound regret. They were to be separated by the great shadow of death—throughout all eternity. It didn't seem fair. Deep in her soul, Mary lamented the providence that having brought them together, now ripped them apart in one great flash of quiet brilliance.

****

A shattering clap of thunder slit the silence of the room. Slowly, deliberately, I opened my eyes. For a moment I was unable to focus. And then I saw Gellis. No, Gail. The dim lights doused the color from her face. She had turned profoundly pale, her chest rising and falling in labored rhythm. She stared at me speechless.

"Welcome back." Anthony's voice was warm salve.

I flung my arm over my eyes, unwilling to remember, reluctant to think. Now I knew. Alexander had loved me, as I had loved him. The deep assurance was like the certainty of returning spring—blades of greening grass, the tiniest purple crocus, the scent of a soft rain.

"Mary, listen to me. Love does not die. It cannot die, for it is not tied to the physical boundaries of time and space."

Hearing his words, but not understanding, I lowered my arm and looked at Anthony.

"But I died." My own words were like shards of glass.

"And you've been reborn," Anthony said to hearten me. "You have a second chance."

"I don't know my black lord. Who is Alexander?"

"Who is your husband in your heart?" Anthony took my hand. His grasp was warm.

"Alex." The word came unbidden like the wind.

"You have your answer."

For once daring to hope, I sat up. "Does Alex know?"

"In his heart," Anthony surmised. "It's your duty to open the window of his heart, to help him remember."

CHAPTER SEVENTEEN

The dark mansion was ominous in its silence. Yet, crossing the threshold with quiet tread, I felt oddly confident and content. *Love does not die.* Hearing Anthony's words again, I gazed at the pristine foyer around me that glowed even in the dimness of the unlit house. It held a truth that thrust daggers of certainty at my soul. For the first time the multicolor tapestries and the shiny coats of armor held reality. These tangible artifacts from the past were keys to my history. They were also fundamental to my future, for they meant that somewhere in the recesses of his mind, Alex must remember as well. *He had done nothing to change his father's medieval decorations.*

The tragedy of my death had happened so long ago, but for some reason, I'd been given another chance. *We'd* been given another chance. That's what mattered. We had been thrown together in the present century to right a wrong—an injustice prompted by misunderstanding.

Gazing at the largest tapestry—the knights and ladies, the hounds and stags, I thought I had been a part of it all. This had been my world. Somehow that faraway world had gone terribly askew. Fortunately, Alex and I had been allowed to finish what we had left undone.

Pausing at the staircase, the wooden handrail hard and slick to my grasp, I wondered where to find Alex. With a tremble of anticipation, I knew he was near. I closed my eyes, and gave myself up to my feelings. Some sixth sense jarred me. Like a fisherman slowly reeling in his catch, I felt the pull of him, as if some invisible line linked us together. It was not the first time I had felt this attraction. I didn't fight it as I once had, but went with it. My steps took me to the library, shut tight against intrusion. Someone was inside, for I saw a faint glow emanating from under the door. I licked my lips as I experienced a growing anxiety tight within my body. My stomach burned. With a swallow, I gripped the knob in my hand. Turning it slowly, the door opened inward, letting me see a comfortable blaze in the fireplace, the only light in the room. Alex, silhouetted against the muted illumination, sat motionlessly in the overstuffed chair. His hand on an empty bourbon glass, he gazed rigidly at some unseen specter in the flickering flame.

Suddenly my confidence evaporated like a tiny puddle of rain water disappearing on a hot summer's day. *Alex will think I'm crazy.* How could I convince that stern man of anything? He hadn't believed me about Munster. How could I relate a tale that sounded too unbelievable to be true?

I approached him slowly, ill-at-ease, like a child going up to talk to a teacher.

"Sit down, Mary." His dulcet voice was hardly loud enough from me to hear. "I turned up the air conditioning. I thought a fire was somehow appropriate on a stormy night."

He remained motionless. How had he known I was there? Compelled to be near him, I settled down on the floor at his feet, pressing as near to his legs as I dared without touching them. Hugging my knees to my chest and resting my chin on them, I waited. The only noises in the room were the occasional crack and pop of the fire, and the soft rhythmic breathing of the man I loved.

"I've always had a longing, an unsatisfied hunger."

I strained to pick up his words. When he placed his right hand on my shoulder, I stiffened a moment, and then relaxed as I responded to the clear connection between us. Turning my head, I rested my cheek on my knees, so I looked up at his grave and drawn features. The line of his jaw was taut with tension, and his gray eyes, so dangerously beguiling, glittered with unnamed emotion.

200

"I don't understand why that has been so, but it has been for most of my life. As a younger man, I tried to cure my melancholy with vigorous exercise and my school work. Then I tried to distract myself by my career. Nothing worked." He lifted his left hand and swept back his black locks from his forehead. "I found relationships with women to be trivial. When my father wanted me to marry Allison, I did what I always did, and followed his instructions." Alex shrugged.

I sensed he was trying to explain his actions to me. Gently, I reached up to my shoulder and laid my hand on his. His skin felt cold to the touch. The minutes ticked by while I quietly anticipated his next disclosure.

"When I reached my thirties, life was monotonous. It lacked significance. No matter what I did, I couldn't shake this despondency which gripped my soul." His fingertips pinched my shoulder. His face was grim. "I think I've always felt the loss of my mother, the lack of a mother's love."

I longed to tell him he was already dearly loved, and he had been for over six centuries. How was I to convince him? How could I make him remember?

"You love Elizabeth." My words fell like inescapable showers. "You have her now."

Ignoring my remarks, Alex removed his hand from my shoulder, stood up and began to pace the room. "Look, in my own offhand way, I'm trying to find a way to apologize."

"For what?" He paused and our gazes confronted each other.

Alex turned away first. Picking up the heavy poker, he jabbed the burning logs into a brighter blaze. "Since meeting you, Mary, I've been like a man deranged. You've tormented me, and I can't explain it." Swinging around, he leveled his provocative gaze at me. "I don't like mysteries. I'm used to scientific facts. Reasons. Cures. Logic, cause, and effect."

"You don't like being out of control," I said with a knowing smile.

"Precisely." The frenzied look in his eyes eased because of my empathy. "I shouldn't have forced you to marry me."

"But you didn't, Alex."

"I used your need for money. I manipulated things to suit myself."

"What has happened to you, Alex, has been out of your control. There's a reason for your feelings."

He glanced at me sharply, not understanding. "Want something to drink?" Taking up his glass and going to the side table, he picked up the decanter of bourbon. "I should have never married you so soon after Allison's death, but when I saw you again at the funeral, something snapped in me. I remembered you immediately. From the miscarriage. It's as if you possessed me." His gray eyes flared.

"In a way I have. Just like you've possessed me."

Alex frowned as he gulped down several swallows of bourbon. I imagined the sting of the strong liquor. He still didn't understand.

"Then those threatening incidents happened. It was all my fault. I should have put a stop to them...." His voice trailed off as he took another drink and put down the glass.

I stood up and went toward him. The electricity in the air between us sparked. "You know who slashed my suitcase and killed Munster? I thought you didn't believe me."

Alex turned to face the fireplace. I watched the shadows and the light flicker across his troubled countenance. When he spoke again, his hushed words filled my heart with sadness. "No, I don't believe you, but what matters is that you believe it. If I hadn't married you and brought you here, you wouldn't have been under such pressure." He turned to look at me.

I blinked at his statement. "You're saying stress caused me to dream up those strange things? Stress killed my cat?"

He shrugged and glanced back at the fire as if he were unable to look at me. "The point is, I'm going to let you go. I'm going to divorce you. Don't worry, I'll still pay your debts and keep my part of the bargain."

The conversation slipped away from me. I felt paralyzed, unable to utter the words I needed to justify myself. The seconds ticked away.

"What if I don't want a divorce? What if I want to keep *my* part of the bargain?" I felt like hitting him. I wanted to smash my fist right into his handsome face. My hands curled in anticipation. I was impotent, and frustrated. Just as in the past, I had no control over this man, and consequently, no control over my future.

Alex's gaze roved over my face, his eyes flickering back and forth. He must have seen my anger. He must have known how much he riled me. He took a step toward me. For a moment, I thought he would touch me. His eyes kindled with desire. And then his gaze deserted me. Like hot air seeping from a popped balloon, his manner deflated. He ran his hand through his black hair, leaving it untidy and wild-looking. The gray in his eyes darkened, and his facial muscles echoed his despair.

"Look, I admit my obsession for you is not normal." He shook his head and turned from me to stare once again at the dancing shadows in the fire. "That's why I want to make it right for one of us."

It was hard for me to watch him like that—so full of remorse. The Alexander I remembered would not be depressed. Back then, we had never used the term. People were too busy just trying to survive to worry about our psyches. In a way, things were simpler. Life was too complicated these days. I told myself all this, while I stared at his broad back, the firelight giving him a phantomlike appearance. Maybe I was still dreaming. No matter Anthony's assurance, maybe this whole thing was a cruel joke. Dejected myself, I lost my earlier contentment, and sadness overpowered me.

Alex's wide shoulders tapered downward to trim hips. His long-legged frame gave him a commanding height, his torso muscular and taut. I wanted to intermesh myself with him, run my hands around his waist and push my own body up against his. I wanted to lay my cheek against his shoulder blades, and feel the cadence of life in each breath he took. I longed to unite with this man I called my husband, now and in the past. In sorrow, I just stood behind him, daring not to touch him. Irresolute, I licked my lips.

"Alex, I need to tell you something." My voice was quiet. I raised a hand to touch him, but afraid, left it poised in the air. "I believe you and I are reincarnated. That's why you felt the need to marry me. It explains our attraction to each other." I took a deep breath, drawing courage from within myself in face of his silence. "We were once married. Back in 1327. You were a marcher lord in England and I was your second wife. I gave birth to our child, but I died afterwards, never knowing you loved me for myself. I thought you cared for me only because of my ability to bear you a son."

Until that moment, I had failed to notice the growing tension in his stance. Twirling around, he directed his furious gaze at me, his face flushed and eyes bright. "My God, Mary. Do you know how insane that sounds?"

"But it's true." I straightened my spine, my conviction giving my carriage an air of confidence.

Swiping his hand through his hair again, Alex shook his head. "No," he said in an impatient tone. "It's just another example of what my recklessness has done to you. You're a practical woman. Now you're spouting inanities about reincarnation. This is even more reason for you to leave."

"I don't want to leave you, Alex." I was aware of the pleading note creeping into my voice. "We belong together."

His grimace wrenched my heart. "We don't belong together. Whatever relationship we had or have is based on a sick premise—a purely business arrangement."

"No, it's based upon our love." I defied his denial with the truth.

Rolling his eyes toward the ceiling, Alex shook his head, and then turned away from me once more. Confronted by his back again, I was appalled by my inability to make him understand. The barrier he had raised was formidable. I swallowed convulsively, my mind a mayhem of indecision and disbelief.

"What about this afternoon? Was it a business arrangement on the side of the cliff?"

"Go on to bed, Mary." Alex's voice was low and sorrowful. "You'll be free of me in the morning."

"I don't want to be free of you, Alex. Can't you understand?" I ventured to lay my hand upon his back.

He jerked away from my touch, lashing out at me

with his words, "Can't *you* understand I don't want you around me?" He turned again to face me, his gaze vicious. "Can't you understand I'm having a hard enough time coming to grips with my own reality? It's difficult for me to admit my whole life has been a lie."

"A lie?" I felt incredulous disbelief.

"Yes!" He spat the word at me with venom. "I've spent my whole life trying to make my father happy. Now I know my thinking was faulty."

"You can't make someone else happy, Alex. Happiness comes from within," I told him, despite my awareness of how trite it sounded.

"Thank you, Ms. Psychiatrist. Your words of wisdom really give me comfort."

Suddenly I was overcome by a feeling of failure. I felt sick, my stomach churning and my head aching. I raised my fingertips to my temples, swaying slightly on my feet. He was rejecting me, my efforts thwarted. I had taken enough. The joust had ended. I withdrew from the field, my banner lowered to signal defeat. I gazed at him a moment longer, and then turned away.

"I'm tired. I suppose I will go to bed."

I left the room, walking out of Alex's life, walking away from my destiny.

****

I didn't know where to go or what to do. Somehow, my steps carried me upstairs, past the gawking knights and rich tapestries. In the hushed and darkened hall, I saw the small form of Rufus. Before I could call his name, the little man nodded once in acknowledgement and darted through the door to his master's wing. I hesitated, perplexed, and then turned into my room. Allison's room. I belonged nowhere else.

Resting my hand on the hard surface of Allison's wooden dresser, I steadied myself. My heart ached with regret. I had been better off not knowing the truth of my past nor the depth of my former love. Not knowing, I had been blindly happy most of my life. In my oblivion, I had pursued a career and hobbies with quiet delight. I had known who I was and who I wasn't. I had been content.

Don't lie to yourself. Gazing back at me through my reflected image, my blue eyes admonished me. Ever honest with myself, I recalled with intensity my deep-seated longing, my feeling of loss, my own unsatisfied hunger. These feelings had been a part of my present life for as long as I remembered. Now I understood Alex's melancholy, for it had been mine. The thin line that had tied us together through the vicissitudes of the ages had a strong pull. Our past loss manifested itself in our modern lives, causing us to make decisions that affected our present. I took a deep breath and gazed back at myself. *Without resolving this with Alex, I will never attain abiding peace.*

So what was I to do? Should I try again? What could I say or do differently to make Alex believe me? How could I reach the realm of his emotions that he held away from even himself? I turned from the mirror, away from the steely blue eyes that challenged me to do more. I had failed not once, but twice. Today and in my past. Reconciled to my fate, I wandered to the bed, my dejection like heavy weights pressing down upon my soul.

That's when I saw the gown. It was spread out carefully on the coverlet as if someone had painstakingly laid it in place. Rufus? An insidious fear began to gnaw at my inner core. Licking my lips, I stepped forward. The canary yellow color had faded to a pale ocher, yet the heavy brocade embroidered with an intricate floral pattern was the same. I recalled the hours of work that had gone into sewing those stitches. With great hesitation, I reached down and touched it. There was something comfortable about its feel—like a familiar friend. I closed my eyes, swaying ever so slightly as I stood next to the bed. *This is my gown.* My heart thudded with certainty, and my palms grew wet with anticipation.

With my eyes still shut, I began to unbutton my sleeveless summer blouse. Slowly, deliberately, I opened the shirt and took it off, dropping it unheeded on the floor. Next, I slipped out of my leather riding boots, and zipped down the side of my jodhpurs, stepping out of them and kicking them away. I stood in my bra and panties, the cool air of the room soothing my bare skin. Rocking backwards and forwards, my breasts rising and falling in the rhythm of my breathing, I opened my eyes. My gaze locked on the gown. I touched my tongue to my lips, and reached down and picked it up.

Kirtle. That's what we had called it. I remembered the name of the gown as I slipped it over my head, put my arms through the tight sleeves and let the fabric slide over my body. The undergown fit firmly around my figure, flowing from my hips in heavy graceful folds. Struggling, I laced up my back, wishing for the experienced hands of Gellis. It took a long time, my arms aching, but when I was done, the clinging lines of the garment further enhanced my lanky form. Next I buttoned my sleeves from the wrist to the elbow. The tedious task took more precious moments. I bit my lower lip in concentration.

When that was done, I gathered my surcoat from the bed. The weighty garment was like a coat with a tippet attached to each sleeve at the elbow. The fabric of this part of my overstated sleeves dangled three feet. Trimmed in rabbit fur, the whole surcoat smelled musty and old. My mind in a mist, I touched the softness of the fur...remembering. Sluggishly, I put on the raiment from the past, the tightness of the sleeves constricting more than my arms, for my heart felt taut with misery. I swallowed and turned to face my image in the mirror. Treading quietly to the dresser, I blinked again at my reflection. All wasn't right. As if by rote, my fingers lifted to my hair, and I began to pull out the pins, my honey-blond tresses falling in waves around my shoulders. Next I brushed it free of tangles, each silky strand sparkling. Then I began again, parting my hair down the middle and plaiting it into two long pigtails. For a moment I remembered my childhood, my modern one. I thought about my mother and the pleasure she took doing my hair. Then my memory swiftly traversed the centuries and I recalled the tender touch of Gellis' hands as she tended to my needs. It was a curious feeling, to have two sets of memories.

Taking up the plaits, I wound each around my ears, affixing them in place. The ornamental net mysteriously left on my dresser fit perfectly, enabling me to secure my whole medieval coiffure. The final piece of my ensemble was a thin, cream-colored veil which I wore loosely on my head. When I glanced into my mirror, I saw Mary de Mandeville.

It was eerie. I blinked again, but nothing changed. Mary Adams and Mary de Mandeville were indeed the same woman. I needed no other proof. Cocking my head to the side, I stared at my reflection, a sensation of hope springing into my breast. If I recognized myself, so would Alex. Rufus had given me another chance.

Frantically clutching at my skirts, I raced, realizing only briefly that I was barefoot. The carpeted stairs were mere impediments to my flight. I grasped the post of the railing with my right hand as I slung around the end of the steps and sped toward the library. The coats of armor stood silent sentinels to my passage.

Alex was gone. The firelight burned low, the coals glowing red under gray ashes. I skidded to a halt. My breathing was raspy and my chest heaved as I stood staring about the empty room, trying to comprehend my new dilemma. *Where can he be?*

Don't give up Mary. The voice came from my subconscious. It sounded so much like the voice of Gellis that my heart lurched. As if in a trance, I went to the front door, opening it with ease. The rain had diminished. I stepped out into the yard, the grass cold against my bare toes, and was immediately enveloped by a mist of white. Like the faint imagining of a dream, the fog swirled around me cutting me off from the everyday world. Alone in the vastness of the universe, time held no meaning. The only force was love. It swelled within my breast as I walked toward the stable. The love I felt for Alex surged once more within my soul.

My instincts had been correct. A faint yellow radiated from beneath the stable door. I pushed it inward, and for the second time since midnight found Alex.

I was afraid. My heart thumped. The palms of my hands were wet as well. I found him brushing Knight Fox, the massive gelding passive under Alex's ministrations. The horse snorted when I approached. Alex turned his head, eyes wide with disbelief. I saw him blanch. I saw the muscles in his jaw jerk. And then he had the gall to turn from me again.

"Go ahead. Deny it." I knew he recognized me. The certainty was within my heart. I held my chin high and stepped nearer. The horse pawed the ground as if he too had seen a ghost.

"Go away, Mary." With great, long strokes, he raked the hard brush through the inky black coat.

"No." I breathed deeply of the earthy animal smells. "Look at me."

He refused, stubbornly turning his head aside as if brushing that damn horse was the most important thing in his existence. I tried to swallow my anger. I tried to remain calm.

"You can't reject our reincarnation. Look at me and tell me I'm not the Mary you once loved."

Sweat beaded on his brow. Yet with arrogant confidence, he ducked under the cross ties, dropping the hard brush into the grooming bucket, and stepped out of the stall. He was tall and commanding, like the great lord he had once been.

"Why are you dressed that way?" His gray, smoldering eyes were mesmerizing. I could not shift my gaze from them.

"You know," I said with a defiant lift of my chin.

"No, I don't." He stood inches from me. His breathing was labored.

"I'm trying to get you to admit the truth."

He laughed, but the laughter missed lighting his eyes. It was a melancholy laugh. "You've been tormenting me ever since the funeral."

I met his gaze head on, daring him to look away again. "There's a reason."

He dismissed my statement with a wave of his hand. "Now after I agree to let you go, you come to me dressed like you're going to a Halloween party."

"How dare you mock me? You have no right." I was breathless in my anger. "You know who I am. You know why we've come together, and I will make you admit it. You will tell me that you love me—now and in the past."

"My God, you are a lunatic!" He spoke his accusations softly, the muscles along his jawline tense.

"I am *not* crazy." I drew out my words deliberately.

Our gazes jousted with each other, fighting for control. I wouldn't stand down. Not again. Alex lifted his hand, and I thought he would strike my face. His jet-colored lashes flickered ever so briefly, shadowing the grayness of his eyes. As he paused, I opened my mouth slightly, spellbound by his movements, daring him to hit me, but then he flicked his hand upward and removed my veil. I shivered within myself but remained still. He fingered the gauze-like material, bringing it to his nose to smell its musty scent. I swallowed. *Take up my favor, my lord. Wear it proudly at the tournament. Honor me with a win.* The words came unbidden. Instead of the modern man, I fancied I saw his medieval counterpart clad in black armor, plumed helmet held under his arm. *Come kiss me, my wife. Come bring me luck.*

Did Alex have the same vision? His gaze shifted from me and he swiped his free hand over his face. "No." The intensity seeped from his voice. "You're trying to trick me."

"Alexander, Earl of Mountjoy," I whispered. My heart was doing double time. I could hardly breathe.

"No!" His denial was loud. Suddenly, his gaze focused on me, and dropping the veil, he grabbed me by the upper arms, his fingers burning through the layers of my ancient garments. "What are you trying to do? I told you I'd pay your damned debts."

His lips assaulted mine. Like the shock of battle his touch jolted me. We grappled together, locking our tongues in a fierce stab of longing. His mouth tasted of bourbon, heady and light. His breath came in sharp gasps. Alarm, I watched his eyes shut for a moment, his heavy lashes shuttering out whatever feelings they possessed. Then it was too late for rationality, and I succumbed, Alex the victor, once more.

"What do you mean wearing that dress?" He barely lifted his lips from mine.

I was unable to answer with words. Responding with my body, I hoisted my arms around his neck, the fur-edged tippet swaying from my elbows. I pressed my thighs against his, and felt my hip bones rub his. As the friction of my action grew, I pushed myself ever nearer, arching my back so that my very femininity, swathed under layers of material, touched his swelling manhood.

"Oh, Mary, don't," he said into my mouth. "Don't make me lose control."

All at once, as I was about to lose control of myself, I

understood the profound power of my gender. For centuries it had been the same, even though some modern feminists chose to ignore it. During this one moment, during this intimate act, women had the ability to slay the mighty dragon of manhood.

"My husband," I murmured. "We shall be one."

Alex groaned against my mouth, as if losing an inner battle. He grabbed at my buttocks, tugging them forward so that my hips and my abdomen pressed even closer to him. Then he moved his own hips, simulating the act, and the inner recesses of my body exploded in flames.

Now I moaned against his lips. I tangled the raven curls at the nape of his neck. My fingers traced upward, over the line of his jaws, up to his temples, across his black brows, to finally rest at the peak of his hair. My fingers tumbled backward, through his heavy locks, in an erotic massage of love.

"Mary."

"Mary de Mandeville. Remember?"

"You witch." His own hands began to mimic mine, racing over the features of my face.

Our bodies were so near to each other, and hot with growing passion that it consumed all my concentration. Yet I pursued him, my words coming in gulps. "Remember our wedding night, my lord? Recall how kind you were to me. How I sat in your great marriage bed, naked and defenseless, and you chose not to ravish me but to comfort me. We slept together that night, and you won my confidence."

"Stop it." He took my mouth with his to hush my utterances.

But I wouldn't quit. When he paused for breath, I spoke again. "Remember how much fun we had when all the castle was asleep? You were quite randy, my lord, for an old man of thirty-five."

"Mary," he protested, eyes hooded by desire.

His hands began to rove over my netted hair, and as he began to kiss me again, I felt him remove the beaded net. He took out the pins that I had so carefully used and one by one, the two braids fell.

"I like your hair long and loose." He pressed his fingertips to my temples and moved them up and

211

backwards over my sleek blond hair, pulled tight against my head where the plaits began. His eyes held a haunted look.

"Remember under the flowering trees of our garden? I was ever afraid the servants would see."

"Stop!"

His increasing anger meshed with an increasing need. I saw it in his eyes and felt it with my body. To prevent me from saying more, Alex scooped me into his arms, and carried me to an unused stall, clean and fragrantly filled with new straw. He carefully lay me down. I stared up at his handsome body, so poised for more. He met my gaze with one of bewilderment and simple lust. I lifted my right hand in petition, the tippet swaying from my elbow. Alex blinked, undecided, but the pull of the tie that bound us was strong.

"Remember on the cliff above the river. You said we belonged together. You didn't know why, but you accepted it then. Accept what I tell you as true, Alex, for you and I are destined to be reunited—together throughout eternity." Our gazes joined in a timeless duel.

"It's not right." His words were rough-edged like a sword.

"It *is* right." My voice was low and bewitching. "Our souls have been joined for six hundred years."

"It's not right," he muttered again and fell on his knees by my side. "You were ever so beautiful."

Now he began to speak with his hands, brushing the loose strands of hair from my eyes. He touched my eyebrows and my chin. He stroked my neck with feather-like fingers.

"Mary," he said, eyes clouded, voice husky.

"We belong to each other." I could barely pronounce the words, so heavy did I feel with wanting.

"No." His speech denied what his actions declared.

He grabbed at my wrist and made an effort to release the buttons. His every movement drove me to a frenzy, so hot did I feel between my legs. I knew him as well as I knew myself at that moment, and I understood the reason for haste.

"My lord." I stayed his hand, bringing it to my lips and gently caressing it. "There's no time. I shall explode for wanting you." I brought his hand down so that it touched my skirt.

He understood my message, and swiftly lifted the skirt, the material bunching around my middle. We had managed this way once six hundred years before, and so the pattern repeated itself. First, Alex stripped off his clothes, standing strong and manly above me. Next he relieved me of my modern nylon panties, and began to pay court to my body. Although I longed to be unclothed lying wantonly naked in his arms, I soon forgot the wish. Alex made me forget, pushing me higher and higher into a world of sensation. His hands tormented me. His lips beguiled me. His rough legs against my wet thighs were a tender torment. I couldn't speak. I couldn't breathe. I couldn't think. When we were joined, the pure validation of the act drove me into a delirium of pleasant pain. Alex sensed it too. Our gazes intertwined, just as our bodies, just as our inner beings. In the past, now and forever.

"Mary!" he shouted my name as the life-giving fluid surged from his body.

I wrapped him in my embrace, pulling him nearer, feeling so hot, so out of control.

"Alex!" I answered his call with my own, and then his body relaxed upon mine, hunkering down as if he never wanted to move.

I shut my eyes in perfect contentment. His breathing grew steady. The thump of his heart slowed. He brushed back the hair from my face. Replete and self-satisfied, I took a deep breath. I had been absolved, my suffering justified. All was to be made right.

Alex stirred, shifting his weight. Somehow, my peacefulness vanished. Like the sun hiding behind the clouds on a rainy day, the light left my mind and it grew dark with trouble once more. For he had not spoken. He had not said the three little words. He had not acknowledged our deep and abiding love.

CHAPTER EIGHTEEN

"Dr. Dominican!" The terrified staccato of Mrs. Garrity's voice stabbed my heart.

Alex's hold on my hand strengthened. "Helena? What's wrong?"

"Elizabeth's gone!"

Lightning seared the dark morning sky as we entered the medieval foyer, and Alex dropped my hand to comfort the distraught woman.

"It's terrible. Terrible. I went to her crib, and there was this bloody body. I thought it was Elizabeth."

"Oh, my God, Helena!" Alex abandoned us, taking the red-carpeted stairs two at a time.

"It isn't Elizabeth in the crib, Mrs. Dominican," the housekeeper said to me. "Thank heavens for that, but I do believe it's your cat."

"Munster?" A slick fear slid through my being as we hurried after Alex.

The death smell assaulted my senses when I entered the infant's Mickey Mouse-papered nursery. Frozen by disbelief, Alex stood at the crib with his head bowed. Going to him, I touched his immobile shoulder, and glanced into the crib. When I saw the remains that I thought had been my darling gray cat, I was unable to control a shudder. Jabbing a fist into my mouth, I struggled to stop the scream rising to my lips.

"I thought about calling 911," Mrs. Garrity said from the door, "but I was afraid. What should we do, Dr. Dominican?"

214

"Guy."

Unsure I had heard him right, I looked at my husband's pale face. Fine marks of strain touched the corners of his eyes and grazed the thin line of his lips.

"But, Dr. Dominican, he's your father." Mrs. Garrity's tone expressed her doubt.

Alex whipped around. "Who else could do this, Helena? You're standing right here, and Rufus wouldn't. You know my father hasn't been himself since I remarried."

Dread knotted in my throat. Had Guy Dominican killed Munster? Had he been responsible for the threats to me? But why? The question loomed over us like a specter.

"He didn't seem like the kind who would hurt a child," I offered to no one in particular.

"What did you say?" Alex turned angry eyes on me.

"When I met him, he seemed like a nice enough old man."

"I thought I told you to keep away from him." Alex's gray gaze dug sharply into my soul.

I shrugged. "The door was open. I just went inside to see what was there."

"Mary, I told you to stay away for a reason."

"What reason was that? Did you know he was threatening me? Did you know he killed Munster?" My own accusations rang through the room. "You let me think you didn't believe me."

I felt betrayed, the dark vortex of my mind seething with anguish. He must have seen it in my eyes. He must have seen my withdrawal from him—the lift of my chin to bolster the eroding foundation of my life. Alex had not spoken his love for me in the centuries past. In the present, he respected me so little that he had lied. Apprehensive about my future, I was like a wounded bird with an alley cat near.

"We'll settle this later. Now we must find Elizabeth." Alex turned from me. "Helena, do you have the key?"

Mrs. Garrity shoved a hand into her pocket, and shook her head. "I don't know where it went. I had it this morning."

"Never mind. Where's the spare?" Alex slung a hand

through his tousled hair.

"In the kitchen."

"Show me."

Left alone in the once cozy nursery, the horrible stench in the crib haunted me. Staggering, I escaped to the long, dim hallway. As the darkness outside was shattered by another burst of thunder, my heart thundered with all I had remembered and experienced in the past twenty-four hours. The tragedy of my death had happened so long ago, but for some reason, I'd been given another chance. That's what mattered. That and finding Elizabeth. Alex would soon make amends for his inability to express his feelings. He had to. We had been thrown together in the present century to right a wrong—an injustice prompted by misunderstanding.

In my preoccupation, my steps carried me to the shut and locked door of Guy's private wing. Without conscious thought, I touched the forbidding knob. The door opened easily, and I was drawn into the portrait gallery by some strange compulsion. Cool air and a tart scent of perfume engulfed me. Allison's perfume. Frightened, I paused, straining to see into the penetrating darkness that enveloped me. The massive house complained as wind battered it. *Had I heard a baby's cry?* Or was it just the wind? Moving by instinct, I found my way down the hall to another shut door. Palms wet, muscles tense, I gripped the doorknob and turned it.

As I entered, a jolt of lightning illuminated the room that I had once been drenched with sunshine. A shadowed figure stood with his back to me at an open window. White drapes blew inward like strange phantoms and rain slammed into the room through the opening. Fear clutched my heart. For some reason, I wasn't surprised to see him standing.

"Come in, my dear Mary." The malice in Guy's voice startled me.

I stepped forward, drawing on whatever courage I could muster. "We're looking for Elizabeth. Have you seen her?"

He turned to look at me, his face wet with rain. The weight of his animosity was like a great albatross. I staggered beneath its burden. And then I saw Elizabeth in the crook of his ancient arms. Thank heavens she slept, unaware of the danger.

"You look so pretty in yellow. The color has always become you, my dear." Guy's slow smile was terrifying.

The smile halted me. I watched him like a house cat watches a bird from a window. It was hard for me to believe the pleasant man who had served me tea would want to do harm to me or Elizabeth. Then I thought about the slashed suitcase and pillow, and the bloody body of my cat. My brain reeled with the horror of it. I suppressed a shudder. My chest begged for air. I drew my fingers into a knot as I stood staring at my adversary.

But why? Why did Guy Dominican look at me like a cat ready to pounce? What had I done to him?

"Let me have Elizabeth," I said. "She needs her diaper changed."

"You'd like that, wouldn't you?" His voice held a strange high-pitched quality. "He loves her just like he loves you."

"She's just been sick. Elizabeth shouldn't get wet. Let me take her back to her crib."

A laugh as sinister and gut wrenching as any bad horror movie echoed throughout the room. The erratic light from the window showed me the amusement in his eyes. It froze me in place.

"You really play the innocent don't you, my dear?"

"I don't know what you're talking about."

"I've been waiting for you." He seemed pleased with himself. "After the other one died, I knew you would come. As long as he was married to that one, you couldn't have him."

Guy shrugged his shoulders and took a step backward, closer to the open window and the steady drill of rain. Outside the thunder sounded like a timpani. I drew a deep breath and waited.

"The first one didn't give me a son. Such a shame." He glanced at Elizabeth who stirred in his grasp.

"Guy, what are you talking about?" I ventured a step nearer.

"She loved him, don't you know. Such a shame too for her sake. *He* didn't love her though. I knew he wouldn't, but I didn't count on the child. The other one ruined everything."

There was nothing now in his eyes but a strange lunacy. His smile broadened as he pierced me with his unusual stare. Elizabeth began to whimper.

"Then he brought you here. I knew it was you, Milady, from the very first."

His use of the medieval address drew me up short. My stomach churned and my legs shook as I gaped at him. Was there a connection here to the past? Did the thin thread of time that tied me to Alex tie me somehow to my father-in-law?

"Guy!"

Alex burst into the room like a knight in battle. Mrs. Garrity was hard on his heels. I glanced back at him and saw how he quickly assessed the situation. Mrs. Garrity remained at the door, shock and fear in her face.

"What are you doing, Father?" Alex asked as he came up even with me.

"Don't you touch that whore," Guy warned.

"Are you talking about my wife?" Alex's voice was soft but full of threat as well.

"You had to marry her. I warned you against it, but you didn't listen to me. You never listened to me."

Elizabeth screamed in protest, her small fists flailing the air. "Give us the child, Father." Alex stepped nearer, his hands outstretched.

"You'd like that wouldn't you? You love her. Never me."

"You're not making any sense," Alex said, moving another step.

"Stay away."

The threat entered my heart like a sharp lancet, painful in its intent. Did Alex know about his father? Did he know that the threat today had somehow come from the fourteenth century?

"Alex, he's reincarnated too. He called me 'Milady,'" I whispered above the bawling infant and the pouring rain.

Alex glanced back at me. "Mary, this isn't the time to talk nonsense."

Guy laughed again, a sidesplitting, rollicking laugh— a laugh that chilled the marrow in my bones. "You play the innocent so well," he said to me, and then threw his son a deadly glare. "It's all your fault."

"What have I done, Father? What is this all about?"

"Don't you know? Don't you remember? You've never done what I wanted." His rambling was demented.

Alex's jaws moved and his lips grew firm. I saw the tenseness in his stance and his shoulders. "All my life I've tried to please you. The only time I've gone against you was when I married Mary."

"It's all your fault." Guy's smile was now controlled, cruel.

"I'm tired of it being my fault," Alex spat out. "I'm tired of feeling guilty for my mother's death. I was an infant when she died in that car crash. I had nothing to do with it, but I felt you always blamed me for it because she was going to the drugstore to buy medicine for me. That's why I always tried to please you, as if I owed you something. I married Allison because you wanted me to, and all I did was make her life miserable. So now you say what I've done is not good enough for you, *madam, please.*"

Alex's use of address startled us both. He glanced back at me perplexed. In the moment our gazes met, I understood all. My heart pounded in my chest and sweat beaded between my breasts. Now I knew why the odd odor of mustard and aged wine when I kissed Guy goodbye had been so familiar.

"Alex, he's your mother," I whispered.

Visions of my jealous medieval mother-in-law swirled in my mind. I remembered her graceful hands and tapering fingers. I remembered my hatred and my fear.

"My mother?"

"From the past."

Alex thrust a hand through his hair. "I don't know what you're talking about, Mary. You're confusing me."

Guy lowered his eyelids, assessing his son with a lazy nonchalance. "You loved her, that snippet of a girl from the North," he said, his words now coming quickly. "You loved her more than me. Yet she gave us the male heir we needed, and he was a good boy. Richard. He was more kind and loving to his old grandmother than his own father had been, don't you know."

Guy's words held me hostage. My laboring breath

loud in my ears, I strained to hear the strange mixture of old and new in his words. Another shock of lightning dazzled the sky, throwing strange shadows of hate across the old man's face. Out of the corner of my eye, I saw Rufus enter the room.

"What did you do, my dear lord?" Guy continued. "After that woman Mary died in childbirth, you left us. You left Mountjoy Castle and spent the rest of your life in that Dominican monastery. Such a waste. Such a damn waste."

With slow motion movements, the old man reached into a pocket and pulled out a tiny knife. A knife that could slash a suitcase or a pillow. A knife that could kill a cat. He pointed the sharp blade at me. "It's your fault, Milady. You made him love you so he wouldn't love me."

Alex stepped forward once more. "Guy, this doesn't make a bit of sense. I've always loved you. You're my father, for heaven's sake. Put that knife down and give me my baby. We'll talk this through. It's not worth getting angry about."

"Don't come near me." Lightning punctured the room, and pricked the edge of the blade as Guy brandished it in the air.

Overcome by the senseless situation and weak with fear, I swayed. "Love never dies," I said going toward Guy.

"Mary, don't!" Alex tried to hold me back.

"Give me my baby, Guy. You can't change what's happening. If you try, we'll just come back in some other time, some other place. You can't change destiny." My words were meant to be soothing, but prophetic.

"No!" His gaze riveted on me, Guy backed another step. "He never loved me or Richard."

I inched nearer, my hands outstretched.

Guy screamed, "It was always you—you. He'll not have you again!"

It all happened so fast. Somehow I found myself grabbing for Elizabeth. We fought over her like two children fighting over a favorite toy. Elizabeth wailed her fear and pain. Alex joined the struggle behind me, reaching for his father. He knocked away the knife. I clutched at the baby, gathering her into my hands, but I now felt the hard fingers of Guy gripping like talons into my arms. He pulled me backward toward the open window. His strength was that of a madman.

"Alex! Take her!"

I gave up Elizabeth into her father's arms. Intent on supporting his daughter, Alex let me go. Cold rain stung my face. The phantomlike curtains whipped around us as we went back—back toward the open abyss. I strained with every fiber of my being. Like the raging storm outside, my stomach raged with fear.

In one great jerk, I felt myself drawn forward. Guy's icy eyes burned into mine as he started to turn, angling me toward the window. His hold on me was endless, like the years.

Rufus emerged by my side. With sturdy strength, he forced his way between us, grappling with my father-in-law. Suddenly, they were gone out the window, and I felt myself topple backward into Alex's waiting arms. A scream like a damning curse froze my heart with horror.

CHAPTER NINETEEN

Both of them were dead. Rufus had saved my life and lost his own in the process. It all seemed so senseless. As Mrs. Garrity, who had fortunately taken Elizabeth to enable Alex to help me, now helped me settle Elizabeth into a spare bedroom. Alex called the police. He would tell them a story of a demented old man, confused by age, and a tragic fall from an open window. He wouldn't lie, but he wouldn't tell the whole truth. How could he? No one would believe him about being reincarnated. After all, I wasn't sure he fully believed me himself.

"Mrs. Dominican?"

I turned to notice a grudging respect in Mrs. Garrity's manner, and wondered about it. If she was curious about my plaited hair and strange yellow dress, she had not mentioned it.

"Mrs. Dominican, I want to apologize to you."

Stunned, I stared at her. "What did you say?"

"I haven't been very kind to you," she said, glancing away. "There are many reasons for it—my loyalty to my former mistress, my jealousy of your place with Elizabeth. Still there was no excuse for my behavior toward you. I know you could never hurt Elizabeth."

I didn't know what to say. Alex's housekeeper had said so many cruel things to me. Now she wanted me to forgive her.

Mrs. Garrity looked back at me, her face pinched sharper than usual. "I just want you to know, I didn't do any of those things you accused me of."

"I know. It was Guy." I glanced back to Elizabeth.

"Yes, we know that now. I wanted to tell you I think you've been a good mother to Elizabeth. You're not her real mother, but I think you love her as if she were your own."

"Thank you, Mrs. Garrity. I know that was hard for you to say."

"Yes, ma'am."

Suddenly, I was overwhelmed by exhaustion. "Will you finish here? I need to lie down."

I left my child in capable hands, and returned to Allison's bedroom, my mind a muddle of dismay.

Once a long, long time ago, Rufus had told me all would work out. All would be okay. Now I doubted his prophecy. All wasn't okay, and Rufus, my ghostly protector, was gone. Somehow I needed to convince Alex about our past. Our future.

I stared at myself in the mirror, straw clinging here and there to my archaic yellow gown. It adhered to strands of my hair. *I like your hair long and loose.* Stepping up to the dresser, I removed the bands holding my braids, and began to un-twine the locks of hair. When both sides were free, I ran my fingers through the unbound ends, from the top of my head to my back. I didn't brush my hair. It didn't seem to matter.

Nothing. I felt nothing. No hope. No despair. Just a blankness within my mind and soul. I walked to the great canopied bed, and stared at the slightly rumpled covers. Heavy with fatigue, I swayed a bit as my eyes refused to focus. In my mind, I saw Munster as his soft gray body wrapped around my leg and he welcomed me with a purr. I trembled. Then I gave in to the tiredness permeating my body and lay down.

Plainly, I had no control over my destiny. I could not change the past by recreating the present. Although Lord Mountjoy had loved me in the past, in the present Alexander Dominican had never said the three words. I was alone in a senseless sea of nothingness where life was trivial and shallow. With lethargy so deep, I shut my eyes and refused to ponder the whys and wherefores of this futile, paradoxical existence of mine.

Almost immediately against my shuttered lids, I saw

our child. Richard, the fifth Earl of Mountjoy. He was a tall boy with his father's striking black features. I saw him as a youngster at play, already learning to fight with cudgels and swords as boys of his day did. I saw him in attendance to another great lord, a lanky lad of fifteen, the blush of his newly awakened manhood on his cheeks. He was a young man taking a bride. I saw everything I had missed, and my heart ached with regret.

Slowly, willing it, I felt myself mesh into the mattress, as it seemingly opened itself to engulf me. I began to float effortlessly within my mind and body, so comfortable, so secure in a weightless, gray-white haze. I felt at peace with myself at last.

"Mary!"

Alex pulled me back out of the grip of my strange lethargy. He hauled me into consciousness by a bone-rattling jerk that snapped my head back and forth. A vise-like grip clutched my upper arms, hurting them, the pain making my eyes fly open because of the pain.

"My God, Mary! What are you doing?" Alex's eyes were wide with fright, his face ashen and drawn.

As he shook me, I fancied he was the Alex of old. The same devotion suffused his glace.

"My lord, you do harm me."

"Oh, Mary." He swathed me in his huge embrace.

His heart kerthumped against mine, doing double time with mine. His breath came in great gulps as the tears began to fall. The torment of the ages was unleashed in that moment. Alex sobbed into my shoulder, rocking me back and forth, hardly letting me breathe. Startled and unnerved, I lifted my hand to his black head and gently smoothed his untamed hair. The fur-trimmed tippet dangled awkwardly from my elbow.

"You look so pale," he began to mumble. "It seems I've seen you this pale once before. You frighten me. Oh, Mary, what's going on?"

"You did see me like that Alex. When I died. Six hundred years ago." My chest rose and fell with labored breaths.

He sat me away from him then, not far, but just so that he could look me in the eyes. Red-rimmed and wet, his own gray eyes held great worry and longing. Tenderly, he sandwiched my face between his hands, forcing our gazes to meld into one.

"Had I not come to you now would you have died?" His words sounded blade-cold.

"No. I am tired. So much has happened." I couldn't move my head, but, uneasy because of the ancient pattern of his speech, shifted my gaze away from his. "Why did you come?"

"Rufus."

I looked at him again and swallowed the lump in my throat. "But he's dead."

"I know. It doesn't make sense. I just had this feeling he was telling me to find you."

Rufus had intervened again. I stilled the kindling of hope that had begun to burn in my breast. No, I wouldn't believe Alex loved me just yet. Too many times my expectations had been dashed like a run-aground ship held fast in barren sand. I wanted something more concrete. I wanted words as well as actions before I would satisfy myself that maybe....

"When you died before, I couldn't do anything about it." His gray eyes captured my gaze and flickered uneasily. "Why did I say that? Mary, am I going crazy like my father?"

"No, you just don't have the far memories I have." My voice was small like that of a timid child. "We're both reincarnated. I tried to make you understand. Guy was your mother in the past. She hated me, as I hated her. Today, Guy tried to kill Elizabeth and me. He wanted to kill anyone you loved."

Still cupping my face in his hands, Alex rubbed my eyebrows with his thumb. "If I hadn't witnessed Guy's madness, I could never believe you might be speaking the truth."

"I am telling you the truth, my lord." I fell back into the familiar way I had addressed him.

"You call me 'my lord.' Tell me," he whispered. "Tell me all of it."

I nodded, and lifted my hands to grasp his, pulling them down and holding his big fists in my small ones. "I was your wife. I died in childbirth."

"They had so little knowledge of medicine back then,"

Alex said, his brows furrowed.

"Yes, and when I think of that ineffectual midwife, I just want to put my fist through something."

Alex's hands escaped my clasp. Taking mine up in his, he turned both of my palms face upward and kissed them. The feel of his lips singed my flesh, causing me to grow wet in more places than one.

"Guy said something about a son living," he murmured, looking up at me.

"Richard lived—our son. Surely, that was a miracle in itself."

"Somehow, it seems to me he was a fine boy." Alex looked away, his jaws set. Standing up from me, he began to pace back and forth, crossing in front of me as I sat on the edge of the bed.

"Can you really believe all this?" Turning, he caught my gaze, an incredulous light in his gray eyes. "It's so improbable. I still resist trusting what you tell me, even though deep in my heart I know it must be true." Alex raked his right hand through his raven hair.

"I know. I didn't want to believe it myself," I told him. "But the dreams were so real. I didn't remember anything but the dreams at first. After Gail's boyfriend regressed me, I accepted the reincarnation. Then I could remember other details."

Alex sat down beside me on the bed. Turning slightly to face me, his look was ernest. "You never had those dreams until you came into this house?"

"No, not until I married you."

"And you remember everything now?"

"Yes, but you don't?" Quietly, I raised an index finger and traced the tracks of his tears down his cheeks. He jerked as if stabbed. Capturing my hand, he pulled me onto his lap, my yellow skirts enveloping his legs.

"No. I don't remember it. I just have this deep feeling of guilt, and sometimes I see little scraps of scenes that I suppose happened to me." He shrugged, and then tightened his arms around me. "I know you've spoken the truth, God help us both."

"Maybe you should see Gail's friend. Maybe he could help you remember, " I said.

Silently we sat that way for some time. I cherished

the feel of his muscular arms and broad shoulders. The rise and fall of his chest comforted me. The moisture on his cheek was a heady reality. Somehow fate had brought us together again. For many moments I was content to savor the happiness I felt just being in Alex's embrace.

"I was very much in love with you back then," I finally ventured to say. "But I didn't think you loved me, not until I died and saw you at my death bed."

He kissed the top of my head, and tucked it tightly under his chin. "Saw me?"

The coldness of memory blew across my eyes. I saw once more from the high white cloud of death how Alexander, my husband, had knelt in misery by my bed. I remembered the regret I had experienced because he had not spoken sooner—the potential for enduring love lost, never to be regained, until now, until this very minute. I sat up and away from him, my heart beating erratically. We had left so much unsaid, and now we had one final chance. Carefully, I straightened my shoulders and lifted my chin. I gazed at him directly.

"After I died, you were alone with my body. You cried out that you loved me, but you had never told me. You were afraid of something. Something I never understood."

"I was afraid you didn't love me because of your first love." His words startled us both. His skin was like paste, his eyes wide with bewilderment.

"My first love?" I asked.

"The young man killed at the tournament."

"You mean Richard?" I was astounded by what I was hearing.

"Yes, that's why I named our son Richard," he said, his gray eyes hooded by dark lashes. I sensed the tension within him. "Mary, how did I know that?"

"Because you lived it once," I told him.

Too troubled to sit on his lap, I left him to begin my own pacing. The long skirts were no problem, for instinct aided my strides across the room and back.

"But I never really loved Richard," I revealed. "Today, we would call it a teenage crush. You were my only love, my lord. I thought I told you that with my actions."

"No," he replied quickly and then shook his head.

"Damn it. What am I talking about? I must be crazy."

Standing, he came toward me, capturing me once more in his grasp so I was made to look up at him. Our gazes never wavered. His words fell heavily around me. "I don't know how I know this, but I do know I felt guilty because of your death. I died a bitter and lonely man in a monastery."

I swallowed hard. "You married me, my lord, to bear you a child. Back in the fourteenth century that was the way of the world. Yet in my heart, I wanted more. I wanted your acceptance of me as a woman, a lover, a wife. I wanted you to love me for myself."

Alex released me and turned away. I couldn't speak. I swayed as I looked at his broad, but slumped shoulders. My fingers curled and my breathing came in heavy gasps as the turmoil in my mind played itself out. Alexander had loved me so much that he had felt profound guilt and grief at my death.

I shut my eyes. So, in our former lives we had failed to tell each other of our love. What about now? What about the present we found ourselves rudely thrust into? We had another chance, and now that Alex knew about the past, maybe we could change our destiny. My heart lurched at the thought. I opened my eyes, renewed in my purpose. Stepping forward I laid my hand on his shoulder, the knots of his muscles hard beneath my grasp.

"What are we going to do about it?"

He stiffened but didn't pull away. "Do? What's there to do?"

"We can't change the things that happened to us in the past," I told him, my voice hushed by emotion. "But we can do something about today."

Alex whirled around to face me, the look in his eyes frenzied and confused. "What do you mean?"

I lifted my chin and secured his gaze to mine. "I love you. If you love me, maybe we have the ability to recreate our future."

"Love you? My God, Mary, I burn with love for you, but it won't work." He backed away from me, halting when he hit the post of the bed.

"Why won't it work?" I challenged him, advancing.

Alex shook his head as if to stop me from coming

nearer, but I ignored him, feeling for the first time in so many, many years that I was in control. When I was a heartbeat away, I lifted my hand and caressed his cheek. He shuddered at my touch.

"Tell me, Alex. Why won't it work?"

"I can't let myself love you." His words were barely audible.

"Why not?" I was relentless.

His breathing strained, he stared into my eyes. "I might cause you to die again."

"That's stupid," I objected angrily. "You know as well as I do that what happened to me was because of the sorry state of medical knowledge. We have modern hospitals and competent doctors today. Things like that rarely happen."

"It happened to Allison."

"Cancer killed Allison."

"If I'd been a better doctor, more perceptive...." his words trailed away.

Sliding away to the left, he moved across the bedroom, his strides long and full of passion. I turned, and followed his movements with my gaze. I had come so far. *We* had come so far. Damn it all. I wasn't going to let it slip from my grasp again. But how could I convince him that his fears were irrational and his thinking faulty?

"Alex. Until today you were living your life without understanding your past. That ignorance probably caused the depression you told me about. It's the root of your guilt—today as well as in the past."

He stopped his pacing and dared me with his gaze. "Is that so?"

"Yes," I answered him, my eyes bold in their challenge. "I know that was true for me." Lowering my lashes, I continued thoughtfully, "I was always depressed too, but I never put my finger on the real reason. Not until I found out about you. Not until I realized I had loved you so much, and you had loved me, and we had been cheated out of our happiness together."

"So you're saying the guilt I felt because of your death in the past carried over to today?" Alex stepped nearer, trying to accept.

"It makes sense. In this time, you were drawn into

obstetrics because of what you couldn't do for me then. You felt guilt because of Allison's death, because it was so much like my death in the past. You had no control over any of it, Alex." I quietly watched the emotions joust across his face.

"But why did I always try to please my father?" He shook his head as if to clear it.

"Guy knew your guilt. He played upon it to control you in this time, making you think you were somehow at fault for your mother's accident." I took a deep breath, my certainty increasing as I spoke. "He wanted your undivided love, now as in the past."

"It's so unfathomable."

"So is reincarnation."

"What are we to do about it now?"

I shrugged. "What do you want to do?"

"Marry you."

I set my jaw. Although those were almost the right words I wanted more. I wanted some sort of assurance, an absurd wish in a world where no certainty existed.

"We are married," I reminded him.

"No, we have a business arrangement." Alex came closer, a familiar and welcome gleam returning to his eyes.

"Why do you want to marry me? Because you feel guilty?"

"No." He was so near I smelled the male spiciness of him, mixed with an earthy scent of horses and straw. I heard his heavy breathing, and imagined I heard the wild thumping of his heart. Deliberately, Alex lifted his finger and placed it under my chin. His touch was magnetic, drawing us even nearer. "I want to marry you because you are beautiful, honest, kind, and you are the most persistent woman I know. I want to marry you because I love you—now, in the past, and for the rest of my life."

I could not have envisioned how I would feel when he spoke those words to me, but the reality was beyond my imagination.

My heart swelled, and as I lifted my arms to circle them around his neck, Alex lowered his lips to mine in a kiss of reconciliation.

"I sure would like to get you out of that dress," he

murmured against my mouth.

I smiled and then jabbed my tongue playfully at him. "You're welcome to try."

As Alex lifted me in his arms to carry me to the canopy bed, I thought I spied the small, jaunty form of Rufus at the open door. Oddly, he was dressed in a red gown, with a tasseled hood on his head. He saw me looking at him and winked—a big, saucy wink. Bemused, I stared at him. I blinked and he was gone.

Then my mind and body were too saturated by the compelling presence of my husband, who, kneeling over me as I stretched out on the bed, began to unbutton the many buttons on my left sleeve. It was a tedious task, but one he accepted with relish, his own hair disheveled and falling into his eyes—his own gaze smoky and love-filled—his touch erotic. I closed my eyes, the erratic catch in my breathing belying the abiding peace I felt. With the far memories untangled, despair in my heart sealed shut for all time.

A word about the author...

I've dreamed of being a writer since I reported on freelance writing for a career project in the ninth grade. After majoring in English at Western Kentucky University, I taught high school English for five years. Since 1982 I've made my living as a writer—a technical writer! But I didn't have the nerve to make my real dream come true until after a life-threatening illness in 1988. I've enjoyed my process of becoming a published author. As a member of the Romance Writers of America, I've been active in my local Kentucky RWA chapter and am a member of Novelist, Inc. My best friends are fellow writers. Who else will check a point plot for me or understand GMC and POV? I live in Louisville, Kentucky, along with two dogs and four cats. I enjoy taking riding lessons on American Saddlebred horses. I'm a member of the American Saddlebred Horse Association. I also belong to the Louisville Thoroughbred Club and the PBR fan club. Believe me. Dreams do come true! On January 2, 2000, I married Bill, my soul mate.

Visit Jan at http://www.janscarbrough.com/

Breinigsville, PA USA
24 February 2010
233128BV00003B/2/P